TEEN JUSTICE:
JUSTICE HAS A CURFEW—BOOK TWO

TEEN JUSTICE

JUSTICE HAS A CURFEW
BOOK TWO

C.A.GORDON

ACKNOWLEDGEMENTS

WE'RE HERE AGAIN ALREADY? OKAY, LET'S DO THIS.

Many thanks to my wife, Katrina, for putting up with me again while I shifted between Reality and Maker Mode. Reality is more fun because I share it with you.

To Debbie Copeland, a loving mother, talented author, and superhero in her own right.

To the real Albert(on) "Butch" Ford(sworth) Jr., my father and my friend. You're only a villain in fiction, and I promise that you won't be forever.

To the twins, Iggy and Will. I've known you longer than anyone who doesn't share my DNA, and you've always exuded a natural maturity and charisma that it took me *years* to achieve.

To David Massey and the MiraCosta Community College faculty. Thanks for a lifetime of memories. And for letting me destroy the theater.

To the memory of the Ruby's Diner formerly located at the end of the Oceanside Pier. Similar sentiments as above, and a special Thank You for being the only edifice capable of bringing my kids together as a team for the first time.

To the real Lindseys and Andersons. *(Psst—Hey, Brandon, I told you I'd give you a lil' page time. More to come!)*

To Nurse Alley Mason, McKinnon Galloway, Emilee Segura, and the entire deaf community.

To Granddad and Mom. You both get another shoutout, and that's probably enough.

And, finally, to Dr. Michael Haas. I ain't quite fixed and may never fully get there, but I'm thrice the man I was before you entered my life. Thank you.

—C.A. Gordon

PROLOGUE

Center for Enhanthrax
Research and Treatment
Keaton Layer—12:45 am

DHS-EX SPECIAL AGENT GEORGE ANDERSON STOPPED the recording. He took a few silent minutes to add some quick yet meticulous notes to the notepad on his server, allowing the room's occupants time to come down off their collective adrenaline high from listening to the Gordon kid's narrative. Lord knew *he* needed to.

Eventually, Anderson locked his device and looked up. His face was stern. "You killed him."

The first teen, Cameron Gordon, looked him directly in the eyes, and Anderson suddenly found himself host to a litany of conflicting feelings ranging from primal disgust to admiration.

"I had to," the teen said simply.

Douglas and Debbie Andrews and Jasmine Haynes looked at him with their own blend of shock, disgust . . . and a tinge of fear.

In Jasmine's case, the experience was strikingly fresh; she'd only just laid eyes on Cameron and her little brother's other friends for the first time two hours ago.

Back then, they were merely a group of teenagers possessed of a host of unique abilities as the result of a shared viral infection. Four teenagers, one short of the original group of five, who'd supposedly taken some stupid joyride earlier that evening, a joyride that somehow turned into a total disaster.

Now, however, Jasmine knew that (at least) one of them was a confessed murderer.

The tension in the room was finally broken, perhaps remixed, by Zack Haynes' next words:

"Good on you."

"*Zack!*" Jasmine exclaimed.

Zack turned his head upward slowly and deliberately until his eyes met his sister's.

"Good. On. You!" he repeated, accentuating each syllable.

Anderson saw Cameron glance over at the blonde girl, Taylor Andrews.

"Tay—" the teen began.

"I know," Taylor cut in understandingly. "So am I."

"Come on, I'm not trying to keep us all here 'till dawn, so . . ." Anderson said, making a *wrap-it-up* motion with his server.

Cameron's face remained stoic. "If you want the last six months in the life of an entire city boiled down into a single account, you need to *stop* with the interruptions. *Sir,*" he added forcefully.

"I'm only looking at the five of you in this room. *Four* of you," Anderson corrected himself. "And the specific events that led to *tonight's* incident."

To the surprise of everyone, Taylor exploded:

"Then *shut up* already and pay attention!"

She let the silence linger for several long seconds, ignoring the verbal lashing from her parents that ultimately never came.

Finally, she pointed at Zack, then at Nova Stevens, then at herself.

"We're up next."

Silence.

Zack looked around the conference room at the dozen armed agents lining the walls like statues, at the grownups sitting across the conference table, and at the other teens seated next to him on both sides.

"Um . . . Which of us *specifically* is We? I mean, 'cause if we're going down the line here, then technically *she's* up next," Zack said, pointing a charred glove in Nova's direction. "But the whole 'she can't talk right now' thing might stretch this out even longer, so . . ."

Sixteen heads turned to look at the thick metallic collar strapped around the girl's throat, the collar that inhibited her ability to produce the slightest vocalization.

Taylor sighed. "I'll go next."

"You'll go next. Of *course* you'll go next," Zack repeated with relief, nodding his head in agreement. "Right, 'cause she actually *was* next in all of this, so it makes perfect sense for her to . . ." He sacrificed his last two words to the overwhelming awkward silence and sat back in his chair, resting his folded hands on the tabletop.

Taylor took a deep breath. Then she went next.

PHASE 2/5: REPLICATION

CHAPTER 1

Benson Preparatory School—Stadium
Kilmer Layer—11:40 am

SHE COULDN'T KEEP UP WITH HER ANYMORE. SHE WAS just too slow.

Taylor Andrews had already endured four hours of individual dashes, hurdles, and team relays. Then *more* relays and more hurdles. Hundreds of meters worth of accumulated track dust on her three-week-old Mizuno trainers. Of course, there'd been a few great heats and plenty of photogenic accomplishments. All the prior months of hard work had led to this exact moment, and Taylor was giving her all and then some.

But she couldn't keep up with Her anymore. She was just too *slow*.

It wasn't like Taylor was being continually outpaced by any of her teammates or rivals. Certainly, her name and achievements would be among those listed in the next edition of the *Charter Pulse*, the school's official blog. Her performance wasn't being affected by any asthmatic triggers, either. Despite last night's showers, it was a perfect morning. The crisp late spring air complimented a sky full of tungsten stratocumulus clouds that would certainly fade to nothing with the approaching noon heat. As a precaution, Coach Kern insisted that Taylor take a peak flow reading immediately before and after every event. And, just in case things got dicey, her parents were sitting just off the edge of the field with her rescue albuterol inhaler at the ready. So far, Taylor had caught nothing but green lights all the way, all day.

But she couldn't keep up with Her anymore. *She was just. Too. Slow!*

The Other Her, that is.

Initially, the Other Her was nothing but a figment of Taylor's imagination: a healthy mental fabrication of her ideal athletic self, one designed to help the asthmatic teen overcome her limitations out on the track. She was invisible and intangible to everyone, everyone but Taylor. She was also identical to her in nearly every way, albeit slightly *faster*.

This morning, however, the Other Her decided to become *real*.

For the past nine consecutive events, Taylor had perceived a faint azure outline of her phantasm, a baby blue projection that appeared the precise moment before Taylor started running and vanished the moment that she crossed the finish line.

At first, she chalked it up as mental exhaustion, a side effect of residual toxic emotional waste. After all, she and Cameron never *did* have that follow-up conversation last night. Cameron's inexplicable memory loss of what happened between them at the party Friday night combined with his behavior yesterday morning was still a painful mystery to be solved. Even so, after Taylor texted the request for solitude, he remained uncharacteristically silent for longer than usual. Their friendship had lasted long enough for Cam to know that *I need some space* really meant *Let me stew for an hour and cool down for a couple more, but let's not allow this minor rift to fester overnight into a chasm.*

But overnight came and went, and Taylor still hadn't heard from him. And when her alarm went off the next morning, *this* morning, all her thoughts coalesced into a single maxim: *Run fast today, everything else tonight.*

That maxim had served her well throughout the morning. So well, in fact, that she averaged second place in the first three events and managed to shave a crucial one point eight seconds off her personal best time during the 4 x 100 metres relay. The sentiment "That extra boost of speed was *just* what Summer [Codi] needed to bring home the win!" was echoing among Taylor's Pulse Charter track teammates, which was perfectly fine with her. From the moment she conceived the notion of trying out for the team up until twenty minutes ago when she last crossed the finish line, it was never EVER about winning. It wasn't even about the camaraderie (read: the forced integration with an intellectually inferior yet socially elevated peer group) she was experiencing. It was all about keeping up with the Other Her. And now she was *literally* in front of her!

Under normal circumstances, Taylor would've been able to conduct a proper self-analysis to determine the true nature of this phenomenon. But not even polymaths are completely mentally sharp first thing on a Sunday morning. So she'd toughed it out, all the while ignoring a growing alarm in her right amygdala that something was about to go terribly awry.

*   *   *   *   *

Cameron shuffled down the stairs and across several rows of generic aluminum bleachers. His bleary eyes struggled to focus on the trio of Douglas and Debbie and Barton Andrews, all of whom were situated at the bottom near one of the gates that allowed entrance onto the track. Cameron wasn't entirely sure how to approach Taylor's parents but he knew that he had to. There was no way on earth they hadn't seen the scandalous video by now, and there was only a slim possibility that they wouldn't eviscerate Cameron with their bare hands on sight. But Cameron was honor-bound to make things right. *Try.* Try to make things right.

"Hey Taylor! Love you baby!" Debbie Andrews' voice rang out across the track like a cat with its tail caught in a bear trap. In characteristic teenage fashion, the blonde on the field ignored her.

One of the parents standing near Debbie looked out at the obviously Caucasian teenager avoiding eye contact. Then she looked back at the dark chocolate-toned woman, and, finally, at the blonde man sitting next to a small mixed-race boy.

"Don't worry," the mother offered with assumptive sympathy. "She'll come around. It took my husband's daughter *years* to call me anything other than 'The Usurper.' Just keep assuring her that you're not trying to replace her mother and you'll be fine."

Debbie stared at the woman with genuine confusion that quickly turned to irritation.

Not this *ignorant nonsense again,* she thought.

"I am her mother," Debbie said simply.

"Of course you are!" the other woman said earnestly, her face shining with a wide, dumb smile as she placed a supportive hand on Debbie's shoulder.

Debbie removed the hand with a thumb and forefinger as if she was discarding a stray hair or a spider. "No, you *don't* get it. *That* is my one and only husband and *she* is our only daughter. The sex was *wild* but the four days in labor? Out of this world!"

The woman turned pale.

"Tragically, she came out of the oven a bit *undercooked,* so we waited a few years to try again and the next one ended up *medium well,*" Debbie continued sarcastically, pointing a thumb at Barton. "Think we'll get it right with Number Three, or will he/she end up *well done?*"

The woman slowly backed away, nearly tripping over the closest bleacher seat.

Moments later, Debbie was rummaging furtively through her purse. She finally offered a subtle shake of the head to her husband, who got up to leave.

"Hey, there's Romeo," Debbie said with a smirk as Cameron approached them. Douglas whipped his head around, saw the teen, and narrowed his eyes. "Not funny," he said to his wife.

Cameron remembered to keep his posture low, deferential. "Good morning, Mr. Andrews, Debbie." He glanced down at Barton and added: "Hey, dude."

"Hey, Cameron," the boy returned. Then he looked up at his parents with a pair of large aquamarine eyes that complemented his cappuccino skin and asked: "Who's Romeo?"

"Never mind," Douglas responded. Then, to Cameron: "What are you doing here? She doesn't need this today."

Cameron had spent the last twenty hours mentally preparing for just such a cold reception, but his response was preempted by an exasperated interjection from Debbie: "Come *on*, Douglas. Don't *start*."

"No, I'm serious," Douglas countered with equal force.

Cameron found an opening in the exchange and dove in. "Mr. Andrews, I'm really sorry," he said with absolute sincerity.

From the corner of one eye, Cameron saw Debbie's face soften. Unfortunately, her husband's face only hardened. Fat beads of sweat formed on his brow as if he was straining to keep from exploding. He was only partially successful.

"Sorry for what, huh? For what *exactly*? For humiliating my little girl on the internet? Or for leading her on for so long while you shamelessly chased some random skirt who barely knows your name?"

Okay, *that* stung, and Cameron felt his jaw and fists clench. The new feeling of his Enhanthroid abilities—or, as Dr. Gosland had clarified—the feeling of hundreds of thousands of EX ions coursing among his cells washed over him, and Cameron fought hard to suppress the instinct to shock some sense into the enraged father. But, after considering the chaotic events of last night (including the five-hour stint rotting in DHS-EX custody and the *incredibly* invasive E-roid intake exam), Cameron realized that even so much as lifting a finger in retaliation now would be tantamount to signing his own death warrant.

So he didn't.

"Mr. Andrews," Cameron began calmly, but he soon realized that no one was paying attention to him.

"Douglas, not the place and *really* not the time!" Debbie said with unmistakable urgency as she tapped the small ornate watch strapped to one wrist.

Douglas was not to be deterred. "No, Deborah! I've been telling you for years that they're too *close*—"

Several bleachers away, a few parents started to take more interest in the blossoming marital squabble than in the adolescent athletics on the field. At the same time, Barton looked up from his seat and thought he saw a dark blue wave of energy rise up Cameron's neck, spiking his hair a little bit.

Cameron finally snapped. "Hey, hey! You know what? *Forget it.* I'm *not* sorry."

"What?" Douglas asked incredulously.

"What?" Debbie asked confusedly.

Cameron took a calming breath. "I mean, yes, *of course* I'm sorry if I hurt her, she means the world to me! But I'm *not* sorry that we shared that moment. I just wish that I could remember it! And before you ask *how come you can't?* it's because someone else who *doesn't* care about your little girl humiliated her on the internet. Humiliated us *both.*"

Before Douglas could object, Cameron added: "So, to answer your original question . . . I'm here to support my best friend."

There was a long, awkward pause that was eventually broken by the eight-year-old's innocently profound query: "Is Cameron a bad guy now?"

Both adults and the teen answered simultaneously:

"No!" said Debbie.

"Yes!" said Douglas.

"Kinda," said Cameron.

Barton opened his mouth to ask for the right answer but was preempted by the sudden beeping of his mother's watch alarm. A split second later, his father's watch joined the chorus.

Debbie rose and grabbed her husband's arm. "Honey, your sugar. We're *done* here," she said with inarguable finality. "Barton, stay here with Cameron, we're going to the car for a quick snack." With that, she guided Douglas forcefully down the bleachers and out of the stadium to the rear parking lot. Cameron noted that the expression on Douglas' face did not change.

"But he's kinda a bad guy!" Barton called out.

The last thing everyone in the entire stadium heard was the echoing screech of his mother from beneath the bleachers.

"No he's not!"

Cameron took a seat next to Barton and looked out at the track, where several boys were currently on the last leg of some relay. Down on the field, clusters of boys and girls from Pulse and the seven other tricounty-area high schools were engaged in a variety of warmups, cooldowns, and other activities that Cameron couldn't identify.

He mentally shuffled through a few talking points, took note of Barton's red *Mighty Morphin'* hoodie, and settled on something benign:

"So, what's going on with you, T-Rex? How long until school's out?"

Barton's head was buried in his server. "Nothing much. Two weeks," he said plainly.

"Nice," Cameron said with a nod. "I'm sure you're gonna miss the other Rangers . . . Summer can feel like it lasts forever." He suddenly remembered the incident that occurred at Lake Kilmer a while back.

"Hey, how's the little girl who fell off the swing? Kimberly, right? Is she back in class?" he asked.

The third grader answered with a casualness that would make any crisis negotiator proud. "Her name's *Ashley* and her parents won't let her come back. Not yet. Mrs. Vivaldi says it's because they're afraid Ashley will hurt us."

"Oh," Cameron said. Now the full memory was fleshing out, and the teen realized that good ol' Mrs. Vivaldi, easily his favorite elementary school teacher, had been feeding her current batch of students a false positive narrative.

Cameron recalled a recent article in the *Nascent* about Ashley Whatever-Her-Last-Name-Was. It reported that Ashley's mother had filed a lawsuit against the Kilmer Unified School District for discrimination following her daughter's involuntary expulsion. There was some controversy because the allegation hinged on Ashley's Enhanthroid abilities being classified as *disabilities;* which, if determined to be true, would guarantee Kilmer Unified's liability under the terms of the Americans with Disabilities Act. (It would also guarantee the handsome seven-figure award.) Another complication was the fact that Title Whatever of the ADA had not yet been amended to specify *if* and *which types* of E-roid 'side effects' were considered to be *legal impairments.* Plus, there was the potential civil uproar from the burgeoning E-roid community to consider, and . . .

Laws aren't subjective, but the people who interpret them *are*. Cameron mused that poor little Ashley would be well into her teens before this case was resolved.

"We went on a field trip to visit her in the hospital last week," Barton continued. "The doctors kept coming in to take her blood and look at her hands. We all signed a Get Well card. I brought her a box of Whoppers. A *big* box of Whoppers, since it looks like she's gonna be there a while."

"That was nice," Cameron said.

"Yeah." Barton finally looked up at Cameron, his eyes full of intrigue. Without reservation, he asked The Question:

"Are you a superhero?"

With an equal lack of reservation, Cameron gave him The Answer:

"Maybe."

Then he held out both hands, palms facing upward, and Barton could hear and see another soft crackle of energy radiate through Cameron's fingertips. Again, his black hair uncoiled and stiffened. Barton's eyes widened.

Cameron felt the sudden impulse to have some fun with his Almost Baby Brother—and, at the same time, scare the daylights out of him.

He closed his hands into fists while keeping the energy flowing, leaned in close, and whispered menacingly:

"*You gonna* tell *on me?*"

He could practically taste the terror as it wafted over his victim, which made the eight-year-old's simple "Nah" all the more anticlimactic.

Cameron frowned, doubled down and hissed:

"You're not afraid I'll hurt you?!"

Barton's face went wry, a word Cameron was sure the boy wouldn't learn for at least another five years.

"Not a chance, your powers *suck*," he said dismissively before shifting his attention back to his server.

Cameron recoiled as if he'd been slapped. The energy in his hands vanished and his hair returned to its normal state as if in retreat.

"Hey! No fair, I just got 'em!" he said weakly, but the entreaty fell on deaf ears as the next girls' running event was announced.

*   *   *   *   *

"On your mark!"

Taylor secured her goggles to her face and placed both feet against the starting blocks, resting her right thigh perpendicular to the brick-red polyurethane surface of the track. As practiced, she took special care to keep her head and neck relaxed as she leaned forward, positioned her shoulders slightly above her hands, and formed a bridge by spreading her fingers apart. She was aware of the seven other girls flanking her on both sides. She knew they were going through an identical set of motions, but, as of this moment, they didn't matter to Taylor. Nothing mattered outside of the forty-two-inch wide lane that comprised her entire universe.

"Set!"

She raised her hips slowly, keeping her shoulders in place while locking her right leg at a ninety-six-degree angle to ensure the maximum amount and most efficient expenditure of energy.

CRA—

The Other Her registered the starter's gunfire a split second before Taylor and took off.

—CK!

Taylor exploded forward. The twin golden French braids whipped out and behind her head like serpents on amphetamines. Her arms sliced neatly through the chilly late morning air as her legs pumped like twin ivory pistons. Not a single external sound reached her ears—neither the cheering crowd of spectators nor the rattle of footsteps on the track. The rhythmic pumping of her heart formed an internal metronome that centered her thoughts and kept her firmly in pursuit of her ethereal opponent.

This was good. This might even be *great.* As Taylor came out of the turn and settled into a steady pace on the straightaway, she allowed a small part of her consciousness to reflect on her current output. She concluded that, barring any sudden catastrophes, she was sure to complete this two hundred metre dash in twenty-six seconds, maybe even twenty-*five.* She certainly wouldn't medal, but it would still constitute another new personal best.

Directly ahead, the light blue visage of the Other Her glanced behind and sneered at Taylor with silent contempt. This time, Taylor ignored her, focusing instead on the muted yellow numbers of the finish line that were fast approaching. Then she summoned that inexplicable last burst of speed . . .

This was good. This might even be *great.* As Taylor came out of the turn and settled into a steady pace on the straightaway, she allowed a small part of her consciousness to reflect on her current output. She concluded that, barring any sudden catastrophes, she was sure to complete this two hundred metre dash in twenty-six seconds, maybe even twenty-*five*. She certainly wouldn't medal, but it would still constitute another new personal best.

Directly ahead, the light blue visage of the Other Her glanced behind and sneered at Taylor with silent contempt. This time, Taylor ignored her, focusing instead on the muted yellow numbers of the finish line that were fast approaching. Then she summoned that inexplicable last burst of speed . . .

This was good. This might even be *great*. As Taylor came out of the turn and settled into a steady pace on the straightaway, she allowed a small part of her consciousness to reflect on her current output. She concluded that, barring any sudden catastrophes, she was sure to complete this two hundred metre dash in twenty-six seconds, maybe even twenty-*five*. She certainly wouldn't medal, but it would still constitute another new personal best.

Directly ahead, the light blue visage of the Other Her glanced behind and sneered at Taylor with silent contempt. This time, Taylor ignored her, focusing instead on the muted yellow numbers of the finish line that were fast approaching. Then she summoned that inexplicable last burst of speed—

Wait. Something's not right.

Taylor stole a glance to both sides and was surprised to see that the other track lanes were utterly void of her competitors. Beyond the track, up in the stands, several people were only partially up and out of their seats, frozen in mid-cheer. Their frenzied expressions and gaping maws were an equally comical and frightening sight to behold. One of those maws, she noted with slight relief, belonged to Cameron.

Further to her left, back on the field, Taylor could perceive the image of a boy from Guajome Tech suspended in mid-leap over the high jump bar, moving through the air as slowly as if he were floating in a sea of custard. Through the polarized lenses of her goggles, Taylor could somehow make out the individual drops of sweat flying away from his face.

Taylor fought the urge to panic. What was happening? Why was everything around her happening so *slowly?*

The Other Her crossed the finish line. Less than an instant later, so did Taylor.

A piercing alarm went off in Taylor's brain. With horror, she finally registered that it wasn't that everything around her was moving *slowly.* The Other Her—and, by extension, Taylor—was moving *fast.* Incredibly fast. Some faint, unidentifiable sense told her that they'd already crossed the finish line once, twice . . . *forty-six times?!* and were still running.

The Other Her crossed the finish line. Less than an instant later, so did Taylor.

It was now evident to Taylor that she was deep in the throes of an Enhanthoid manifestation, one apparently tied to her affinity for running. The realization was mildly soothing, albeit academically.

The Other Her crossed the finish line. Less than an instant later, so did Taylor.

But now her anxiety was rising, which would only trigger the inevitable sequence of wheezing, moderate to severe coughing, and, finally, total constriction of her pulmonary airways. She knew the symptoms better than the geometric genus.

The Other Her crossed the finish line. Less than an instant later, so did Taylor.

Ohmigodohmigodohmigodohmigodohmigod, Taylor thought with a sudden, dreadful irony.

I'm an asthmatic with superspeed.

Back in real time, everyone on the field and in the bleachers felt a sudden, intense gust of air blow past them. Then another. Then forty-four more blasts of air, each of them occurring in such rapid succession that it felt as if twin industrial wind machines had been stolen from a movie set and placed directly on the field.

Spectators were slammed down onto their butts. The runners, together with their field teammates, coaches, trainers, the judges, the water stations, the speakers, the audio/video tents, and even the digital scoreboard were all knocked over, smashed into each other, and utterly blown away. Later, much later, the people who weren't completely blinded by the flying dust and debris would only kinda recall catching a glimpse of a baby blue blur. A baby blue blur shaped vaguely like a *person.*

The Other Her crossed the finish line. Less than an instant later, so did Taylor, but this time she attempted to stop running. Unfortunately, stopping was *not* an option for the Other Her, and Taylor felt herself being pulled against her will around the track over and over and over and—

Against my will? She only exists because I let her!

Taylor's brow furrowed with cold determination.

That ends now.

Except it *didn't* end now. In fact, the Other Her dragged Taylor across the finish line another thirteen times before the teen could clearly form the words *SLOW DOWN, STOP,* and *GO*

AWAY in her head. None of her mental commands were obeyed, but Taylor did detect a minute shift in her doppelganger's forward momentum. Almost like the entity was considering the notion.

Utilizing an area of her brain she didn't know she possessed until this exact instant, Taylor mentally repeated those five imperative words while simultaneously searching for an external solution to her situation. Her options were few and almost certainly life-threatening.

The Laws of Physics are predominantly and overwhelmingly immutable. Throughout history, those legions of individuals who accidentally break or are ignorant enough to flout said Laws always end up broken themselves.

Taylor was keenly aware that, given her current rate of speed, any sudden contact with any hard surface would result in the forces of Momentum, Inertia, and Impact all conspiring to *end her,* no doubt in a most painful manner.

The Other Her crossed the finish line. Less than an instant later, so did Taylor.

The lightbulb finally came on in her head.

Sand is soft! she reasoned.

And right now there were two hundred eighty-eight cubic feet (roughly 2,154.39 gallons) of sand in the long jump pit on the field, minus whatever amount had been displaced throughout the morning's activities or during this most recent maelstrom. The sandpit was the natural choice.

SLOW DOWN, Taylor screamed internally. *Slow down. Take a left. Sandpit.*

The Other Her crossed the finish line. Less than an instant later, so did Taylor.

Her antagonistic apparition snarled in protest but finally acquiesced, and Taylor Andrews enjoyed a microsecond of relief.

Then she fought The Laws . . . and The Laws won.

At the moment Taylor's sneakered feet came into contact with the bed of tawny washed river silica, the surface of the pit was superheated into a river of molten glass and then flash-froze more solidly than an Arctic lake. A lake that was sleeker than a freshly waxed bowling lane.

The Other Her vanished an instant before Taylor slipped, lurched forward, and cracked her face on the glistening raven surface of the former sandpit. Her unconscious body hurtled onto the field like a runaway buzzsaw for another forty feet before coming to a stop with a final, devastating explosion of grass and earth.

*   *   *   *   *

The roar of the wind was abruptly cut off by a sonorous sonic *BOOM* that echoed across the track and field, knocking down the few remaining upright spectators in the stands.

Silence.

Cameron rose slowly and cautiously to his feet, blinking profusely. Instinctively, he gave himself a quick pat down and was pleased to learn that he was still in one piece. Then he took a cursory survey of his surroundings: the track was completely empty, with the runners and everyone on the sidelines reduced to a sprawl of writhing bodies intermingled with the remnants of athletic and A/V equipment scattered on the field. Nobody looked happy . . . but nobody looked *dead*, either. Whatever that freak occurrence of nature was, it had lasted only a few seconds.

Cameron closed his eyes and breathed a sigh of relie—

Bedlam erupted in the stadium. A swarm of humanity bolted for the exits, their collective shrieks and footsteps sending impact tremors across the bleachers more powerful than a Serengeti stampede. They were soon joined by the occupants of the field. Every man, woman, and child knew exactly what a terrorist bombing looked/sounded like and wanted to be Nowhere Near the scene of a potential second attack. Or, even worse, another E-roid outbreak.

Cameron grabbed Barton and shoved him through the widely spaced horizontal bars of the bleacher guardrail before hopping over the gate and shielding the boy with his own body to prevent them both from being trampled. Thankfully, Barton complied with minimal resistance.

As the masses teemed and fled, Cameron's attention gradually turned to the center of the field, where a giant mound of dirt was piled up at one end of what looked like a meteorite impact trail. In the center of the mound was an inert, porcelain-tinted body wearing the familiar colors of the Pulse High track team uniform. An inert body with *blonde hair pulled into a double French braid . . .*

"Tay!" Cameron screamed, but his voice was drowned out by the chaos.

He knelt back down to face Barton, careful to obscure the boy's view of his motionless and, in all likelihood, severely injured sister.

"T-Rex!" Cameron exclaimed. "Listen to every word I say to you. *Carefully*. Call 9-1-1 and tell them that there was an explosion at the Benson Prep track meet. Tell them that someone got hurt and we need an ambulance but that it has to come *on the field.* Not in the parking lot, Barton. On. The. Field. *Understand?!"*

Barton nodded furiously, recalling the similar instructions he'd received from Mrs. Vivaldi when Ashley had her accident. Right now, Cameron looked and sounded the same way his teacher did.

"Great. Stay here, I'll be right back." Cameron gave Barton a quick, reassuring pat on the shoulder and ran off toward the middle of the field.

Douglas and Debbie Andrews were standing beside the open trunk of their weekend SUV in the Benson parking lot when they heard the sudden gust of wind and accompanying explosion. Both adults locked eyes, the same thought in both their heads. Douglas tossed the last fragment of his peanut butter and banana sandwich back in the cooler and slammed the trunk door shut, even as his wife was already running back into the stadium.

At the entrance, they were met by a sea of fleeing people. Some were yelling, others were screaming, but all of them shared the same expression of complete and utter *panic.* In the midst of the cacophony, Debbie was able to decipher the dreaded words *E-roid* and *attack,* and that was enough to make her redouble her efforts to reach her babies.

Cameron powered his way onto the field and past the debris, eventually reaching the crumpled figure of Taylor. She was lying motionless in a shallow crater. For a brief moment, Cameron marveled at how no one at all had bothered to render her aid. But then he chalked it up to the basal self-preservation instinct in all humans and decided to set aside his irritation to focus on his best friend.

Taylor looked horrible. Nearly two-thirds of her exposed skin resembled a deranged abstract artist's canvas of grass stains, dirt smudges, fresh bruises, and—Cameron let out an involuntary gasp—dried *blood.*

"Tay? Tay! *Tay,*" Cameron shrieked hysterically. He placed one ear on the center of her chest, expecting to hear or feel the accelerated heartbeat that was characteristic of one of Taylor's asthma attacks (*tacky car,* tachy-*something,* he couldn't remember the term right now). Instead, he was dismayed to observe the exact opposite—the absence of *any* discernible heartbeat.

Cameron grabbed one limp wrist and felt for a pulse: nothing. He put his head back to her chest and listened again, more intently. This time he was able to make out a faint, irregular flutter.

She was alive. *Alive!*

"Yes!" Cameron exclaimed to the universe.

Then dread settled deep in the pit of his stomach. Cameron had absolutely zero training to properly assess Taylor's condition and even fewer resources on hand to treat her injuries. The only medical insight he'd picked up from a steady diet of television and movies was that it was dangerous to move Taylor's body on the chance that she'd sustained a neck or back injury. Not to mention any internal damage.

But the heart thing . . . Maybe he could do something about *that . . .*

Cameron was not a trauma nurse like Zack Haynes' sister Jasmine, but even *he* knew that the second basic function of an automated external defibrillator, commonly called an AED, was to shock an erratic heart back into a proper rhythm.

Cameron didn't have an AED. But he *was* an AED.

Debbie Andrews found her son standing safely on the other side of the bleachers just in time to hear him say "—on the *field*, okay? Thank you!" Before the boy could close his server, Debbie grabbed him by the shoulders and unleashed a barrage of barely intelligible questions:

"Barton! What was that? Who was that? Where's your sister? Where's Cameron? Why'd he leave you?"

Douglas was at their side a moment later. Without hesitation, he knelt down and clutched his son to his bosom in a warm bear hug.

The perpetual litigator flame in Debbie's eyes cooled a few degrees. Her maternal pilot light intensified, and she joined her husband in the embrace.

Barton endured the ordeal as long as he could before finally squirming out of his father's arms. "Okay, come on, enough! He's on the *field*, they're on the *field*. I think he's helping Taylor."

Taylor!

Douglas bolted to his feet and ran onto the nearly vacant field, leaving Debbie with their son, who tried his best to calm the crazy situation and his crazier mother.

"Mom! It's *okay*, it's okay, I called 9-1-1 and they're on the—"

His words were interrupted by the piercing wail of multiple rapidly approaching sirens. Then there was a sickening metallic

CRUNCH and four emergency vehicles—three DHS-EX cruisers and a Kilmer County EMS ambulance—poured onto the field.

"See? They're already here," Barton said, crossing his arms in triumph.

Cameron placed his left hand on Taylor's chest, just beneath her right collarbone. He followed suit with his right hand but remembered at the last moment to drop it down to the lower left chest, which resulted in a brief brush across one modest breast.

Ignoring a brief flush of embarrassment and the approaching noise of what sounded like a thousand clarions, Cameron forced himself to concentrate. He had no time to question whether his next move would revive Taylor or kill her. If she died, Cameron would willingly spend the rest of his life in remorseful torment. But he would just as soon end his own life before sitting back and doing *nothing*.

A faint burst of energy pulsed from his fingertips. Taylor's body jerked.

Cameron placed his ear back to her chest, hoping desperately to hear or feel a new, normal heartbeat.

No change.

He was about to administer a second shock when two powerful arms enveloped him in an iron grip from behind and yanked him away from Taylor. The next thing Cameron knew, Douglas Andrews was shouting at him just as three federal cop cruisers and an ambulance pulled up.

The paramedics rushed onto the scene first, carrying jump bags and trailing a gurney. A heartbeat later, Douglas and Cameron were surrounded by DHS-EX agents armed with guns aimed at their heads. The agents shouted orders for them to show their wrists.

Amidst his screams of "Let me go let me *go, that's my daughter!*" Douglas was puzzled at such an oddly specific order. Still, he raised his hands and slid back the long sleeves of his windbreaker to reveal a simple digital timepiece with a faded brown leather strap around his right wrist. The guns trained on him lowered a fraction . . . to the center of his chest.

When Cameron lifted the sleeves of his own designer jacket, Douglas was surprised to see a thin, narrow, fluorescent yellow band strapped just below the teen's left wrist joint. Before Douglas could inquire, the band's significance was made all too clear with the agents' next words:

"On your *face,* E-roid! *Now* or you know what's coming!"

E-roid? thought Douglas.

Cameron lay flat on his stomach, his arms and hands still splayed out. One of the agents immediately knelt, grabbed his banded wrist, and placed an armored knee into the small of his back. Cameron squirmed in pain as the agent took a small device from one belt pouch and scanned his bracelet.

E-roid! thought Douglas.

One of the first responders was waving a similar device over Taylor's arms and legs. After a couple of seconds, she announced:

"Her ion count's over eight seventy-five and climbing; this girl's clearly manifested. Put out a call to get Gosland or one of her people to meet us in the ER and be sure to have a band ready!"

The other paramedics finished applying a cervical collar to Taylor's neck and rolled her gently onto a spinal board before strapping her securely to the gurney.

Douglas went rabid. "You're one of them! E-roid! You! The hell did you *do* to her?!" he shouted. The agents quickly placed the man's flailing hands in a pair of cuffs.

"Get away, get him *away* from her!" Douglas kept screaming.

Meanwhile, the agent detaining Cameron double-checked the reading on the small device in his hand and held it up to his partner for confirmation, who nodded and lowered her weapon.

"All right, he's stable. Let him go," she said. "Stay put until we're done, kid."

The first agent rose up off the teen, who immediately scrambled backward and away from his captors and the thrashing Mr. Andrews.

"No! *No!* Don't let him go!" Douglas hollered over and over, but no one listened.

One of the agents tapped a switch on his lapel radio and the noise of the sirens ceased, mercifully, only to be replaced with the sound of a different klaxon: a female voice ringing out in panic and protest.

Douglas and Cameron whipped their heads around to see Debbie rushing the field with Barton in tow a few steps behind her.

"No! *Don't!* Let him go!" she hollered over and over. Then she saw Taylor's body being lifted into the ambulance and ran toward it, but she was quickly intercepted and restrained by two agents.

Debbie went rabid. "That's my daughter, you have to let me *go* with her, she's my *baby*, my Taylor—*Taylor!*"

But the doors were already shut and the ambulance was pulling away from the stadium with its lights and sirens flashing again in the midday sun.

"Ma'am, we know, we *know*, we're gonna take you right to her," the agent said. "Calm d—*calm down*. Okay, *come on*, come with us."

The agents "escorted" Douglas and Debbie into the back of one cruiser and removed their handcuffs. Barton hopped excitedly into the back of another cruiser and was buckled in nice and snug. One of the agents in charge of the Andrews parents slammed the door shut on them and took a deep breath, savoring the few blessed moments of silence before he climbed into the driver's seat and zoomed off.

Cameron jumped to his feet. "Wait, wait! You gotta take me too, take me with you, please!" He started to run after the two remaining agents but was shoved back on his ass by a stern hand and an even sterner face.

"No way, Gordon. You didn't do anything wrong this time, don't press your luck. Go finish getting checked out, okay." It was not a request.

Cameron persisted, but the agent shoved a sausage-sized index finger directly in his face, which was somehow more terrifying than the gun.

"Trust me, kid. *Stay. Down.*" With that, the agent joined his partner in the cruiser and then they were gone.

Silence.

Cameron gazed, depleted and dazed, at the utter carnage of the track meet strewn about the empty field around him. His eyes finally settled on the highlighter yellow shackle on his left wrist: the permanent symbol of the end of his old life, the beginning of something new and horrifying.

Not just his life. Now Taylor's.

A seething rage born of helpless frustration finally boiled over, and Cameron let out a primal howl, pounding two fully energized fists into the earth beneath him. The nonelectric current sent up a spray of sparks and soil but did nothing to ease the teen's anguish.

Silence.

At length, a car horn sounded behind him, and Cameron turned to see Dr. Gosland's sedan idling in park. He noted the solemn expression on the scientist's face but could sense that she wasn't genuinely upset with him—even though, given his actions earlier this morning, she had every right to be.

Gosland opened the passenger window. "Are you finished?" she asked in a neutral tone.

Cameron opened his mouth but couldn't utter a sound for fear of bursting into tears. All he could do was point behind him at the mound of dirt that had nearly served as Taylor's final resting place. Eventually, he lowered his head and nodded once.

"Good," Gosland said without emotion. "Local police and fire are right behind me for crowd control and cleanup. I'd rather not have to talk your way out of a second mess in less than twelve hours. So let's get you taken care of, then we'll go to her."

Cameron looked up at Gosland. The absolute *last* thing on his mind was tending to his own welfare, despite the agent's order to do just so. Besides, every second that Gosland spent examining Cameron was one that could be spent by Taylor's side . . .

Gosland's face softened. "I know. We'll *go to her*, Cameron," she repeated, almost pleadingly.

Silence.

"I promise."

It took every remaining ounce of Cameron's physical, mental, and emotional fortitude to stand up and take the eleven steps to Gosland's car.

CHAPTER 2

Ford Solutions General Hospital
Critical Care Unit (CCU)
Kilmer Layer—5:32 pm

MANY HOURS LATER, DR. GOSLAND OPENED THE DOOR to a private waiting room in the CCU, where Douglas and Debbie Andrews were sprawled across several vinyl-coated pews that could barely be classified as *seats*. In one corner of the room, Barton flailed about like a fiddler crab during a mating dance, completely engrossed in the video game on the large flat-panel television mounted on the wall in front of him. Mercifully, the adults were spared the play-by-play audio assault, courtesy of a giant, immersive headset strapped around the eight-year-old's face.

Douglas and Debbie popped up in their seats with fresh anticipation masking the exhaustion plastered on their features, but Gosland held up a hand to preemptively quell the inevitable torrent of questions.

"Please," Gosland began. "It's a lot, so let me get through as much as possible without interruption first, then I'll answer your questions and fill in as many gaps as I can."

Douglas and Debbie looked at each other, then at Gosland, then nodded slowly.

"First things first: Taylor is a fully manifested Level Two Enhanthroid with inverse inertial abilities. The number of EX ions in her PTG has stabilized at nine hundred fifty-three thousand and there's no indication that she's going to manifest again anytime soon. We've given her a mild sedative that should suppress the . . . *being* . . . responsible for awakening her abilities." Gosland paused to acknowledge the pair of glazed and confused looks.

"I didn't understand anything you just said," said Douglas. "I mean, I think I know what all those words mean separately, but *together . . .*"

"Why Level Two? Is that good or bad?" Debbie asked, which was a great question in Gosland's opinion.

"It's not as good as Level One, not nearly as bad as Three," Gosland said simply. She extended a manila file folder labeled *Andrews, T. EX #21595* to Douglas, who opened it and stared at the contents like they were hieroglyphs.

"What's this?" asked Debbie, snatching the folder from her husband.

"Homework," Gosland said. "Read it, sooner before later."

Debbie flipped through several pages of notes and charts while Gosland continued: "Aside from a mild concussion, most of the injuries she sustained on the field were superficial and have completely healed."

Douglas was flabbergasted. "What . . . *How*?"

Without looking up, his wife pointed an index finger to a highlighted phrase on one page and said:

"Accelerated . . . healing? Accelerated healing. I think."

"You *think*? That's physically *impossible*—"

"Mr. Andrews," Gosland cut in sharply. "Mr. Andrews, you have to understand that Enhanthrax forced *traditional physics* out of the conversation long ago and no one knows when or *if* they'll be invited back. I'm not going to stand here and narrate my entire report verbatim to you; suffice it to say that Taylor can now somehow manifest a being who can move at incredible speeds. That being *somehow* pulls her along at the same high speeds while *somehow* protecting her from the normal adverse effects that such speed produces on a human body. Her capacity to control this being depends on the quality of her mental and emotional health—both of which are extremely delicate right now."

Debbie closed the report and set it on the seat beside her. "How can we help her?" she asked.

"You can start by accepting the fact that her condition is permanent and her abilities are irreversible. We forwarded her information to the DHS-EX and installed an EX-ion band on her right wrist."

Both Andrews parents screamed, almost in unison: "You did what?!" The outburst was so loud that it momentarily distracted Barton from his game.

"We did *not* consent to that!" Debbie insisted.

Gosland's face remained neutral, unfazed. "Your consent wasn't necessary. Nor will it ever be anymore. The latest federal EX protocols supersede parental consent for any EX-positive person over the age of six with respect to medical or criminal affairs."

"So you're saying they make this shit up on the fly!" Debbie spat.

"It's more like they're crying 'genetic terrorist' in a crowded trauma ward to justify flouting HIPAA," Gosland sighed. "But until a comprehensive and considerate policy is drafted and adopted, please understand that any information I divulge to you has to be approved in advance by your daughter. And . . . anything I do *to* or *for her* from now on doesn't strictly concern you."

Both parents glared at her with a combination of murderous intent and helpless incredulity.

"I'm sorry," Gosland added sincerely.

Douglas looked at his wife. Then at Gosland. Finally, he relaxed his jaw.

"Can we see her?" he asked.

"Soon. She's finishing up a treatment."

*   *   *   *   *

In the glaring fluorescence of one of the CCU patient rooms, Taylor was seated upright on the edge of her bed. One hand balanced the nebulizer delivery device in her mouth while the other hand, a tightly closed fist, rested on one thigh. A long, narrow tube connected the apparatus to a lunchbox-sized jet nebulizer hub resting on the counter beside her bed. The hub emitted a steady, dull *hum*. With each slow, deep breath, a thinning wisp of excess vapor trailed out of the rear port of the clear coiled tube of Taylor's mouthpiece while faint droplets of the remaining albuterol solution danced balletically within the small, emerald-shaped translucent chamber.

Taylor hated this cold, clinical dance with every fiber of her being. She had hated it every day for as long as she could possibly remember, and some of those memories stretched back to the playpen. The asthmatic nebulizer treatment was worse than the rescue inhaler, worse even than the myriad of arterial blood gas tests she'd been subjected to as a toddler. Back then, after being stabbed repeatedly in the radial artery with a hypodermic syringe as thick as a chopstick . . . at least she was given a sugar-free lollipop afterward.

To Taylor, a treatment signified a total loss in the battle between her awesome mind and pathetic body. Setting aside her new and ironic abilities, no amount of straight-A report cards accumulated throughout a lifetime could ever replace the feeling of abject powerlessness that accompanied the shattering reality that, once again, two of her major organs just . . . weren't that good at their job.

"Come on, a little more."

And, to make things worse . . . okay, *better* . . . Cameron was standing right by her side, had been there from the moment she regained consciousness, and was at this moment cheering her on during the final moments of her humiliation.

Taylor jerked her head to one side in defiance and uttered something in between a toddler's whine and a donkey's bray.

"*Tay* . . ." Cameron intoned, his intense almond eyes locked firmly on her with no indication of leaving.

Reluctantly, Taylor matched his look with one of impending surrender and let out another unholy whine. Then she took one final, Not-Quite-Half-Assed deep breath and held it for a few seconds.

Cameron leaned in to check the solution chamber attached to her mouthpiece for any lingering droplets of the dancing solution, and his face was only inches from Taylor's. The girl involuntarily flushed, and one last bit of vapor sputtered out of the rear port.

Cameron smiled, removed the mouthpiece with one hand, and caressed her cheek with the back of the other.

"There we go," he said softly as he set the apparatus down on the counter next to the nebulizer and switched off the machine. He kept his eyes trained on her as he uttered the same phrase he repeated after every one of Taylor's treatments he'd witnessed over the years:

"Now, you're back to better."

The warmth in Taylor's cheeks spread downward to her chest, briefly dampening the residual increase in her heart rate that was the hallmark of a successful treatment.

"Thank you," she said simply, which meant *Thank you for being with me at my lowest. Again.*

"Always," Cameron replied, which meant *I'm always here for you. Always.*

A long moment passed, during which time both teens silently considered and rejected several potential bits of small talk before accepting that Nothing would suffice, and that was totally okay.

For his part, Cameron was just as exhausted as Taylor and Dr. Gosland. He had the dark circles beneath his eyes, a lump the size of an apricot on the back of his head, and a mild delirium resulting from an acute psychologically traumatic event to prove it. Over the last twenty-four hours, the teen had (1) endured the painful dissolution of his first significant romantic relationship; (2) participated in and lost his first fistfight (wait, did he win? He couldn't quite remember), and; (3) survived an intense DHS-EX exam-turned-interrogation that lasted long into the wee hours of this morning. At the end of it all, the feds and local uniforms drew the same conclusion it took Douglas Andrews less than an instant to reach: Cameron was one of Them.

At three in the morning, Cameron's options for a phone call were limited. Dr. Gosland answered her server on the seventh ring of his second attempt but she was at the station in a jiffy. With a flash of her Gordon Industries corporate ID badge and a swipe of Cameron's emergency credit card, the scientist bailed out her hapless intern on the strict condition that he undergo a complete physical and psychological evaluation to certify his Enhanthroid diagnosis within the next twelve hours. The alternative was incarceration pending his first appearance before a magistrate.

The fact that Cameron was both EX-positive and recently manifested all but guaranteed that such a stay in county lockup would end fatally, so Gosland dropped the teen off at his house just after five a.m. She gave him explicit instructions to be on the front porch at ten-thirty so that she could escort him to Gordon Biogen for a full litany of tests. Cameron grunted his agreement, trudged up the steps, and vanished behind the front door before sinking into the plush cushions of the formal sitting room sofa.

Less than four hours later, the memory of Taylor's first official track meet jolted the teen out of an already light sleep. He quickly showered, dressed, and boarded the Levitt Hoverail up to Kilmer, all while ignoring several calls and furious texts from Gosland.

As for Taylor . . .

"She's pissed that we're stuck here," the girl said.

"Which She?" Cameron asked with both eyebrows raised in confusion. "'Cause right now our moms and the Doc are probably taking turns."

Taylor opened and closed her mouth a few times, unsure how to proceed. She knew that whatever came next, no matter how genuine, would come across as utter nonsense. So she opted to avoid direct eye contact while delivering her next words:

"I never bothered to name her because she was never *real*. Now she is, and she's *me*, but she's *not* because she's pure energy, pure speed, and she can do everything I can't, but I . . . I . . ."

She clenched her jaw and forced herself to lock eyes with Cameron. She *needed* him to understand, even if she didn't fully herself.

"I've still got my asthma," she concluded. "Just not when we run."

Cameron gave a slow, solemn nod. "I get it. For real. I got my own reservoir of energy inside me, just waiting to be released, but I don't know how to do it right. And that's not all. Every single piece of tech in this room—" He pointed to the various medical devices scattered about the room, from Tay's nebulizer to a pulse oximeter on her index finger to the electrocardiogram.

"—is calling out to me, almost begging me. To play with it, to take control of it, and even to . . . *end* it."

There was a faint, wicked glint in Cameron's eye.

"Part of me wants to."

"Start with *that*," Taylor said, indicating the hated nebulizer.

"Nah. It takes a lot outta me, and I'm already running on fumes," Cameron said with a smirk. He suddenly realized the bad pun and winced. "Sorry," he added.

Silence.

Both teens searched in vain for a suitable change of subject.

Silence.

After a while, Cameron said: "Last night, me and Aiden . . . It finally went down."

Taylor was grateful for the diversion. "I know. Dr. Gosland told me. How are you not in a jail cell?"

Cameron responded with an intensity that, for the first time in their lives together, actually *scared* Taylor: "Because *I didn't kill him!* I mean, not *totally*. He's laying somewhere in a coma and I'm out on bail until my detention hearing next Wednesday."

The girl's intellectual curiosity overwhelmed her unease. "We don't have the right to bail," she pointed out.

Cameron held out both hands as if in resignation. "According to the feds, I'm not a juvenile anymore. They don't have to worry about me skipping town, I'm tagged. I'm just another E-roid, right?" He pointed to the highlighter yellow strip around the girl's right wrist.

"Like you."

Taylor examined the ion bracelet in detail for the first time. She was unconscious when it was applied, no doubt by some anonymous EX specialist during triage. It was a simple device, nearly identical to a Synth tech wristband in design, right down to the small light-emitting diode (LED) display. However, in addition to tracking the wearer's routine biodata such as heart rate, sleep patterns, and body mass index, this micro machine also kept a running count of the number of active EX ions in the wearer's PTG.

Taylor briefly mused on the possibilities of hacking the band's firmware. Then she resolved to do exactly that.

Cameron mistook her intense focus for a look of reluctant acceptance, and he held up his own banded wrist in a gesture of solidarity.

"There you go, look at that. We're bracelet buddies!"

Taylor raised an eyebrow. "That's what they'll call us?"

"Not at first," Cameron allowed. "But at some point, they gotta run out of synonyms for *freak*. And even if they don't, there are too many of us to ignore. We're five seconds from becoming a protected class. So from here on out, anyone who gives you crap is gonna get *expelled* or *fired*." A sudden look of cold fury darkened his features.

"Unless I get to them first."

Taylor smiled and shook her head before stating the obvious:

"You won't. Not ever again."

Silence.

Cameron finally smiled and let out a deep breath, searching vigorously for any object to focus on except Taylor as he mustered up his next words:

"So . . . We can't have the Us talk right now, can we?" It was only partially a question.

Taylor shook her head, the smile still brightening her face.

"But we're still *us*," Cameron continued, almost pleadingly. "Just not . . . *Us*."

Taylor nodded slowly in agreement, and nothing more was said about the matter, but neither teen was truly satisfied.

*　　*　　*　　*　　*

Douglas ran one hand through a swath of his honey golden hair, hair that'd long since faded to dishwater blonde in the heat of the day's intensity.

"Let's talk next steps. Are we—"

His words were cut short as the door to the waiting room blasted open. L'Tanya Gordon bounded in, followed a split second later by her father Perry. Both of them looked as riled as the Andrews were emotionally depleted.

"Vivian!" L'Tanya exclaimed.

"L'Tanya," Gosland said, offering the other woman a hug. She preempted the next eruption with the words "I know, I tried to call you last night but you were probably in the air." She extended a hand to Perry but was met with a rare look of irritation that caught her off guard, so at the last moment she joined both hands behind her back and adopted a professional posture.

"*Where's my grandson?*" Perry demanded. "None of the nurses can give me a straight answer, and the only thing the uniformed agents are saying is that 'he was processed, assessed, and added to the registry.' What I want to know is *who* assessed him?"

Posture be damned; Gosland held out both hands in gentle restraint as she said, "He's fine, Perry. *I* assessed him. He's fine, we're done. I'll give you the details later. Right now he's in with Taylor—"

Douglas leaped to his feet. "What? No! How could you let him anywhere near her? Get him *out* of there, now!"

L'Tanya rounded on him. "Hey! *Watch* your mouth, Douglas! That's my *son* you're talking abo—"

"No, that's your little *sex offender* I'm talking about!" Douglas countered with an angry index finger shoved an inch in front of L'Tanya's face. The single mother's eyes blazed with anger and then went suddenly cold, lifeless. Like a great white shark's.

"Douglas!" Debbie shrieked, but her husband's rage would not be quelled.

"No! *No.* We all saw the video, right?" He glanced over from his wife to Perry, then back at L'Tanya. "You saw the video. But you didn't see him on the field today. He broke her heart and gave her the virus two nights ago, but that wasn't *enough* so he had to come back and finish the job—"

"Stop it, Douglas, and sit down, you *know* that's not how it happened!" Debbie insisted.

"No, I *don't* know that! What I know is that he's *one of them*, and he put his hands on her—*again*—and she almost died, and now she . . . she's . . ."

Douglas' voice cracked, and suddenly everything that had transpired over the last forty-eight hours sank in all at once. His vision went blurry, and he dissolved into a puddle of whimpering sobs.

Gosland took the opportunity to speak up. "Please, stop! Everyone, just stop. She's *alive.* And if it weren't for her son she *wouldn't* be. *Yes*, he's 'one of them.' But so is *she.* And that quasi electric shock he administered bought her enough time for my people to stabilize her." Gosland pointed to Barton, oblivious in the corner.

"Without Cameron, right now he'd be an only child."

Silence.

Debbie and Douglas Andrews exchanged a reluctant look of shame before extending it to L'Tanya and Perry. Douglas lowered his eyes remorsefully.

"Sorry," Debbie offered weakly.

"Damn right you are!" L'Tanya returned without hesitation. Then she saw the stern expression on Gosland's face and noticed the subtle softening of her father's features. She remembered the thirteen years of warm friendship that the Gordons had enjoyed with the Andrews family before today. Finally, she considered that, as of this moment, her son and their daughter shared a permanent bond incomprehensibly more unique and stronger than any other in history. The adults might as well get onboard now or risk losing their children forever.

L'Tanya cleared her throat and tried again.

"We're good . . . We'll get there. Together."

*　　　*　　　*　　　*　　　*

Cameron had just slipped the thinly soled hospital moccasin onto Taylor's right foot and was in the process of helping her off of the bed when the door to the patient room slid open. The teens were suddenly joined by Douglas, Debbie, Mom, and Granddad. An instant later, Barton squeezed his tiny frame between the adults to reach his big sister first and gave her his best attempt at a bear hug. Taylor knelt down to receive it and bathed in the little monster's expression of pure, unadulterated love.

Conversely, Cameron saw Douglas charging toward him like a runaway bull again and instinctively backed up a few steps. In doing so, the teen accidentally slammed into Tay's intravenous pole, rattling the hanging bags of saline and supplements.

"Mr. Andrews, *I swear*—" he began before he was silenced by another of the patriarch's engulfing embraces.

"*Shh, shh*, it's okay. I'm sorry, Cameron. *Thank you.* I mean it. I'm so sorry and Thank You. *Thank you* for saving my little girl, Cameron," Douglas blubbered with glassy eyes.

Cameron relaxed his rigid body . . . a fraction . . . and reached his left arm around Douglas, gingerly patting him on the back in a gesture of simultaneous forgiveness and *Please-make-it-stop*-ness.

After another few moments, Douglas relinquished. He was immediately replaced by Cameron's mother and grandfather, both of whom offered similar displays of affection, and suddenly the room was full of incomprehensible parental blather:

"—God you're okay, the report said—"

"—*last* time I fly business class. A five-hour and change flight turned into ELEVEN, stupid layover in Kansas City—"

"—straighten this out in the morning, but you have to answer for this, Cameron—"

"—protection? I promise, sweetie, I'm not *mad* at you for what you did (I'm not even sure *what* you did), I just want to make sure—"

"All right, enough," Gosland said in a weary tone that still commanded attention. Then she rattled off a set of instructions to the teens:

"You both have prescriptions to fill downstairs and followups to schedule. Taylor, you can go home tonight, but I expect you at the lab first thing tomorrow morning. Cameron, you can come by anytime after lunch."

Gosland next turned her attention to the two sets of parents, focusing on the Gordons in particular.

"They're *done* for the semester. I need them here all day every day until further notice. Figure it out with the school."

L'Tanya and Perry nodded silently, then everyone shuffled out of the room.

Barton suddenly called out: "Hey, wait!"

Everyone paused and looked at him eagerly, even though his question was directed to his sister's best friend.

"Is Taylor a bad guy now, too?"

Both teens answered simultaneously:

"No!" said Cameron.

"Yes!" said Taylor.

"Okay," Barton said.

And later, as the lobby elevator doors closed on him and the other grown-ups, Barton contented himself with the real answer.

Kinda.

CHAPTER 3

The Corsican Towers, Milano Suite
Kilmer Layer—9:42 pm

THE MOVIE WAS DREADFUL, BUT NO ONE WAS PAYING attention to it.

With two sets of lips and four hands engaged in a vigorous exploratory expedition of their bodies, Maximus Sylvester and Nova Stevens waged carnal warfare atop the Chesterfield sofa in Nova's darkened living room.

It was certainly a more enjoyable scene than anything in the action-adventure romantic comedy playing on the sixty-five-inch smart television mounted above the fireplace. It was also a scene that'd been playing on a loop for the last several weeks but was steadily racing toward an equally explosive climax.

During the few intervals of post-coital lucidity, Max reflected on the caustic nature of this whirlwind relationship. Nova was self-centered, self-indulgent, and condescending on her *best* day, which was easily mistaken for any other day of the week. On top of all that, she was an unapologetic snob, which Max would have found intolerable were it not for her taut cleavage and advanced linguistic abilities. Twice already he'd invited Nova back to his place to meet his foster parents, and twice she'd laughed off the offer with a short and brusque "I left my cradle at eight months and have no desire to see *yours.*"

Consequently, their nocturnal trysts always took place in Nova's penthouse bedroom. Or in her penthouse private elevator. Or, like now, among the supple cushions of her penthouse *couch.* And, through them all, Max fought hard to deaden any emotional whispers of genuine affection for this girl. Instead, he focused on the seven words that defined their unholy union each time he put his hands up to her waistline and her back into a slow grind: *Let me get mine, you get yours.*

Of course, both teens knew what they'd signed up for, and both of them were savoring every moment. Though they'd never admit it to each other or anyone else, Max and Nova were two classic self-destructive souls who'd stumbled across a funhouse mirror version of "love" in the *wrongest* of places. Their inevitable internal combustion would be a magnificent sight for innocent bystanders to behold; but, for now, Max was content to enjoy as much of his girl's body as he—

A quick, dull *buzz* emanated from the coffee table in front of the Chesterfield. The sound echoed across the glass surface, louder than the trite dialogue spewing from the soundbar beneath the television. It was followed by a second, then a third *buzz.*

Nova's right hand suddenly appeared from somewhere inside Max's jeans. It wandered aimlessly across the tabletop for a few seconds and eventually landed on her server. She lifted it into view and immediately saw that the notification hadn't originated from her device. So she replaced it and grabbed the server next to it, the one that belonged to Max, pressing the side button to illuminate the display.

Whatever cheap third-party texting app Max was using only showed the names of new message senders on his lock screen but omitted the message itself; Nova could only see the three letters that, in recent weeks, she'd come to utterly loathe: *MsV*.

Nova rolled her eyes and muttered an indistinct curse before tapping the back of Max's head with her free hand.

"It's Her."

Without a moment's hesitation, Max lifted his head from where he'd been licking Nova's exposed ucipital mapilary and reached for the server.

"Thanks," he said simply.

Nova pulled the device away, just out of arm's reach. "Now?" she asked with moderate vexation. The idea of bringing that ethereal stranger into her living room perfectly fit the dictionary definition of *mood killer*.

Max's face wrinkled in confusion, then irritation. "Really?"

Nova's expression did not change.

Max's face hardened. "Yeah, *now*," he said firmly. He snatched the server out of Nova's hand and climbed off of her and the sofa, the muscles of his bare chest and arms glistening in the dull television light.

Nova scowled, flared her nostrils, and let out a low groan.

She muted the movie playing in the background and rose to her feet, clad only in a hunter green lace bralette, a matching pair of boyshorts, and Max's short-sleeved casual button-down. On her petite frame, the oversized garment hung exactly three inches below her bikini line, accentuating her thighs.

Nova yawned and took a few moments to stretch out her back. Finally, she grabbed her empty highball glass and walked briskly upstairs to the kitchen for a refill. As she flipped a switch above the bar and bathed the kitchen and surrounding area in blinding LED light, Nova mused sourly that she would have ample time to sip and seethe. Why? Because Max had effectively taken two steps away from her and into another universe for Who Knew how long. Just like he *always* did whenever he got a message from that mysterious bitch.

MsV (apparently pronounced "Miss Vee") was the name of someone who'd been a part of Max's life ever since the loss of his biological parents at age seven. Someone Max had never actually *met*. She wasn't a social worker, or a court-appointed guardian, or a juvenile probation officer, or even a Boys and Girls Club mentor. As far as Nova knew, MsV wasn't even a real *person*, just a series of pen pal exchanges between itself and Max that spanned an array of media over the years.

From the snippets of information Nova had been able to extract from Max, who was insanely guarded about the topic, she learned that their "relationship" began with a small sympathy card sent from an anonymous post office box to the group home where Max was staying during his late mother's overdose investigation. Soon after, the boy received his first handwritten letter, to which his first set of foster parents, the Stewarts, were more than happy to help him respond. More letters were delivered at random intervals commemorating seemingly random events.

They often came with gifts, but never in celebration of birthdays or holidays.

One package, received after Max's eventual graduation from elementary school, contained a simple cord of tightly braided black leather with a magnetic screw clasp. The necklace featured a small brushed nickel dog tag with the same words that ended her letters—*I'll always be around. Sincerely, MsV*—inscribed on one side.

From that moment onward, Max wore that necklace all day, every day of his life. In the shower, in the swimming pool, in Juvenile Hall. Max never removed the treasured piece of jewelry, regardless of the special maintenance it required, inconvenience it created for some people, or physical pain it inflicted on others.

Nova guided her thoughts on a brief detour back to the first time she and Max were intimate, and her fingers unconsciously traveled to the skin of her right cheekbone; where, in the frenzy of the moment, one edge of Max's tag had sliced her open. Only superficially, thank God, but a *physical wound* nonetheless.

Initially, Nova's pleasure mollified the temporary pain. Over time, however, she came to view the since-faded scar as the work of a faceless, psychotic puppetmaster who'd spent too much time and too many resources in an effort to groom an already damaged young man into willingly submitting to a lifetime of psychological torture. And that was unacceptable . . . especially since that was already *Nova's* gig.

Anyway, in recent years, the handwritten letters from MsV gave way to emails and, now, text messages. All of them were delivered from an anonymous source, each one signed with the same cryptic cipher. And, the instant they were received, Max stopped in the middle of whatever and *whoever* he was doing to read and reply to them. To Nova, who had never considered herself the jealous type, it was mostly annoying.

Tonight, however, it was both insulting and maddening. So, this time . . . she decided to even the score.

"What does It want with you this time?" Nova asked with extra scorn as she took a bowl of ice out of the freezer and placed it on the counter next to the bottle of Kentucky rye. She used a pair of tongs to add several cubes to her glass and measured out two shots of whiskey before topping it off with a bottle of Australian craft ginger beer. A wedge of lime completed the cocktail.

Across the room, Nova could see Max completely absorbed in his server; he might not have heard her.

Nova took a generous sip of her drink, careful to let the alcohol dissipate the carbonation a bit before swallowing. She was taking every conceivable measure to preserve her voice for the vocal and dance show this coming weekend.

(Every measure except, of course, for the obvious one of Not Drinking—she was reasonable, not *masochistic*.)

"I bet this guy's been paying off his house with the ad revenue from trolling you all these years," she muttered derisively.

Again, Max didn't look up. But this time, Nova noticed a slight narrowing in the corner of one eye, a clear signal that he had indeed heard the insult and was trying to ignore it.

Nova was in mid-sip when she had a flash of inspiration.

"*Mmn,* ask if They can get me a pair of earrings to match your little collar—"

"Goddammit woman, silence!" Max barked, the words echoing through the penthouse. *"Please!"*

Behind her glass, Nova smiled in satisfaction.

Max finished composing his response and closed his server before turning to face Nova, his expression fierce. He stabbed an index finger at her as he growled the words:

"And I *told* you to watch your mouth about her."

Nova was not the slightest bit afraid of Max, and now it was her turn to erupt.

"About *who?!*" she screamed. "She's a random *voice*—one you've never even heard! She's words on a *screen*, a . . . a weird-ass *font* on a couple love letters!"

Surprisingly, Max's features actually brightened, as if he'd just discovered the answer to the Question of Life.

"Not anymore. She wants to meet."

Nova was momentarily stunned speechless. She hadn't expected to hear *those* words in retaliation. Her brain searched frantically for a suitable retort and finally landed on:

"Well . . . That only took eleven years. Why now?"

Max shrugged his broad shoulders. "I don't know. I don't care. It's happening."

"She say when?" Nova asked, betraying her curiosity.

"Not yet, but it doesn't matter." Max ended the conversation by tossing his server onto the couch before disappearing down the hallway, en route to the bathroom.

Determined to secure the last word and, simultaneously, to remind Max of his priorities, Nova affected a passive tone and said:

"Whatever, as long as it's not this weekend."

She heard Max pause, no doubt thinking.

"You owe me front-row flowers on Saturday?" she added. It wasn't so much a question as it was an expression of surprise at his sudden onset of ignorance. Nova had long since secured Max's ticket to *Shapes and Refractions*—in fact, the two of them had been out earlier that day shopping for Nova's after-party outfit.

Max's voice was indifferent. "We'll see. You know she means more to me than anything."

"Including—?"

"*Especially* you!" The words were punctuated with the firm *shut* of the bathroom door.

Behind her glass, Nova Stevens fumed.

The transition from conception to execution took less than a heartbeat.

Nova knew how sensitive Max was about his privacy. It was another symptom of his self-consciousness as the result of living with extremely limited means. The way he rode that adorable refurbished motorcycle and carried that third-rate mobile device with his head held high was irrefutable proof of his dignity. In fact, Max's struggle to quell his overinflated sense of self-worth was one of his most endearing qualities. To date, Nova never even gave serious thought as to how he could afford to attend Pulse Charter for the last four or five years. There were tons of ghetto scholarships available, probably.

Now, however, she was beginning to wonder if good ol' MsV had been floating Max's tuition the entire time. And paying his server bill. And keeping his rust bucket gassed up. After all, she *did* mean more to him than anything and any*one*, as he'd made painfully clear. Maybe the feeling was mutual. Maybe Max and MsV were meant to be.

And so it happened that Nova found herself back in the living room with Max's server in her hands, typing in his 6-digit passcode. Of *course* it was *6-7-8-6-7-8*, a.k.a *MsV-MsV*.

Then, Nova found herself opening his texting app.

Reading his last conversation with MsV.

Hi Max

Hope it's not too late, but I've been thinking about you a lot lately

I'm ready to meet if you are

From Max, Nova read:

Hey

It's not too late, I got nothing special going on right now

Nova's cheeks flushed crimson with anger. *Nothing special?!* she thought. Then she read the second half of Max's response and snorted at his pathetic attempt to keep it cool:

Sure, whenever

No wonder he was taking so long in the bathroom. He'd probably been fighting the urge to crap his pants with excitement as he carefully composed and then swiped each word.

Without warning, Max's server buzzed again in Nova's hands. In her surprise, she nearly dropped the device onto the table, but she recovered quickly before reading the new message from MsV:

How does this Saturday sound? I'm free after 6:30 pm
I owe you dinner and an explanation

Nova collapsed onto the couch, the wind knocked out of her. The heat in her cheeks rose to her ears.

Saturday. This Saturday.

Her Saturday.

No! Absolutely, unequivocally, emphatically *NO* . . .

Later, Nova would feel a twinge of regret over her next actions. Much later, that regret would turn into *remorse*.

But neither of those emotions was anywhere to be found in the room—nowhere, in fact, on the entire Kilmer Layer—when Nova opened the texting app and composed the following:

Cool

Davatini's on Keaton is pretty good

How about 7:30?

Nine words, three digits, and one suggestion. Together, they added up to one missed encounter. And guaranteed one bouquet of front-row flowers.

Seconds stretched on like hours until MsV finally answered back with:

Okay then! I'll be there
Thank you for your patience, Max
I really look forward to seeing you

The muffled *flush* of a toilet echoed from the bathroom up the hallway, followed almost immediately by the sound of the faucet running.

Hastily, Nova sent one more text to MsV: the thumbs up emoticon, signaling Max's confirmation of the plan. Then she deleted the message from Max's history, along with everything else in between his *Sure, whenever* and MsV's *I really look forward to seeing you.*

Nova closed the app, locked the server, and replaced it in its haphazard location beside her on the couch just as Max walked back into the room. He walked past in silence without giving his server or Nova a glance, making a beeline for the massive fridge in the kitchen. A minute later, he killed the light and returned to the couch with a freshly uncapped red ale in one hand.

Nova leaned up against Max, snaking one arm around his waist. With her other hand, she began gently rubbing the inside of his right thigh.

Max took a long swig before grabbing his server to check his message thread. Then he relocked it and set it face down on the coffee table. Nova couldn't be certain, but she thought she caught a flash of disappointment on the charming bastard's face. But the look vanished as quickly as it appeared.

Nova unmuted the television and put honey into her own voice: "Are we good to go?"

Max finally looked at her as if suddenly remembering that she was in the room with him.

"Yeah," he said simply. "We're good to go."

CHAPTER 4

Davatini Enoteca
Little Italy Neighborhood
Keaton Layer—7:15 pm

SEVERAL DAYS LATER, THE WANING LIGHT OF THE LATE spring sun bathed the streets of Silver City in an almost aurorean glow that prompted drivers to put on their sunglasses and activate the anti-glare feature in their windshields. In short, every motorist on the city's upper three layers was forced to slow down, pay more attention, and generally Drive Better.

Every motorist except two.

The sport bike was electric orange, with custom fiberglass fairings, a modified 600cc engine that could give the douchiest 1000cc owner a run for his money, and a wireless media interface that boasted crystal-clear helmet acoustics.

It was also stolen. And currently being chased by a DHS-EX cruiser.

Andy "Tweak" Tindall knew that he was making the latest in a long line of stupid mistakes. But, at least this time, the reward outweighed the risks. Just a few more miles and he'd *be there*, long before the feds caught up with him, long enough to get It *off*. Jail always sucked and the prospect of detox was even worse, but both outcomes were a slap on the wrist compared to the God-awful bracelet that was currently *stuck* on his wrist.

And he really, *really* hoped that those two lady cops weren't that badly damaged. Not because he was afraid of the additional charges, but because he honestly *hadn't* meant them any harm. They just happened to be in his way at the wrong time. Same with the owner of the bike.

Tweak slowed to a complete stop at the intersection of West Date and India Street. It was pedestrian rush hour on a Saturday night: people flooded the streets of Little Italy in search of their favorite pre-cocktail lounge meals, and Tweak had no stomach for vehicular manslaughter. He brushed a strand of unruly hair out of his face before revving the engine and running the red light, narrowly avoiding a pair of bare legs wearing sensible yet stylish heels crossing the intersection on its way to Davatini Enoteca.

As Tweak zoomed past the restaurant, the woman to whom the legs belonged gave her name to the server, was escorted inside, and reappeared a few seconds later at a table out on the patio. The woman ordered a lavender Italian soda and perused the main menu. She was mentally debating the merits of ordering the newest house cabernet versus her favorite pinot grigio when the unmistakable wail of police sirens suddenly filled the air. The sound moved closer until the woman finally saw the flashing lights of a DHS-EX cruiser as it sped past the restaurant, no doubt in pursuit of that maniac on the motorcycle.

*   *   *   *   *

"—license plate number One Apple X-Ray Two Zero Niner. Suspect is EX #20597—Tindall, Andrew S., a.k.a. 'Tweak.' Level Two Enhanthroid with extreme dissociative identity replication abilities—"

"It's that stupid crackhead who makes copies of himself!" shouted DHS-EX Agent Falacci angrily.

From inside the passenger seat, SCPD Officer Lauren Finney quickly muted the cruiser's comm mic and snapped her head up from the center console, where Tindall's file was displayed beside a GPS map tracking the stolen motorcycle in real time.

"Really?" she hissed.

"Don't *really* me, Barbie. Just keep talking," Falacci spat.

"Then just keep driving!" Finney responded with equal force, momentarily ignoring the chasm that separated them in terms of rank. Falacci didn't seem to notice.

"And he's a *meth*head," Finney clarified before unmuting the mic to resume her relay: "Repeat, suspect is Andrew S. 'Tweak' Tindall. Level Two E-roid with dissociative identity replication abilities. DHS-EX supervisor assistance requested—"

A voice on the other end of the comm interrupted Finney: *"Was that Falacci?"*

Finney saw the federal agent's features lighten a fraction.

"Anderson!" Falacci exclaimed.

But Finney was determined not to screw up her role in the chain of communication. And now she was acutely aware of the pecking order. So she continued, in as professional of a tone as she could muster:

"This is SCPD Finney, sir. I'm with Agent Falacci, who is, ah, *stable* at the moment but will require medical assistance. EMS personnel are tracking our location and will rendezvous with us once we've recaptured the subject and cleared the scene."

There was a pause, then DHS-EX Special Agent George Anderson said: *"Medical? What happened to her?"*

Falacci shot a glare at Finney. Finney opened her mouth, but nothing came out.

It started out so simple. Then everything went . . . insane.

Finney had spent her week shadowing Falacci as part of the blossoming DHS-EX/SCPD Exchange, commonly referred to as "Orca Apprentice" by the feds. The program was designed to familiarize local police officers—the derisively nicknamed *orcas*, referring to their standard black-and-white vehicles—with official DHS-EX enforcement protocols. There was an overwhelming dearth of agents available to investigate the surging number of EX-related incidents, and the Exchange was the first of several proposed efforts to cross-train exceptional SCPD candidates in preparation for future DHS-EX recruitment.

(Of course, given Finney's relatively short yet *colorful* tenure with the department, it was safe to conclude that DHS-EX leadership entertained a liberal view of the term *exceptional*.)

Less than twenty minutes ago, Falacci and Finney responded to a "shoplifting in progress" call at a small hardware store. Upon arrival, they discovered recently released E-roid offender "Tweak" Tindall standing in the middle of the plumbing aisle attempting to unpackage a set of utility snips with—get this—a pair of *pliers*. Tindall bolted and led Finney on a brief and uneventful chase through the store before he was stopped at an emergency exit by Falacci. Specifically, by her outstretched gun arm. A second later, Finney tackled Tindall to the ground.

As Finney secured Tindall in a pair of cuffs, Falacci handed over her EX-ion override, a bioelectric device the size of a roll of fifty-nani coins. The override was an experimental nonlethal compliance tool that temporarily reduced the ion count of an EX offender to a level that inhibited manifestation of any abilities, effectively rendering that person a *Neutral*. As a bonus, the drop was so sudden that it produced a physiological effect on the body similar to the one experienced during a full taser ride.

Finney tapped the ion bracelet on Tindall's right wrist with her override and the felon melted into a puddle of dead weight.

Out in the parking lot, Falacci kept her Glock 22 trained on Tindall as Finney prepared the override to restore enough EX ions to get him ambulatory enough to hop in the back of the cruiser. But she had some trouble balancing Tindall's body with one hand while operating the device with the other, and, ignoring Falacci's firm and repeated warnings, Finney accidentally restored too many ions.

That's when things skipped *bad* and went straight to *insane*.

Suddenly, three additional Tindalls—none of them wearing cuffs—appeared. Before Falacci could react, one of them slammed her head into the cruiser's rear quarter window. The tempered glass shattered and the agent dropped to the pavement. A second

Tindall shoved Finney down to the ground and held her in place while a third quickly rifled through the pouches on her belt, eventually finding the key to the cuffs. The duplicates freed the original Tindall and all four of him took off again on foot . . . but not before Falacci squeezed off two shots.

As Falacci and Finney recovered from the ambush, Tindall and his duplicates snatched a man off his motorcycle at the entrance to the shopping center, stole the bike, and tore off. The owner ran over to the women and gave them a frantic albeit concise description of his Baby, which included the *glorious* tidbit that he'd recently installed a tracking chip in the steering column. Moments later, ignoring Finney's firm and repeated objections, Falacci was behind the wheel of their cruiser in hot pursuit.

And now . . .

"Never mind, Boss. Bad override," was the only explanation Falacci offered Anderson. "Tweak is headed southwest toward the Industrial District, we're a minute and change behind him. I got off a couple shots, think I tagged one of 'em." (She did *not*, in fact, tag one of 'em.) "We've got files on his girl and old crew—Barbie's sending some uniforms to their locations for possible intercept."

"Barbie" rolled her eyes as she tapped the console and sent some uniforms to those locations for possible intercept.

"Industrial District, got it. I'm en route," said Anderson. Another pause, then: *"How bad is bad, Falacci?"*

From the corner of her eye, Finney saw the agent reach behind her head and gingerly pat a section of red hair with one hand. When she lowered it, the palm and several fingertips were still red. And shiny.

"I'm fine," Falacci said stubbornly.

"Fine?!" Finney exclaimed, extracting a napkin from the glove box. "You're driving with a Category Two concussion and need stitches, at least!"

Falacci hastily muted the mic, snatched the napkin from the rookie's hand, and shot her another death glare.

"I know, Barbie! I *know* . . . Let's hope by the end of this you *won't.*"

*   *   *   *   *

Back at Davatini, the woman made up her mind and selected a limited edition sauvignon blanc. After all, tonight was special, and new beginnings were always an excuse for a new wine.

*   *   *   *   *

Falacci took a corner at fifty miles per hour and the cruiser fishtailed, sending Finney's stomach into her throat for an interminable instant. They straightened out and continued south toward the Industrial District, where boutique shops and eateries gave way to wholesale furniture warehouses and dilapidated 24-hour storage facilities.

Anderson's voice came through the comm again. *"What was he after?"*

Finney was still feeling the effects of her own mild cranial trauma, so it took her a little bit to jog the memory loose. She finally responded: "Nothing of value, sir. Just a fifty-nano pair of wire cutters . . . Presumably to remove his ion bracelet," she added as an afterthought.

"*He did* what?"

Finney didn't think her comment warranted such an outburst, but she still acted quickly to clarify it. "No—not *yet*, sir, but he's been trying to for a while. During the arrest, I observed several recently healed cuts in the flesh of his wrist as well as burn and, ah, *bite* marks on the band itself."

Falacci snorted. "Surprised the *meth*head's got any teeth left." Her eyes suddenly widened. "Oh, shit."

"What?" Finney asked.

Anderson apparently shared the sentiment, because his next words carried imminent urgency:

"*Falacci, call off the other units, get everyone over to—*"

"Already on it, Boss. Where you at?"

"*Coming up on Thirtieth and Donnelly.*"

"Okay, you'll get there first."

"Get where first?" Finney asked.

"*Gotcha,*" said Anderson, and he cut the connection.

Finney turned to Falacci. "Get *where* first?" she asked again. She *hated* when senior officers spoke their shorthand language while exchanging critical information.

But Falacci was focused on navigating a complex maze of one-way streets. "You heard him, reroute any available backup to Thirtieth and Donnelly!" she barked.

Finney clenched her jaw and dutifully obeyed. Her fingers flew across the display console as she updated their destination and relayed it to the appropriate recipients.

After a long minute, Finney said: "Done. Now, are you going to tell me *where* our perp is going?"

Without looking at her, Falacci said: "The *bracelet*, Barbie! He's heading for a chop shop, and not for the *bike*."

At that moment, Finney realized that she was also bilingual.

"Oh, sh—"

*   *   *   *   *

Fifteen minutes was late, but not enough to warrant a call.

The woman mentally ran through every probable scenario to justify her anticipated guest's delay—heavy traffic, parking woes, even simple last-minute nerves—as she absently twirled her server between one thumb and forefinger. Ultimately, she opted to wait a bit longer, at least until her focaccia di Recco and honeycomb appetizer arrived. Then, perhaps, she would send a text.

*   *   *   *   *

Tweak shoved an elbow into the grimy window pane with a loud *CRASH* that sent glass shards tinkling to the floor. A second later, the deadbolt unfastened, the handle was turned, and another Tweak swung the door open from inside the nondescript auto body repair shop. Tweak gave his mirrored companion a look of confusion laced with scorn.

"What?" Tweak said to Tweak. "It was cool!"

A third Tweak, the original, frantically pushed his way past both of them into the shop, which had already darkened in the fading sunlight. Outside, the sound of cop cars was getting closer and louder with each passing moment. He didn't have much time.

As Tweak shut and relocked the door, several other Tweaks fanned out across the dim expanse of the shop in search of a suitable light source . . . and any remaining workers. A few *thumps* and muttered curses echoed across the shop, courtesy of the Tweaks who tripped over repair equipment or banged their heads on raised cars.

At last, one Tweak emitted a quick, chirping whistle and flipped a switch, illuminating a long work table set up along the rear wall. The table was littered with auto part diagrams, bits of scrap metal, nuts and bolts, and miscellaneous tools. An industrial bench vise was mounted on one corner.

Tweak gave the hint of a smile. *Perfect.*

Several of the Tweaks vanished as Tweak rushed over to the table and hopped onto the cracked leather seat of a rolling stool. He slid up his right hoodie sleeve and placed his forearm into the cast iron jaws of the vise, taking care to leave his wrist exposed and accessible.

He was soon joined by a Tweak holding a cordless angle grinder outfitted with a cutting disc. This Tweak had somehow located and donned a pair of oversized safety goggles.

"For the sparks," Tweak said.

"Just do it!" Tweak growled as he tightened the vise around his arm.

Tweak fired up the grinder.

*　　*　　*　　*　　*

MsV took the last sip of her second glass of the delectable sauv blanc, dropped a few ten-nani bills onto the table, and sent one final text message to Max. Then she rose from the table and walked briskly out of Davatini Enoteca into the warm embrace of a full moon.

Despite the growing protestations from her swollen feet, she concluded that the night was not a total loss.

There was plenty of work waiting for her back at the lab.

*   *   *   *   *

The diamond-tipped blade sliced neatly through the outer layer of Tweak's ion bracelet as easily as if it were soft candle wax. As Tweak predicted, a shower of incandescent sparks burst into the air as the grinder reached the inner core, a densely packed coil of wires and microcircuitry.

Tweak felt a sudden jolt of pain and let out a groan. A spatter of blood flew into Tweak's face and he realized that he'd cut all the way through the device and accidentally nicked the skin of Tweak's wrist. He lifted the goggles to inspect his work: the band had indeed been separated at the junction of Tweak's, um, *inner arm bone* and the lowest part of his thumb. All that remained was to peel off the bracelet from either side.

But something felt . . . off. Tweak set the grinder down and peered closer at Tweak's wrist. The bright yellow band didn't look or feel as if it'd merely been sealed around Tweak's wrist like the docs back in the precinct medical ward told him. It looked like it was *embedded.*

Tweak pulled on one of the severed flaps and Tweak squirmed in the vise, attempting to stifle another guttural howl. More blood flowed, this time from the fresh wound. And now Tweak's own wrist was beginning to ache, along with the rest of his body. He stopped pulling.

Tweak looked up at Tweak expectantly. "Come *on* already!"

But Tweak was already backing away from the table, shaking his head. "Nope," was all he said.

Tweak looked around desperately for the other Tweak, only to find him writhing on the floor in apparent agony. So Tweak tried desperately to create another replicant, but, for some reason, he couldn't.

He heard the screech of approaching tires and the sound of several car doors opening.

Okay, gotta do it myself.

Summoning every last ounce of his fortitude, Tweak Tindall grabbed one edge of his ion bracelet, took a few ragged breaths, and grit his teeth.

Then he let it rip.

Anderson caught the final notes of an otherworldly scream as he burst through the door to the body shop, gun in hand. He was trailed by Falacci, Finney, and several SCPD uniforms, all of whom shouted the standard commands.

"DHS-EX, freeze!"

"Hands in the air! Tweak! *All* of you!"

Silence.

Anderson advanced cautiously toward the light source at the back of the shop until he reached the work table. "Ah, *crap*," he said grimly, lowering his weapon. Then someone flipped the main light switch and the entire shop was flooded with sterile white fluorescence. Finney gaped in horror.

The body of Tweak Tindall lay slumped in front of the table beside an overturned swivel stool. One wheel was still spinning wildly on its axis, indicating a chaotic upheaval. Tindall's right arm was anchored in a giant vise from the wrist to the elbow; a bloody mass of shredded flesh and ion bracelet dangled loosely from the remains of his wrist. A second Tindall was sprawled motionless on the floor nearby, and a third one wearing safety goggles was heaped at one end of the table. Neither of them had any visible injuries matching those of the original, but both were still incredibly dead.

Falacci frowned, holstered her gun, and gave Finney a quick, sororal slap on the back that sent a tremor of nausea pulsating through the young officer's body. Finney immediately clapped a hand over her mouth, fighting a violent urge to retch. Suddenly, a career in independent broadcast journalism seemed like a more effective use of her sociology degree . . .

The distinct lights and wail of the approaching ambulance outside galvanized Anderson to action. "Falacci, get out there and have them check you out. I've got a call to make, then I'm gone and you're in charge." Ignoring the junior agent's groan of protest, Anderson turned to address the gathering swarm of SCPD uniforms and forensic evidence technicians:

"Listen up, orcas! You can tag and bag one of the copies for the morgue but keep your hands *off* my original, the one in the vise—he goes directly to our lab, you understand? *Nowhere else.* DHS-EX press protocols are in effect, meaning no one with a

SCPD badge breathes a word of this into a mic. I *mean* it, I don't wanna see a shred of this mess online later. You have any questions, Agent Falacci's your AIC."

Anderson paused as a blonde female SCPD uniform flew past him on a direct path to the nearest trash can. The officer stopped short, dropped to one knee, and puked her guts up all over an empty patch of yellowing grass.

"And somebody get Finney a roll of Tums!" Anderson added.

*   *   *   *   *

Twenty minutes later and as many feet away from the action, Anderson pulled out his server and placed an encrypted call to an unlisted number. Without greeting or preamble, he said:

"It happened again . . . Angle grinder, got all the way through it. Damn near ripped the whole thing off . . . Of course he's *dead*. Yeah, on his way. You need to get in *front* of this, now. If we keep racking up bodies before you put out the PSA, I promise you that my people will pull the plug and lead the crusade against you for liability . . . So what? *Figure it out!*" He ended the call abruptly, took a calming breath, and walked back to his personal SUV.

Inside the car, he fastened his seat belt and adjusted the rearview mirror. "All right, the side mission's over," he said. "I'm done working. You tell Mom we're on our way?"

From his spot in the rear passenger seat, twelve-year-old Brandon Anderson, the secondborn of George and Bena's three children, looked up from his own server and nodded.

"Uh-huh."

"She mad?" Anderson asked.

"Uh-huh."

Anderson shrugged with his face. "No problem, I'm just gonna tell her it was all your fault."

Brandon gave him a look of profound disinterest. "Really, Dad?"

"Uh-huh," Anderson smirked. He started the car and reversed out of the parking lot.

They cruised through several intersections in silence before Brandon manufactured enough courage disguised as indifference to ask: "Is Agent Falacci gonna be okay?"

"Not if she can help it," Anderson replied nonchalantly. Then he remembered the boy's *unique* interest in his junior agent and added: "Oh yeah, I forgot. She said 'tell Brandon to hurry up and turn twenty-nine so he can ask me out properly. And make sure he takes his meds before dinner.'"

"Already did, Dad. But nice try," Brandon said with an air of confidence not typically found in adolescents. "FYI, she would've rounded up to *thirty*."

Anderson suppressed a grin. He never played favorites, but Brandon was certainly the most insightful and entertaining of his offspring.

"Probably," Anderson conceded, switching the satellite radio to his favorite country station. The sound of acoustic guitars and anguish filled the car.

At length, Brandon asked: "Those guys you were chasing . . . Did you get him?"

"Yeah," Anderson responded tonelessly. "He's done."

*　　*　　*　　*　　*

Two layers below in a modest neighborhood on Clooney, the Lindsey/Sylvester household pulsated with sounds of decidedly more jovial music and merriment.

Joe Lindsey bobbed his head and hands in perfect tempo with the lovely tones pouring from his even lovelier wife Denise's mouth as she completely botched the karaoke lyrics to her verse of their favorite hip hop duet.

Max Sylvester was lounging on the sofa with a can of cream soda in one hand and an open playlist binder in the other. A rare smile of genuine contentment decorated his features. It wasn't often that he reflected on the positive aspects of his life with the Lindseys. But Joe and Denise Lindsey were Good People, plain and simple. They loved each other to pieces and had worked tirelessly to extend that affection to their foster son every day for as long as he could remember. The least he could do was join them for the occasional musical massacre. In fact, Max couldn't imagine a better way to spend this Saturday night.

Downstairs, nestled comfortably on the charging station in Max's basement bedroom, Max's server buzzed again.

At least, it *would've* buzzed, were it turned on.

CHAPTER 5

Pulse Charter Academy
L. Yvette Gordon Theatre
Keaton Layer—7:15pm

IT WAS EXACTLY FIFTEEN MINUTES TO SHOWTIME, AND the main house would soon be filled to the brim with everybody from parents and peers to the general public and the press.

And Nova Stevens had lost her voice.

She'd performed beautifully on stage in rehearsals all week, beginning with the first initial session in the theater on Monday. The final production design review on Tuesday was fine, followed by the infamous Wednesday double-length AV/lighting tech run. Each evening, Nova had belted out her solo with the same energy first exhibited while recording her backup vocals in the studio. And each evening, Professor Massey stood behind the glass of the engineering booth wearing a Cheshire Cat-sized grin on his face as he watched his golden-tongued wunderkind lay down one sublime delivery after another.

Then came Thursday night, a.k.a. Preview Night, and, once again, everything went off without a hitch. In addition to her time at the center stage microphone, Nova was also a featured player in one of her friends' student dance pieces. It'd taken until Preview Night for her to completely abandon all self-manufactured artifice and fully commit to the operatic physical language of Annine's modern choreography. However, the efforts paid handsomely, and when the curtains rose Friday evening, Nova was absolutely In The Zone. And feeling the applause wash over her at the end of that show was the closest she'd ever come to experiencing a dark chocolate-coated orgasm. Intravenously.

When Nova woke up the next morning, this morning, she couldn't utter a sound.

At first, she chalked it up to exhaustion from overexertion. A long stint in the steam room and a sixteen-ounce ginger tea with plenty of honey and lemon were her go-to nonalcoholic remedies for everything from laryngitis to phantom morning sickness. The combination worked well enough to quell her symptoms for a few hours. Even though the Saturday matinee was nothing special, Nova's performance was nothing to scoff at, either. A solid B-minus effort, in her opinion.

Now it was *Now*, tonight, the second Saturday show. The most important show of the entire production, the one that would actually be *recorded* and *sold* to the public to offset next semester's show expenses. It wasn't the final performance of Pulse Charter's *Shapes and Refractions*—that was the always mediocre Sunday matinee, in which the majority of students on stage were either understudies or severely hungover from the post-Saturday night cast party. The cast party Nova was anticipating more than the applause following her final bow tonight.

But, once again, she'd lost her voice.

A spectral figure with exaggerated lashes and overly rouged cheeks glared drearily at Nova from the opposite side of a vanity mirror in one corner of the girls dressing room. Behind and around her, the chorus of backstage hustle and bustle droned on like a field of discharging power lines. The usually soothing sounds of her fellow castmates' guttural tongue trills and the odd clatter of tap shoes on the linoleum were suddenly painful to her ears. Worse yet, it seemed like the more she tried to distance herself from the noise, the louder it grew. At one point, she even popped in her wireless earpieces to dampen the ambience, only to discover that the devices weren't fully charged. Maybe. At the very least, they weren't working nearly as well as they should've; Nova could still hear everyone and every*thing* in the dressing room . . . and in the hallway . . . and in part of the adjoining green room. Maybe in the entire building.

Fan-effing-tastic. I'm a singer who can hear everything and say nothing.

Nova rolled her eyes and mentally retracted the hyperbole. While not completely trite, it was a bit too *clean* of a punishment. Nova was certain that when the time for her uppance finally came, God or Fate or Randomness would definitely use something more . . . artistic.

This new idea of her current predicament being some form of retribution brought Nova's mind sharply to Max; specifically, to what she'd done to him back on Sunday. Or was it on Tuesday? *Someday* last week.

On that night, Nova had dismissed her actions as necessary, even vital. Max Sylvester started out as a fun conquest—a rare, interesting challenge. Unfortunately, somewhere along the line, Max forgot that he was Hers; and, therefore, needed to be put back in his place. Just like the rest of them. Nova was not in the habit of losing, and certainly not to fictitious mommy figures. At the time, she figured that if MsV *was* real, she'd get over the snub and try to meet up with Max again some other time. Nova also concluded that Max—if he ever found out—would probably be butthurt and skip the show that weekend. But he'd get over it, too.

Tonight, however, Nova couldn't help but wonder whether her super-sensitive hearing and blown out vocal cords were cosmic payback for what was, in her opinion, a minor personal foul. If that was the case, if the universe was truly *that* petty . . . it was a good thing Max wouldn't be here to see her bomb.

One of the theater's stage ninjas reached into the doorway and flashed the overhead lights five times in rhythmic succession, signaling to everyone backstage that ten minutes remained before showtime. The motion would be repeated in five minutes as a final reminder for the performers of the first student piece to take their places on the darkened stage.

Nova closed her eyes and inhaled deeply, savoring the breath before releasing it slowly through her lips. The action cleared her mind of everything except the opening lyrics of her song and the first steps of Annine's dance piece. Then, she deliberately pushed those aside as well, opting, as always, to rely on the weeks of muscle memory she'd developed and the emotional bond to her melody. It was a bond that only fully congealed when she stepped into the spotlight.

"Hey, girlie!" Annine's voice rang out from the doorway. "You ready to bring down the house?"

Nova turned around, her eyes sparkling, lashes curled to perfection, cheeks pink with anticipation. Her face gleamed with exuberance while the rest of her countenance exuded renewed confidence.

"Of course," she said in a golden voice fully restored. "Who else can?"

*   *   *   *   *

Fifteen minutes earlier, as the sun began its slow descent beneath the horizon, L'Tanya Gordon drove up to a five-minute loading zone in front of the theater and deposited Cameron and Taylor out on the curb. The teens ascended the massive staircase and maneuvered through dense clusters of chattering teachers, students, and assorted family members all on their way inside. There was a long line to the box office, but it moved forward at a steady pace.

From the corner of one eye, Cameron glimpsed a small group of students standing near one of the raised concrete landscape beds. He took note of a short figure with a large pile of orange hair that was poorly subdued beneath a thin charcoal-grey beanie.

Cameron's nostrils flared.

"I'll be right back," he said tonelessly before walking off.

Taylor looked in the direction Cameron was headed, saw the object of his focus, and, for a moment, considered stopping him. But she knew that the Other Her was still faster than her own sense of impulse control, and the last thing she wanted was to cause another E-roid panic riot in front of her contemporaries.

Between the lingering gossip about her and Cameron's kinda carnal encounter at the ill-fated party last month and some fresh rumors surrounding the incident at the Benson track meet, Taylor had taken great pains to maintain a low profile at Pulse Charter Academy. Even before her parents pulled her out of classes for the last few weeks of the school year, she'd gone so far as to pull the Asthma Card and quit the track team to dispel any notions that she was connected with that disaster or its aftermath.

Taylor knew that Cameron was also endeavoring, with greater difficulty, to remain incognito among their peers, so there was no reason for her to doubt his ability to exercise discretion. In the end, Taylor had unwavering faith that Cameron would keep his cool. Probably.

"Be nice," she called out after him.

Zack Haynes turned and saw Cameron stalking toward him with a look of second-degree murder in his eyes. Zack went pale.

"Help?" he wondered audibly, but nobody around him paid any attention.

Cameron advanced another few steps.

"Yeah, definitely *help,*" Zack said more forcefully.

Again, no acknowledgement from the surrounding teens.

Zack began repeatedly and frantically tapping the arm of the nearest teen. The force of each tap matched the growing intensity of his voice.

"Help, help, help, HELP!"

Bradley Moore turned around. He saw who was approaching

and threw a lightning left fist that connected with the high part of Cameron's right cheek, sending him crashing to the ground. The sucker punch elicited a few *oohs*, *ahhs*, and *hahahas* from the nearest cluster of kids, but no one was dumb enough to start the playground *"Fight!"* chant with so many adults nearby.

Zack winced in sympathy for his fallen, would-be attacker. "Not *exactly* the salvation I was hoping for," he muttered, "but I'll allow it."

Brad was standing over Cameron with balled fists and a look of justifiable homicide on his face. It was clear to Zack that all traces of their friendship had smoldered to ash.

"We gonna do this right here?" Brad snarled.

Cameron raised his head slowly until his eyes were locked with Brad's. "Depends," he said coolly. "You wanna end up like Aiden?"

At the mention of that name, a wave of thick, oily uneasiness rippled throughout the small crowd. Several bystanders recalled hearing reports of a weird incident involving Cameron and Aiden Marcell at the Kameda Tea Garden a few weeks ago. There was something about a fight, Cameron Gordon's subsequent arrest . . . and Aiden's mysterious *disappearance*.

The bystanders suddenly decided to give Cameron and the other two teens some privacy, and hastily dispersed.

Some of the fury drained from Brad's face, only to be replaced with angry fear. Zack didn't move a muscle.

Cameron sighed, rose to his feet and gently rubbed the side of his face. It was already beginning to swell but didn't really hurt.

"That's not a threat," he began in an even, measured tone. "But I'm *done* apologizing, man. You told me we're through, we're *through.* Zack and I are gonna have a few *words*, but that's it." He pointed to a vacant corner of the outdoor waiting area and added:

"Do yourself and everyone else a favor and spend your last few days here somewhere Over There."

It took a moment for Brad to realize just how deftly he'd been dismissed. When he did, the balance of fear to anger started to tip back toward *anger*, and he was on the verge of saying something stupid when Cameron's darkened expression stopped him cold.

"I'm serious, Brad. You got your freebie, now walk away or the next thing I say *will* be a threat."

Brad unclenched his hands and skulked off, leaving Cameron alone with Zack.

Silence, save for the smattering of nearby voices.

"Soooo," Zack said awkwardly. "You wanna—"

"Really, dude?!" Cameron exploded with just enough restraint to keep from alerting anyone in their immediate vicinity. "'No footage, strictly stills,' my ass!"

"—go first?" Zack finished inanely. "Okay, that's a start. But next time, use words that actually convey your feelings. Start with these: *Thank you.*"

Cameron wrinkled his brow in confusion. He hadn't seen or spoken to Zack since the night of the party, and so he'd forgotten that the bite-sized buttmunch operated on an entirely different plane of thought and speech than the rest of humanity.

"Thank y—? For what?" Cameron asked.

Zack shook his head in disappointment. "So close! Whatever, you're welcome."

"Trust me, Zack, I'm giving you way more rope here than you deserve. Just . . . Tell me *why*, okay? Why me? Why *Tay*? She didn't deserve it."

Zack nodded slowly. "I know she didn't," he agreed solemnly. "Collateral damage. But—trust *me*—you're welcome."

"I'm not gonna thank you, you ruined our lives!"

"No, I *saved* them. Yours, anyway."

Cameron sighed and rubbed the bridge of his nose to stave off the beginnings of a stress headache. His patience was running thin.

"Zack, what are you *not* telling me?"

To his surprise, Zack actually grinned.

"Hey, you're saying the thing you said that night!"

Cameron took a few beats to search for the memory of that exchange and, coming up empty, growled in frustration. He felt a surge of *electroneuralytes* (Dr. Gosland's term for his unique EX ions) course from the crown of his head all the way down to his toes. In anticipation of a discharge, the tips of his hair stiffened.

Zack's already animated features went into overdrive at the display. "Yowza!" he exclaimed loud enough to elicit some glances from random passersby. "Okay, you win, I'll talk!" He reached out to grab ahold of Cameron's arm but stopped mid-gesture, thought better of it, and just motioned for the teen to follow him a short distance away to prevent unwanted eavesdropping.

"For the record, you and Tay belong together," Zack began. He saw irritation creep into Cameron's eyes and quickly switched to the main topic:

"But the *video*. You got off easy. It was supposed to go *waaay* worse for you."

"Meaning?" Cameron asked dubiously.

"*Meaning* Aiden Marcell wanted the cops to shoot you down

like a dog while you were on a PCP rager. And he wanted it broadcast live. Super scandal, the Gordon family legacy flushed down the drain, and—oh, yeah—you *dead*."

That was a lot to absorb, and Cameron took more than a minute to parse the revelation into mentally digestible fragments. He finally responded:

"That nearly happened anyway. Just one night later."

"Except it was Aiden who got dead," Zack said darkly.

"Only *kinda*—never mind." Cameron decided that now wasn't the time or place for a detailed explanation of his manifestation. Or its unintended aftermath. Instead, he just stared at Zack, who tried to avert his gaze, crossing both arms in nervous defense.

Suddenly, the fragment of a memory popped into Cameron's head: *the small teen was wearing some kind of cast on his arm that night.*

Cameron couldn't remember which arm or the exact words Zack used to play off the injury, but now it made perfect sense, especially in light of *another* incident that occurred at the party.

While Cameron was in federal custody, he learned that John Porter—Aiden's primary crony who, incidentally, tried to shove a knife into Cameron's back a while ago—was arrested out on the Andrews' front lawn the previous evening. The arrest occurred right around the time Cam and Tay vanished upstairs, and it was later determined that Porter was in the midst of a full-blown PCP rager. Max Sylvester, the only legal adult on the premises, spoke with the police and narrowly prevented the entire party from being shut down. (Cameron recalled overhearing something about the officers not having enough manpower or cruisers to haul off a bunch of intoxicated but otherwise *nonviolent* adolescents, Porter excluded.)

Now, as Cameron reflected on the incident, he marveled at the fact that, initially, those details somehow bothered Doug and Debbie *less* than finding out that he and their daughter had been kinda intimate . . .

Hold up. If Aiden used Zack to frame me but sent Porter to ensure it all went down, then—

"So, your janky arm was 'encouragement' to help him out," Cameron said.

Zack whipped his head violently upward and shot Cameron a venomous look. "No, assclown, the threat to *green light my sister* was the 'encouragement!' The arm was for taking too long to say *Yes*," he said scornfully.

Cameron felt his own boiling anger reduce to a simmer. He realized that, in his own bass-ackward way, this kid risked his own health and the safety of his only family on Cameron's behalf. At the very least, that earned him a second chance.

"Okay, you dosed Porter," Cameron said a bit more softly. "So why bother messing with me and Tay, why not just force me and Anna to get together? I probably would've thanked you sooner! I mean, that's your thing, right—telepathy?" He flashed Zack the same *knowing* look that he now shared with Taylor.

Zack blinked a few times, his face blank. "What? *No*, I'm not an E-roid!" he said as vehemently as if he were denying that he still played with action figures (which he totally did). Then he saw the sense of insult in Cameron's eyes and quickly added: "Not that there's anything *wrong* with that . . . No, you silly goose. I did you a solid and dosed *you*, too."

"You *what*?" Cameron screamed. A few heads turned in their

direction.

Zack frowned wryly. "Come on, dude. We both heard me." He pointed to a passing stranger and said, "*You* heard me, right?"

Without breaking stride, the stranger ignored both teens and continued on his way.

Zack turned back to Cameron. "No, no mind control. Just good ol' fashioned GHB."

Cameron's jaw dropped.

GHB.

GHB!

His mind instantly flashed back to freshman year Health class, specifically that one incredibly uncomfortable discussion on recreational drug use.

GHB, or gamma-hydroxybutyric acid, was one of the most potent and versatile sedatives on the planet. It was also one of the most popular club and, sadly, *date rape* drugs available on the street. Predators used the colorless, odorless liquid to pacify their victims, relying on the lowered inhibitions and memory loss it induced. On the other hand, party poppers loved mixing the drug with alcohol because of the enhanced euphoria and supposed increased sex drive it produced.

Not 'supposed,' Cameron corrected himself bitterly. *Confirmed.*

At that moment, everything that happened with Taylor at the party—every word they exchanged, every action they took, and everything they did and *didn't* remember—fell horribly into place. A myriad of questions and curses directed toward Zack scrolled in front of Cameron's eyes, but the only thing he managed to get out was: "Where'd you *get* it—no. No. Don't tell me."

Without hesitation, Zack answered: "I made it. The internet is a bottomless font of . . . *bottoms* and *fonts*. And, instructions on how to assemble, construct, or concoct almost anything."

Cameron hung his head in both hands, suddenly exhausted by the weight of this conversation. "I said *don't* tell me," he said almost pleadingly.

"And yet I told you. Obviously telepathy ain't *your* thing," Zack retorted. He pointed to the yellow strip on Cameron's left wrist that was giving off a faint neon glow in the dying sunlight and asked, in his own conspiratorial voice:

"So what *is* your thing? A nappy taser?"

"Never mind," Cameron said as he absently reached a hand up to pat down and reshape his unruly hair. Dr. Gosland said it was a lasting side effect of his *elekinesis*. That was his official diagnosis and E-roid classification—he was an *elekine*.

"Of course it was GHB," Cameron mused aloud. "That's why we can't remember anything from that night."

A look of puzzlement decorated Zack's features. "Weird. I only dosed you, and that stuff's non-transferable once ingested. So . . . Either Tay had something else in her system before you two hooked up or she's lying."

The implications of both those options were too much for Cameron to handle at the moment, so he mentally shelved it and refocused on Zack's betrayal.

"But *Anna*, man! You knew how much she meant to me. And Taylor—"

"Hey! *Hey!* First of all, whatever went down between you and Tay was already somewhere inside both of you. All I did was help to bring it to the surface. Second, like I said, I only slipped it to *you.*"

At that moment, a passing teenage girl paused, looked at Zack and Cam and let out a harsh snicker.

"That's not—Erica, I didn't mean it like that . . ." Zack sighed in defeat before being snapped back to the point by the literal snapping of Cameron's fingers in his face.

"And *Fifth*," Zack continued, "better that you broke Anna's heart than every bone in her body."

Cameron's eyes went wide.

"Uh huh, yeah," Zack said with an exaggerated nod and tone. "It took three cops and a K-9 to bring Porter down. And then he went to jail, and your pet Lurch somehow convinced the cops not to kill the party early, and *you* probably got laid, and none of what I just said matters because Aiden *still* put the hit out on Jas." He pronounced those final words like they were hollow-point bullets targeted at Cameron's heart.

Silence, save for a blaring new tension in the warm night air.

"She got jumped the next night, I'm assuming right before or right after you and Aiden got into it," Zack added.

"Oh my God. I'm so sorry," Cameron offered sincerely.

"Yes, that is the correct response."

"How is she, is there anything I can do?"

"Sure, you can kiss my ass upside your head," Zack spat.

Cameron was about to object to the rejection before realizing that the kid was just venting, which he had a perfect right to do. So, instead of reacting negatively, Cameron swallowed his bruised pride, composed his face, and said evenly: "And after that?"

Zack's features softened a fraction. "Nothing, dude. Jas is recovering just fine. Aiden's boys only roughed her up a little, but now she's totally freaked to go anywhere alone. She's probably gonna quit or ask for a transfer, but in the meantime, neither one of those options guarantee that Aiden or his people will leave her alone, so . . ."

"Aiden can't hurt anyone else," Cameron said firmly. "And I'll ask my folks if they can do something for Jas. The legacy's still intact. For now."

"Thank you," Zack said.

Cameron smiled. "That was *my* dialogue, bro."

Zack was taken aback for a moment. Then he also smiled, but with characteristic condescension.

"Aww, how adorable! Your first callback."

Cameron's brow wrinkled. "No, I threw your phrase about taking pics back at you, didn't I?"

"Touché, douche," Zack retorted. There was a pause, then he asked: "Are we okay, Cameron?"

Cameron let out a deep sigh. "We *will* be, Zack. Just don't use the 'be the bad guy to beat the bad guy' plan anymore."

"What?"

"'You don't have to *be* the enemy to *beat* the enemy.' It's one of Granddad's favorite bits of nonsense that, in this context, actually makes sense." With that, Cameron turned to walk away.

Zack had several whimsical retorts loaded and one in the chamber, but he decided to let Cameron have the last word. This time.

Inside the large wall-length windowed lobby of the theater, Taylor emitted a mental sigh of relief as Cameron located and rejoined her. One glance at his face—in particular, the steadily reddening swell on his right cheek—was enough to tell the blonde genius that things hadn't gone as *nice* as she'd hoped. Then she reasoned that, given Cameron's emotional state and his capacity to inflict devastation on others, things could've gone much worse.

Taylor was handing Cameron his ticket stub when L'Tanya entered the building and gazed around, eventually setting eyes on the teens. When she finally joined them in line, Cameron asked:

"Where'd you park, on Lowery?"

"Don't *start* with me, child," L'Tanya said, accepting the stub from Taylor's outstretched hand. "I couldn't find my spot and had to steal one in the teacher's lot."

"You won't get a citation? Or towed?" Taylor wondered.

"Not until they take my name off the side of this building," L. Yvette Gordon replied confidently.

Just then, the house manager flashed the overhead lights five times in rhythmic succession, signaling to everyone in the lobby that ten minutes remained before showtime. Two Pulse Charter student ushers opened the entry doors on both sides of the main theater and beckoned everyone to come inside to find their seats. L'Tanya and the teens fell into line with the growing crowd.

"How did it go?" Taylor asked Cameron. "You seem . . . *other.*"

Cameron gave her a look she'd never seen before, a look she wasn't quite sure she liked. It was slightly mistrustful, almost . . . accusatory.

"Good. I'm good, we're good," Cameron said quickly, placing a hollow smile on his face. "Let's talk later."

Yep, Taylor thought. That look was definitely accusatory.

And *Nope*, she didn't like it.

CHAPTER 6

526 Grant St
Clooney Layer—7:45 pm

JOE LINDSEY PRESSED A BUTTON MOUNTED BESIDE THE light switch on the wall at the end of the corridor leading to his basement. Exactly thirty seconds later, the button flashed green and the pocket door to the basement door slid open. Joe guided his wheelchair onto the 3 x 3.5-foot plank of aluminum diamond tread-coated plywood and locked his wheels with a quick *snap* of his scissor brakes. Finally, he pressed another button on the basement's interior wall to close the door behind him and activate the thirty-second chair lift that would carry him downstairs and into Max's studio bedroom.

Even though Joe could count the number of times he'd used the lift during the last month on one hand, he never missed the opportunity to reflect proudly on the ingenuity with which it had been constructed. The design only required a suitable platform, a few rollers, and a length of cable attached to a simple electric worm drive. Everything was cleverly concealed in the small utility closet next to the water heater. Joe had drafted the plans himself and supervised the installation, but it was Max who completed the bulk of the work. Not a bad accomplishment, considering that the boy was *twelve* at the time. Joe considered the project as the first inkling of a bonding moment for the two of them.

The lift ended its journey at the base of the staircase and Joe wheeled across the polished concrete floor into a warmly lit area the size of a one point five-car garage. The room only spanned the space beneath the living room and half bath, providing enough space for a few furnishings: a full-size mattress atop of a set of dark stained and sealed wood pallets; a small black office chair and matching desk littered with textbooks and school supplies; a tall, dark wardrobe with an equally tall mirror mounted on one door; and a two-drawer nightstand that'd been hollowed out and converted into an entertainment cabinet. The cabinet now housed a small television, a secondhand multimedia receiver, and an infrequently played video game console. A small bookshelf resting against one wall was home to a set of outdated encyclopedias and the shallow glass dish in which Max kept his wallet, spare change, extra batteries, and keys. The walls were devoid of decoration, emitting a utilitarian aesthetic.

Only three items in the entire space offered a glimpse into the personality of its teenaged occupant. They were (1) a minifridge dotted with vinyl stickers and decals of various boy bands and girl groups from all points throughout the ages; (2) a shoebox with a hinged lid resting on the bookshelf containing mementos of the relatively few bright spots in Max's otherwise dark existence; (3) and, of course, his motorcycle, the hybrid elephant docked in one corner of the room. There was no space in the upstairs garage to contain the vehicle and Max refused to store it outside.

Joe loved the sight of that machine. Every time he laid eyes on it, he reminisced fondly about his own adventures as a young and impetuous man racing through the layers of Silver City on his own bike, with the wind whistling through his afro and Denise's white-knuckled hands clenched tightly around his waist. Before the accident, before the paraplegia. Half a life full of Good times, followed—but never *replaced by*—even more years of Less Than Good times.

Joe mused briefly that he was about to reach a significant milestone. Come his next birthday, he'd have officially been using his chair for longer than he hadn't. Not the life he expected, but certainly not a life regretted.

Anyway, Joe never tired of seeing Max's bike. On the contrary, he was delighted to know that the boy—*No*, Joe corrected himself, the *young man*—had discovered the absolute freedom that could only be experienced on two motorized wheels out on the open road. Apparently, the desire to live vicariously through one's son was not restricted to biological fathers.

"Hey, bud," Joe said as he rolled to a stop beside Max's bed. The teen was lying on his back with his arms outstretched and hands interlocked behind his head, a look of deep contemplation on his characteristically pensive face. To Joe, it seemed like Max was either staring at a particular spot on the ceiling or trying to decipher the smell of a particular color.

"Hey," Max returned. "And, before you ask, *No*. I'm not doing backup vocals for y'all again."

Joe smiled. "Oh, come on, son! It's just the intro, you know it's only one word."

"Yeah, *no*. There's no way I can say *bone* nine times in a row while looking you two in the face," Max said. Joe and Denise always closed an evening of karaoke with their favorite ballad, an ode to fallen loved ones originated by a group of harmonious thugs. It was sentimental to the Lindseys but embarrassing for Max since they always wanted him to kick things off with a word that, in the years following his descent into puberty, had become increasingly more difficult to speak aloud without an eye roll.

"So look at the monitor," Joe said without any real conviction. He knew perfectly well how Max felt, but he was enjoying the repartee.

"Still *no*," Max said with clear finality. He finally sat upright in the bed and turned his head to face Joe. "You taking a break?"

"Nah, we're done. The cooling timer just went off—care for a slice?" Denise was a significantly better baker than she was a singer and had just produced another flawless pumpkin pie.

"Not at the moment, thanks. I'll get some later."

"Can't promise any'll be left . . ." Joe's voice trailed off and Max knew that he *meant* it, because Joe was an insatiable and shameless beast when it came to his wife's desserts.

Before Max could withdraw his refusal, the harsh sound of Joe clearing his throat grabbed his full attention. Not because it was a deliberate attempt to secure the teen's focus; rather, it seemed to Max that Joe was having difficulty trying to express something important. A rare occurrence, indeed—and, therefore, worthy of Max's consideration.

"Thanks again for tonight, bud," Joe began. "Your mother and I really enjoyed it."

"Sure," Max replied.

"It wasn't *too* bad, right? We weren't too bad? We figured you could use a little nonsense," Joe continued with more intensity than usual, almost like he was trying to convince himself more than he was seeking validation from Max.

Max shrugged. "That wasn't 'a little.'"

"*Ouch*," Joe said with feigned pain. "I'm just saying, I *get* it. Of course I get it! Tonight was a bit overwhelming, so maybe next time we do it together. As a family."

Max raised an eyebrow. "We just did." He assumed Joe was referring to the evening's frivolities.

"No, not—not *that*," Joe stammered. He mentally flailed about awkwardly for a few moments in search of the least inflammatory way to phrase his next thought. Finally, he settled on: "Your . . . *meet-and-greet*."

What? Max thought, genuinely confused.

"What?" Max asked, genuinely confused.

Joe held up his hands in preemptive defense. He and Denise knew to tread lightly with Max when it came to this subject.

"You're right, we promised not to press too hard. But I gotta say, we were just as excited for you to finally meet her."

Oh, Max thought. "MsV? No, that hasn't happened yet."

"I know, and, again, we're super happy you chose to hang out with us instead."

Max's confusion returned and rose a few notches. "We're—we must be having two different conversations. MsV told me she *wanted* to meet in person, but we haven't set anything up yet."

Now it was Joe's turn to look confused. "But you did! You two set it up for tonight, and then you backed out last minute, and instead you and me and your mother made several rap and R&B legends roll around in their graves for an hour . . . None of whom are actually *dead*," he added as an afterthought.

"*No*," Max said with enough force to shove Joe out of his fog and trigger his paternal concern.

"Hold on, son. You're telling me you *didn't* set up the meeting with MsV for tonight?"

"I'd know, right?" Max's voice was rising with the tension in the air.

Joe retrieved his server from one pants pocket and opened his own messaging app before turning the screen toward Max.

"Then who sent me this?" he asked.

Max took the device and saw an open text thread between Joe and a familiar Private number. There were only a few exchanges spread out over the last year, but the most recent was a screenshot of a conversation between Private and . . . Max?

Hi Max
Hope it's not too late, but I've been thinking about you a lot lately
I'm ready to meet if you are

Hey
It's not too late, I got nothing special going on right now
Sure, whenever

How does this Saturday sound? I'm free after 6:30pm
I owe you dinner and an explanation

> *Cool*
>
> *Davatini's on Keaton is pretty good*
>
> *How about 7?*

Okay then! I'll be there
Thank you for your patience, Max
I really look forward to seeing you

Max read the words over and over. And *over*. As he did, a dark, overpowering feeling of dread slowly wiped every thought from his mind. The psychological sensation quickly turned physical. What began as a dull heat in his earlobes spread downward to his cheeks and neck, finally resting in the center of his chest. Max's heart began to throb uncontrollably.

MsV hadn't said *anything* about meeting this Saturday night, which was *this Saturday* night, a.k.a. Tonight. What was more, Max would *never* have suggested some random Italian restaurant he'd never been to for such a momentous event.

And yet, there it was. In print. MsV's words and Max's words, and a bunch of . . . *something else* . . . in between.

"Where did you get this?" he asked.

"From MsV," Joe responded immediately. "Or, at least, from the same anonymous number I've had for her the past seven years." He saw Max's dark eyes widen and quickly added: "Oh, no, she never *ever* repeats the private stuff. But this was a big event, and she wanted to keep me in the loop."

"*When* did you get it?" Max demanded.

"Right after you did, several nights ago . . . Sunday. Or was it Tuesday? I'd have to ask your mother. Or you could just check the original date stamp."

Max leapt off the bed and snatched his own server from the desk where it'd been left to charge all evening. He'd also shut it off to clear any background app data to improve the outdated device's performance. He quickly switched it on again, opened his texting app, and reread the actual message in his thread.

"I never had that exchange with MsV," Max said, returning to stand in front of Joe. "She just said she was ready to meet up and was looking forward to it, then—" Max saw that there was a new message from MsV, one sent less than thirty minutes ago:

I understand

Let me know when you're ready

Have a good night

Max handed his server to Joe.

Silence, while both of them processed the magnitude of the situation.

Joe shook his head. "I don't know what to tell you, Max. We can talk about upgrading your server when the next stimulus check gets here, but for now you're gonna have to make do . . ."

But Max was no longer listening. His mind was engaged in a rapid but thorough review of the night he'd received the original message from MsV, down to the smallest detail.

He remembered the taste of Nova's neck and navel, and the reflection of the crappy movie in her eyes as they rolled when she alerted him to MsV's first text. He could hear the bile in her voice as she chided him for the umpteenth time about the improbability of MsV's existence. And he vividly recalled the moment he finally vented his frustration at Nova shortly before tossing his server on the couch and going to take a piss—

Max's train of thought came to a crashing halt.

Nova.

Nova, who insisted that Max postpone his meeting until after her little song and dance show this Saturday night. *Tonight.*

Nova, whom he'd left alone for several minutes.

With his server.

"I gotta go." The words were uttered in a tone that left no room for further discussion. Max turned away from Joe to grab a leather jacket from the wardrobe and lace up his riding sneakers. He moved so quickly that he neglected to grab his gloves.

"Now, son?" Joe asked. He recognized the controlled fury in the teen's voice and knew that there was nothing he could do to stop him from releasing it.

"Yeah." Max slipped on his jacket and helmet and moved to his motorcycle. He lifted the kickstand and walked the vehicle out the rear door of the basement, where a small ramp would lead him off the property and into the night.

"Okay. Be back by curfew," Joe offered feebly.

His only response from Max was the loud *SLAM* of the door, followed immediately by the muffled *vroom* of the hybrid engine.

*   *   *   *   *

Leaning forward in her back row center seat in the darkened theater, L'Tanya Gordon squinted to make out the small text on her playbill. Only one performance remained before the blessed intermission—some vocal solo from that reporter Randall Stevens' kid—and soon afterward, the concession stand in the lobby would flood with hungry parents and exhausted siblings in search of a sugar or caffeine fix. L'Tanya was neither party to anyone in the cast, but she was *quite* eager to avoid that chaotic scene. She considered her options for a moment and then leaned forward to grab her purse from beneath her seat.

"I'm gonna get a jump on the coffee before it goes cold, maybe grab a brownie," she whispered to Cameron, who was sandwiched between her and Taylor.

"I'll take a brownie," Cameron said softly.

L'Tanya snorted. "Then come get it!" She rose from her seat and shuffled past her son.

"Wait! *Wait.*" Cameron grabbed his mother's coat sleeve until she paused and bent down within listening range.

"Get me a brownie and Tay a cookie and we'll meet you out there," Cameron said as he pulled out his wallet and extracted a few hundred-nano bills. "Thank you, love you, bye."

L'Tanya snatched the money from her son and scooched out of the row, disappearing up the aisle and out of the theater.

A moment later, the teens heard a haunting yet effervescent melody ooze out of the surrounding speakers. It was accompanied by an otherworldly chorus of despondent voices and synthesized strings. At last, the rhythm track kicked in, the curtains opened, and an overhead spotlight illuminated a single figure standing on center stage in front of a microphone.

Nova Stevens opened her mouth wide and the angels wept in delight . . . At least, everyone in the audience wept.

Everyone except for Cameron, whose mind was occupied with weightier concerns. The recent revelations from Zack about himself and Tay had been prickling his psyche throughout the entire first act of the show. And, because it was impossible to effectively conceal his emotions, Cameron was certain that Tay could see the suspicion on his face, even though she was doing her best to avoid his piercing gaze. The tension between them was growing unbearable, at least from where Cameron sat. Sure, he told her that they'd talk later, but as the evening progressed, he realized that he had to be sure. *Now* was later.

"He drugged us," Cameron whispered into Taylor's ear. There was no easier way to introduce the subject, and he was not surprised at her surprise.

"Who what?" she asked, her face twisted in disgust.

"Zack. He drugged us at the party. Something about a plot to get me killed by the cops, but he changed his mind last minute and sabotaged it—it's why Porter got arrested. But *that's* why we can't remember anything."

Cameron's face was only inches from Taylor's, just like it was that night. This time, however, she looked into his eyes and saw that tinge of doubt again, felt the heat of his scrutiny.

"Cameron . . . He didn't drug us. Just you," she confessed in a low voice.

Cameron's expression was even more harsh in the contrast of the faint theater lights.

"He said *that*, too."

Tay lowered her eyes in shame.

Silence, which was, ironically, the name of the song Nova was crooning.

"Why didn't you just own it the next morning?" Cameron asked, more hurt than angry at the deception. A sin of omission was still, by definition, a sin. "Did you think you took advantage of me? Or maybe . . . Were you too afraid to admit just how much you enjoyed . . . whatever we did together?"

"A little of both," Tay admitted.

Cameron relented a fraction and his face softened. "Tay, you know we—" he began, before someone in the row ahead turned around and hurled a quick, harsh *"Shh!"* at the teens.

"We're not done with this," Cameron whispered, and the two of them went back to enjoying Nova's performance.

But not really.

*   *   *   *   *

This is the greatest moment of my life, Nova thought as she transitioned seamlessly from the chorus into the next verse of her ambient electronica ballad.

The music was flowing freely through her veins. Her backup vocal tracks blended in perfect harmony with Professor Massey's strobe lighting cues. The lyrics had found their way from Nova's heart to her tongue and, subsequently, into the mic without a hitch. Best of all, she hadn't missed a single vocal step yet. In fact, at this moment, Nova was willing to write off her earlier oral and aural troubles as nothing more serious than a random bout of psychosomatic hiccups. A temporary lapse in self-assurance.

She glanced out at the audience and was pleased to not see her father or Max in the front or, indeed, *any* of the rows. That was totally acceptable, even preferable. Max's perpetually sexy scowl would only mess up the vibe in the theater, and Dad already exhausted Nova's tolerance twice—once on Preview Night and the second on opening night. Tonight was *her* night. And this was her moment.

As the instrumental break came to an end, Nova adjusted her posture, placing both feet shoulder-width apart with her knees and shoulders relaxed. The music swelled and she took a quick, calming breath to prepare for the crescendo to her melody, which included a long, difficult high note *and* a bonus glissando . . .

A translucent wave of concussive energy issued forth from Nova's mouth, sailed out across the auditorium, and slammed into the control booth. There was a deafening explosion and a cocktail of drywall, glass, and miscellaneous electronic shrapnel showered onto the audience below.

The music stopped abruptly and the mic feed was cut. When the house lights automatically switched on, Nova Stevens had disappeared from the stage . . . only to reappear a dozen feet *above* the crowd. She hovered in midair with both arms flailing about, each hand somehow emitting a similar beam of destructive energy that was shredding the acoustic panels lining the walls, then the walls themselves. Chunks of the ceiling and rafters rained down around her like hailstones.

Naturally, the audience reacted to this display with dignified aplomb. Disguised as utter pandemonium.

Inside the control booth, Professor Massey screamed as the mixing console combusted in a flurry of sparks and, soon enough, flames. His scream triggered the inevitable stampede of patrons, but the fire spilled quickly outward from the rows of padded seats to the carpeted aisles, effectively blocking both exits to the lobby.

L'Tanya finished drying her hands and was about to exit the women's restroom when a thunderous jolt to the wall nearest the door knocked her to the floor. A second, then *third* jolt came from above. One of the mirrors mounted above the sink shattered. At first, L'Tanya thought it was an earthquake and she quickly moved to seek refuge beneath the sinks. Then she remembered that such a geological phenomenon was physically impossible on this layer and she regained her footing, mentally ascribing the sensations to the theater's recently upgraded (and incredibly expensive) sound system—yet *another* reason her name stayed above the marquee.

The emergency exit doors burst open and people poured out of the theater in a standard disorganized mob fashion as the smoke and flames continued their journey toward the stage.

Cameron knew that there was little risk of damage to either the stage or the massive hanging curtains. *They* were treated with fire retardant chemicals. The greater and more immediate danger was that of smoke inhalation and escapees trampling one another. So, the instant that everyone else ran for the doors, he grabbed Taylor's arm and yanked her down to the ground, shielding her body with his own. Fortunately, their location in the center of the last row ensured that everyone ran *away* from them, buying the teens a few seconds to catch their breath and assess the situation. But only a few, since the flames were fast approaching and would soon enclose them. They had to find a safe way out!

Cameron poked his head up, shook some debris out of his hair, and took a look around. To his left, flames blocked access to the emergency fire hose. To his right, flames blocked access to the emergency fire extinguisher. The smoldering crater of the control booth sat behind him. And Nova Stevens was still aloft above him. Aloft, rising higher, and screaming a hole through the roof of the theater. Clearly, she was manifesting some E-roid abilities in the *worst* way . . .

"Tay!" Cameron exclaimed loud enough to temporarily drown out the roar of the fire and Nova's sonic shrieking.

The blonde lifted her head, her porcelain face dripping with sweat. The heat was immense.

"Can you clear us a path outta here?" Cameron asked, waving his hands back and forth to simulate a fanning motion. For the past few weeks, Dr. Gosland had been teaching the teens some basic mental and physical exercises designed to help them control and focus their new powers into useful tools for daily activity. As usual, Tay was the superior learner. She'd already disciplined the Other Her into obeying her direct mental commands. (More times than not.) Maybe, right now, she could use her superspeed to blow out the flames blocking the main exit.

Taylor wasn't sure she could, but she nodded anyway and rose to her feet.

Just then, the roiling heat finally reached one of the overhead sensors and activated the sprinkler system. A few of the flames were doused, but not enough, and not *fast* enough—the entire auditorium would be reduced to ashes in a matter of moments.

The sudden blast of cold water to Nova's face was so jarring that she instantly stopped screaming and the beams of concussive energy vanished from her fingertips. Gravity resumed control and the girl fell, noiselessly, some twenty-five feet from the sky like a stone. A stone on a one-way collision course to the stage below.

Taylor looked up, wiping drops of water and two long strands of her blonde hair away from her damp face. *No!* she thought, and the thought incited action. Before she could even form the mental command, the Other Her rushed down the aisle, dragging Taylor with her up and *over* several fleeing patrons. She arrived on stage just in time to catch Nova. With Taylor's face.

Nova landed directly on top of Taylor with a loud *thud* that sent both girls crashing to the stage floor.

The pain was so intense it knocked the very taste from their mouths. Taylor was a crumpled pile of bruises trapped beneath the squirming, panicked form of the redhead.

Back in the audience, Cameron hadn't yet registered Taylor's disappearance.

"Any time now, Tay . . . Tay?"

Then he caught sight of Nova plummeting and, a split second later, a familiar baby blue streak directly beneath her.

"No!" he screamed as he rose to his feet and ran to the stage. The water spraying from above may have added another element of hazard for those attendees who had not yet exited the theater, but it was absolutely *invigorating* to Cameron.

Behind him, one of the main doors to the auditorium burst open and an usher ran inside, another fire extinguisher in hand. The stragglers who saw this new way out all turned on a dime and ran upstairs toward the exit . . . toward Cameron.

There was no time to think or curse. Acting on pure instinct, Cameron dropped to his knees and reached for the nearest strip of aisle lighting. He sent a quick elekinetic blast into the lights, shattering them with a smaller yet satisfying burst of sparks and smoke. The action discouraged several would-be tramplers from advancing, thus allowing Cameron to move past them safely. But more *kept coming*, so Cameron had to resort to drastic measures.

A medley of *"Hey!" "Ow!"* and *"What the—?!"* erupted from the crowd as Cameron delivered some elekinetic *encouragement* to a few strategic body parts on his way to the stage.

Back in the lobby, it took two burly L. Yvette Theatre security guards to drag L'Tanya out of the lobby and down the stairs to the designated evacuation area, where she was deposited on the lawn like discarded luggage.

She turned around to see a giant vortex of black smoke underlit with bright orange flames rising from the building. There came a sickening *CRUNCH* and then L'Tanya and the group of coughing and frenzied escapees watched in horror as the entire roof of the theater collapsed inward, sending up a fresh geyser of cinders and smoke.

L'Tanya's scream of anguish was swallowed up in the chaos.

*   *   *   *   *

The sky was falling, and it was also on fire.

Taylor wriggled out from beneath Nova as Cameron stooped to help the latter to her feet. In the crackling, smoke-filled orange glow, he saw Nova's face contort and she let out a howl of pain accompanied by a devastating blast of sonic energy that would've taken Cameron's head off his shoulders if he hadn't jerked it away at the last second.

"No! Stop! I can't! I can't walk on it!" Nova repeated helplessly, pointing to her right foot. It was evident that she'd landed badly

on Tay and rolled her ankle, maybe even broke it. That . . . complicated the situation.

Cameron slung Nova's right arm behind his neck and lifted her up gently, taking care not to place any of the girl's weight on the injured foot. He motioned for Tay to do the same from her side, and together they carried Nova toward the small staircase and awaiting emergency exit located downstage to the right.

A large piece of flaming rafter smashed onto the stage directly in front of them, destroying a corner of the apron and the staircase. They turned to go the other way but were dismayed to see a gaping hole in the stage near the opposite exit. One of the fireproof curtains apparently snapped out of its decidedly *un*fireproof support housing and had also fallen through the stage, effectively blocking any access in both directions.

Cameron's eyes widened.

They were going to die.

Tay . . . Granddad . . . Mo—

"Yo! Over here!"

The words smacked Cameron violently out of his Not Quite Final Thought and back to attention. He looked around and saw a small yet vaguely familiar figure standing in an open doorway upstage. The figure was waving his arms at Cameron in a fervent, beckoning manner.

"Come *on*, let's go, let's *GO!*" screamed Zack Haynes with what sounded to the teen like extreme impatience, almost anger. Cameron allowed himself the wisp of a smile before he and Taylor shuffled Nova quickly yet carefully out the door.

Zack took a single, lingering, *longing* look at the conflagration before leaving the theater to join the other teens.

Mercifully, the green room and dressing areas were free of smoke and fire, but the alarms were still blaring. A few student performers and faculty members ran frantically past the quartet as it traveled down the long corridor to the staff entrance at the rear of the building.

"Annine!" Nova croaked weakly to one of the passing girls.

The girl paused briefly to identify the voice. When she saw that it belonged to Nova, she screamed and took off furiously in the other direction, repeating "E-roid! E-roid!" at the top of her lungs as though she were summoning an exterminator.

Zack pushed open one of the double doors and the four teens spilled out into the night, sweaty with anxiety and gasping for fresh air. They savored a few moments of Actual Silence before the unmistakable whine of sirens announced the arrival of fire engines and ambulances on campus. Law enforcement wouldn't be far behind.

"One of those supposed to be our ride?" Zack asked.

Instead of answering him, Cameron and Taylor carried Nova over to a picnic table near a set of waste disposal bins. They set her down and Cameron disappeared down the concrete stairs into the staff parking lot in search of his mother's car. It was a hunter green full-size sedan this time, another "loaner" from the Gordon Industries executive concierge service. After fumbling around in the minimal overhead lighting, he finally located it.

And that was when he remembered that his spare key fob was, at this very instant, safely housed in his mother's purse. With his mother, wherever she was.

Cameron was not the slightest bit worried about his mother's welfare. If she was anywhere near the lobby when the craziness first began, she was almost certainly one of the first to evacuate the theater safely. In a crisis, L'Tanya Gordon was good at getting *gone*. Cameron was, however, concerned with finding a solution to his current predicament.

He took a moment to consider his options and noted that the car was outfitted with an electronic entry keypad on each front door. He finally settled on an idea that was as absurd as it was without a suitable alternative.

The other teens watched as Cameron tentatively reached out a hand, took a quick breath, and released a concentrated burst of elekinetic energy. His intention was to simply bypass the car's anti-theft alarm and unlock the door. The effort was successful; unfortunately, in the process, Cameron accidentally shattered the front passenger window.

Nova gasped sharply in surprise before clapping both hands over her mouth, afraid to utter another sound lest she destroy the entire parking lot.

"Oh ... *That's* his thing," Zack muttered casually. He suddenly removed his hoodie and tied the sleeves together beneath Nova's right knee, forming a makeshift sling to elevate Nova's bum foot. Then he and Taylor lugged the girl downstairs and over to the car. Cameron already had the rear passenger door open and was now strapped into the driver's seat.

Taylor squeezed backwards into the car and pulled Nova in behind her. Nova, in turn, used her remaining strength to prop herself up with her good foot. Zack placed the bundled hoodie beneath her other foot, which was already red and swollen.

"Shotgun," said Zack.

"Shut up and get the door!" Taylor snapped.

Zack closed the back door firmly and hopped up front next to Cameron. "Can you start this thing without blowing us up?" he asked. It was not a joke.

Cameron closed his eyes and listened to the faint mechanical whispers calling out to him from beneath the hood. Even without the key fob, the car wanted to start for him; it seemed to *yearn* for his touch.

He felt more elekinetic energy flow from his chest down into his fingertips. Slowly, he pressed the ignition button.

Nothing.

Nothing?

Then he remembered to place his foot on the brake and he tried again. The car immediately sprang to life. Cameron let out a half-sigh, half-exclamation of joy at the achievement.

"Okay. You *win*," Zack conceded as he fastened his seatbelt.

Cameron pulled the sedan out of the staff parking lot and drove cautiously to the front of the theater, past the clusters of displaced patrons and emergency response vehicles. Firefighters were busy combating the blaze with water hoses that whipped about like hissing albino anacondas.

As Cameron rolled by, he thought he spotted his mother. He knew it was gonna be *bad* later, but right now all he could focus on was Not Getting Pulled Over before reaching Gordon Biogen. He was, after all, still a few weeks of practice and a final exam away from obtaining his driver's license.

The teens were several miles away from Pulse Charter and on the highway before anyone spoke.

"Oh God . . . Oh my God," Nova said in a soft voice laced with terror. "What did I do?"

Cameron looked at her through the rear view mirror. "Never mind, we're getting you some help."

"Thanks . . . Cameron, right?"

"Yeah. No prob."

Nova looked up at her other rescuer, the blonde. She also looked familiar, but Nova couldn't quite remember where from.

"And Tray . . . lor?" she asked feebly.

"Taylor," the other girl corrected gently. "Don't talk."

"*Taylor*. Right."

"Her pipes seem fine, but she ain't listening so good," Zack observed.

Nova looked surprised, like she just now registered the fourth occupant's existence.

"Who even *are* you?" she asked.

Zack turned around in his seat, his long hair flapping about beneath his beanie in the evening breeze.

"Oh, I'm the best thing that ever happened to you, Sonica," he smirked.

"Sonic-what?" said Cameron.

"Come on, *sound waves*, she's a *girl* . . . Sonic, Monica, it's—it's a play on . . ." Zack slumped back in his chair and sighed in defeat at yet *another* proof that he was a comic aristocrat stuck in a world full of humor-deficient plebeians.

But these plebs weren't so bad . . . the two he knew, anyway. And this Nova dame might turn out to be a great foil someday.

"Be sure to explain that again when she wakes up." Taylor's voice snatched Zack out of his reflection, and he turned around again to see that Nova had finally passed out from exhaustion. Wisps of the girl's dark red hair lay haphazardly across one of

Taylor's outstretched legs. Her closed eyelids fluttered slightly and her ample chest rose and fell slowly with each deep breath.

Zack's eyes widened and he gulped noiselessly.

"That's it," he said to Taylor after regaining his composure. "Next time *you're* up front."

*　　*　　*　　*　　*

Back at the smoldering remains of the theater, L'Tanya pulled her server out from her purse and dialed her son.

<=Mom—=>

"Cameron Alan Gordon, you better bring your ass and my *car* back here before I report it stolen!" she said with all the grace and serenity she could muster.

<=Not gonna happen,=> came the response. <=Nova got her powers and almost died. We're taking her to the lab.=>

"I don't care if she almost—wait, is that the little whore who was on stage when I left? *She* did all of this to the building, *my* building?!"

Cameron's voice was infuriatingly calm and direct. <=Yeah. Anyway, tell the Doc we're on our way. Then hang tight and tell the feds everything you know. Seriously, just tell them the truth and where they can find Nova . . . but leave *out* the part where I took the car.=>

L'Tanya was in no mood to be ordered around, but she couldn't ignore the sensibility of her son's words, and some of her anger dissipated.

"Okay, fine. But you're *done* when this is done, young man. Do you understand me?"

<=Heading into the tunnel, love you bye.=> The call ended.

L'Tanya gritted her teeth and clenched her fist until the nails dug into her palm. Then she called Vivian.

"Yeesh!" Zack exclaimed. The teen's sympathy was tempered only by the residual awe he felt after witnessing Cameron use his shockwavey powers to activate and manipulate the car's phone without so much as pressing a button on the steering wheel.

"She gave you the middle name *and* a 'young man!'" Zack said gravely. "You're screwed six ways from Sunday."

"Whatever," Cameron responded. He stole a backward glance at his unconscious passenger and added:

"Let's just hope Nova *isn't.*"

CHAPTER 7

Gordon Biogenetic Laboratory
Keaton Layer—11:45 pm

A MARVELOUS MOVIE CAME OUT EARLIER THIS SPRING, a movie about a teenager without fear who did something heroic and suffered an accident that robbed him of his sight; but, as a consolation prize, that same accident granted him the ability to hear everyone and everything around him better than anyone else. The scene where he awakened in the hospital and discovered his fate was especially visceral because the filmmakers employed a combination of cutting-edge CG imagery and superb Foley design to depict the cacophony of the kid's first moments experiencing this new and bittersweet gift.

Conversely, Nova Stevens was *not* a hero. And her awakening was only the beginning of her suffering.

When she first regained consciousness, Nova found herself strapped from head to toe on a gurney, surrounded by a battery of strangers wearing lab coats, face shields, and tarmac earmuffs.

She'd been stripped of her performance outfit and stuffed into a hideous patient gown. The strangers poked her repeatedly with needles and prodded her endlessly with sensors and she could hear everything, everybody, everywhere.

Corridors echoed with explosions and screams of terror as the scientists and doctors tried desperately to contain the waves of sonic kinetic energy flowing from Nova's mouth and fingertips. Nova screamed and screamed until her lungs were empty and her vocal cords burned. Then she screamed some more.

When the girl finally paused to catch her breath, someone seized the opportunity to jab a needle into her neck. She spent the next hour basking in the sweet oblivion of sedation.

The familiar cacophony of human speech brought her back online again, but now the pain was somewhere far away. It hadn't totally left her body, it was just . . . taking a break. Even so, Nova decided to take things slowly, so she remained motionless with her mouth and eyes shut. No sense in using *all* of her senses just yet.

Nova recognized the voices of Cameron and that other kid, the little guy—little girl?—coming from across the room. The two of them were doing their best to speak in a low whisper, Nova supposed, out of consideration for her. Unfortunately, it still sounded like they were yelling at each other through bullhorns. On top of that, they were yelling in a foreign language. Nova couldn't pinpoint which one, but it was definitely Asian.

Nova also registered the presence of a fourth person in the room. Judging from the sound of two feet squeaking back and forth across the floor in a pair of foam resin clogs, it was probably a nurse. The shoes made noise but their wearer *didn't*, which was difficult for Nova to comprehend.

It was too much, too much input to process, there were too many voices and too many noises and they were all too *loud* and—

Just as Nova felt herself slip over the edge into insanity, the teen boys reverted arguing quietly in English.

"Seriously, dude? She ain't a *stray* you can just bring home!" the short one said.

"I know that, Zack! Okay? I *know* that," Cameron responded. He sounded exasperated. "I'm not trying to adopt anyone, I'm just saying things are about to suck really, *really* bad for her. Forever!"

The other kid, Zack (who was apparently a boy), seemed to relent a fraction. "Okay, I get it. She needs someone. But, last I checked—and I didn't—she's got two perfectly *alive* parents, more money than all of us combined—"

"Mostly you," Cameron interjected, which Nova had to admit was both true and a little funny.

" —and some third point that makes sense." Zack sighed in what sounded like excruciating frustration. "*Whatever*, I'm spent."

Nova heard the muscles in Cameron's face clench. "You don't get it, Zack. You're on the other side of this."

There was a pause, then Zack conceded: "Fine. But . . . maybe hang back on this one, okay? You can't be everything to every*one*. This time, let the ovaries do the talking."

Ovar—What did he say?! Nova thought.

"Hey!" Cameron's voice thundered with the intensity of a German Shepherd. "Two Don'ts. First, don't you ever talk about her like that again. Second, don't try to shove this off on her, she's got enough on her plate without—"

"Shove what off?" Zack asked with equal intensity. "Was she on that stage with you? *Yeah.* Was she in the car with you? Also *yeah.* She's a part of this now, *deal* with it. And, like you said, as of tonight, Nova's plum out of a peer group, and we both know that Tay needs more friends besides you, me, and her fantasy Science Mom."

"You? She still wants to *kill* you for what you did at the party!" Cameron said with a note of incredulity that Nova recognized long before she could properly identify it. She finally realized that the boys were referring to another *she*, another *her*—the blonde. But what was this talk about them all being *friends*?

Nova decided that now was a good time to rejoin the world.

"My point exactly," Zack said triumphantly, as if he'd just won a debate championship. He glanced to one side and saw Nova, who was fully awake and sitting upright in her bed.

"It lives," Zack said in a normal speaking volume.

Nova looked around and saw that she was in some sort of modern, overly teched-out hospital room. The room was larger than her bedroom suite at home but certainly didn't feel like it was. She was separated from the other occupants behind a wall of one—no, two!—*two-inch* glass. Either it was glass or some kinda composite material. Nova decided that if that stuff was supposed to be soundproof, whoever had it installed should ask for a refund *and* sue the manufacturer for fraud. Thankfully, the machinery on the wall near her, the machinery that was monitoring her vital signs, was silent. So was the digital clock on the wall behind her.

Cameron, Zack, and a young woman in navy blue scrubs (wearing those infernal squeaking shoes!) stood frozen in place. All of them were staring at her with uneasy anticipation.

Nova opened her mouth to respond but nothing came out. Not a scream, not a whisper. *Nothing.* She could feel and hear her tongue rattling against the roof of her mouth and the back of her teeth as she tried, hysterically, to form words. But no sound was produced. Even worse, every attempt produced a soft mechanical vibration against her throat.

Panicked, Nova jerked her chin downward to see if something was still attached to her head. The motion was impeded by something around her neck, and she could hear her heart begin to race again as she reached up to grab and remove the unknown vocal obstruction, only to discover that both her hands were encased in some weird-ass medical *mittens* that were emitting the same vibration that somehow numbed all feeling in her fingertips and *oh God I can't talk I can't feel I can't breathe get it off get it off get them OFF—*

On the opposite side of the transparent wall, the nurse was waving her own hands softly and slowly at Nova in an attempt to de-escalate the situation, to calm the girl down. Her efforts were unsuccessful.

"You don't wanna do that, Nova," Cameron said in a soft but urgent tone. "That gear's supposed to keep you from blasting your own head off."

Nova froze, her eyes wide. Slowly, carefully, she lowered her mitts.

"Plus, you're, like, *incredibly* drugged right now," Zack added. "Adrenal suppressants, the good stuff. Best not to fight 'em."

"This isn't a normal hospital, but I promise you're in good hands," Cameron continued. Technically, it wasn't a *hospital* at all; Gordon Biogen had only recently added a team of cardiothoracic, neurological, and trauma surgeons to its full-time staff to respond to the rise in EX manifestation events.

Cameron decided that Nova didn't need to know that piece of information. Yet.

He pointed to the nurse, a brunette twenty-something who was busy transferring the data from one of the machines onto her tablet. "That's Allie, she's awesome."

After a few moments, Allie looked up and smiled at Nova.

"Taylor's with Dr. Gosland, they'll be back shortly," Cameron continued. "Do you . . . remember us? Remember anything that happened?"

"Dude, she fell on her ass, not her *head*," Zack scoffed.

"Yes she did, Zack, *thank you* for clarifying," Cameron said. He was about to add *Now shut up*, but at that moment, the door to the room slid open and Max Sylvester walked in. The strap of his motorcycle helmet hung from one tightly gripped hand.

Cameron gaped. "Max?" he exclaimed.

"Sure, why not?" Zack said casually, attempting to mask his own surprise. "What's up, Lurch?"

Max ignored both of them and walked directly to the barrier of Nova's enclosure. Nova lept from her bed and rushed to meet him, oblivious to the faint echo of discomfort she felt in her bandaged ankle. She'd never been happier to see or hear anyone more in her entire life.

"She can't talk right now," Cameron offered.

"Sexy, eh?" Zack quipped before darting to narrowly avoid a swat from the back of Cameron's hand.

"But she can hear everyone and everything all at once, so . . . try to speak softly," Cameron added.

Max's locked eyes with Nova. "Okay," he said. "We're done."

The simplicity in his tone hit Nova harder than the words. She reeled in devastation.

Baby I'm sorry, I'm so sorry! Nova mouthed the words over and over frantically, but no one—especially Max—heard her.

"Come *on*, Max. Now?" Cameron asked angrily.

Max whipped his head around. "She *stole* from me, Cameron," he said with unexpected yet unmistakable emotion. He looked back at Nova.

"You *stole* from me. Something irreplaceable, someo—" Max stopped abruptly and took some time to regain his composure. It became evident to everyone in the room that he'd almost revealed something deeply personal.

Baby, please don't do this! I need you right now, I—

"I came from the theater. I heard what happened," Max said, calm again. "You're probably terrified of what you've become. You feel confused, lonely."

Max inhaled deeply and savored the breath for a few seconds.

"I don't give a shit," he said plainly. "You were a monster long before tonight. Now it's official."

Silence.

Nobody moved or dared even *breathe*. Nobody except Nurse Allie, whose attention was focused on recording a set of Nova's vital signs from a nearby monitor.

"Well . . . That's a closer," Zack finally said.

"Stay away from me, Nova," Max continued. "Like I said, I know what you are, saw what you're capable of. But if you *ever* scream, speak, or so much as *look* in my direction again . . ." Max smashed a bare fist into the protective barrier directly in front of

Nova's face. Everyone in the room recoiled. Nova let out a silent shriek of terror, stumbled backward and fell to the ground. A fresh wave of pain spread across her ankle.

Silence.

Max lowered his fist, leaving a small spiderweb of cracks in the composite decorated with flecks of his blood and tissue. Then he turned and walked out of the room, passing Dr. Gosland and Taylor without sparing either of them a glance.

After a while, Zack squeaked:

"Correction—*that's* a closer."

"Max—*Max!*" Cameron called out even though he knew it was pointless.

Gosland snapped her head around to get a second, better look at the teen, but he was already halfway down the corridor.

Back inside her cell, Nova scrambled to her feet and pounded her own protected fists against the clear wall, bellowing mutely for Max. The mittens didn't leave so much as a smudge.

"What was that?" Gosland demanded.

"Typical young adult sci-fi melodrama," Zack said.

Taylor indicated the damage to the barrier. "Dr. Gosland . . ." she began as Gosland rushed over to inspect.

"Oh my God! Nova, what happened?"

Max did it! He *did it, he broke my heart and punched the wall like a psycho and then he stormed off!* Nova's arms flailed wildly as she reenacted the teen's savagery.

Gosland nodded her understanding. "We still need to relocate you. This room's been compromised." Then she turned to address the remaining occupants: "Everyone out, now. Allie, I'm so sorry you had to witness that. I assure you it *won't* happen again. Please go take your break; I'll stay with Miss Stevens." Gosland signed the words simultaneously as she spoke them.

It's okay, Dr. Gosland, Allie replied. *I'm fine, thanks. I understand she's just hurt and freaked out. I'll be back in thirty to help you with the transfer.* Then she left the room, trailed by Cameron and the other teens.

*　　　*　　　*　　　*　　　*

Vivian Gosland needed a drink. Something a lot stronger than white wine.

All those years she'd spent basking in the glow of anonymity as MsV were supposed to have prepared her for this moment. All the letters to Max. The gifts. Begging Perry Gordon to garnish her salary to pay for what turned out to be five years of tuition at Pulse Charter. (Of course, Perry refused her proposal outright and insisted that she apply for one of several available scholarships on Max's behalf. Which Perry then approved without hesitation, even going so far as to forgo the prospective candidate interview.)

Then, there was the decade-long strain Gosland had placed on the Lindseys. And, finally, her insistence that her identity as Max's mysterious patron *not* be divulged until a time and place of their mutual choosing, and not until he was mature enough to handle the revelation. Or, at least, not until Gosland could muster up the courage to lay her eyes on him, which would trigger the inevitable tsunami of guilt.

So, naturally, Gosland was relieved when their grand union didn't happen earlier this evening. She'd known for years that the boy struggled with a litany of psychological issues ranging from a disorganized attachment style to an overdeveloped capacity for self-preservation. She concluded that, after tonight, Max would need some time before he was emotionally ready to try another face-to-face. Until then, Gosland was more than happy to retreat to the shadows and let MsV deal with the consequences.

Neither Gosland nor MsV was emotionally prepared to deal with any of those consequences less than four hours later that same night. At the lab, of all places. They were even less prepared for the first encounter with Max to occur seconds after a violent outburst.

"Doc, that was Max," Cameron was saying from somewhere in the distance.

Max . . .

"He and Nova have a thing. *Had* a thing, and—"

That was Max . . .

"Doc?"

Gosland blinked rapidly and gave a subtle shake of her head to clear her thoughts and collect her bearings. She was standing in front of Cameron beside the empty nurses' station in the hallway outside of Nova's room.

That. Was. Max!

"No, Cameron! *No*," Gosland said. "I don't care *who* he is or *what* he has with Nova, I said I don't want him anywhere *near* this lab again!" Her words gushed forth like water from a fire hydrant that had been bludgeoned open.

"Um . . . no, you didn't," Cameron responded quizzically. "But I agree—no more Max. But, hear me out, I swear he's not a bad—"

"Taylor!" Gosland snapped. "I need you to—"

Before she could finish, a baby blue streak suddenly appeared next to Cameron, followed a split-second later by the blonde.

"What did I *tell* you about doing that on this floor? *What?*" Gosland barked.

Taylor hung her head sheepishly.

Gosland was about to read Taylor the riot act about using her zipheeling abilities in narrow corridors when her server buzzed an alert.

"*Ugh.* Never mind, the DHS-EX and Nova's father are on their way," Gosland said. She heard exhaustion steadily creeping into her voice, but she was unaware that it was coming across as *mania* to the teens.

"Cameron, you have my sincerest gratitude for getting Nova here so quickly," she continued. "Now *go home*. Taylor, I need you to file a report with the security team, tell them that I want that, that—" She snapped her fingers at Cameron, who just sighed and mumbled a faint "max."

"*Max* Sylvester. Tell them that Max doesn't set foot inside this building again without my permission or else the entire team gets replaced. Then *you* go home. And *you*—" Gosland turned her attention to the third teen, the short one who'd just exited from a hallway bathroom a dozen feet away.

"Who even *are* you?" she asked.

Zack stared at her like she was a crazy person.

Cameron stared at her like she was a crazy person.

Even Taylor stared at her like she was a crazy person.

Gosland began to feel like a—

Zack broke the silence with what he no doubt thought was a legitimate question for his two companions.

"Um . . . How exactly does this doc have letters after her name but forgets that we all drove together?"

Before anyone could formulate an answer, and before Gosland could get her hands around the scrawny teen's neck, a familiar voice boomed up the corridor.

"Cameron!"

All four heads whipped around to behold L'Tanya and Perry Gordon marching toward them. Both were visibly upset.

Cameron groaned and threw his head back into the air, as if appealing to a higher power to end his eternal torment. Gosland sympathized.

"Oh, *please*, not now," Cameron said.

"Yes, *now*," L'Tanya said firmly.

"Huh? Oh, I'm sorry, Mom," Cameron said.

L'Tanya appeared to relax her guard a fraction, an action that turned out to be premature.

"You thought I was *asking*," Cameron continued with a wildly uncharacteristic yet unmistakable edge of sarcasm in his words. "Let me rephrase: *Not. Now.*"

Perry said sharply, "Okay, young man. That's *no* way to talk to your—"

"Granddad," Cameron interrupted, "I love and respect you more than anyone alive, but I meant what I said for you, too."

All three adults and the two other teens were stunned silent.

Gosland felt the icy sterility in the air transmute into a boiling tension, one that spread outward to envelop the entire corridor. Her heart was pounding so loudly that, for an irrational instant, she thought that she'd gained Nova's enhanced hearing.

L'Tanya appeared more confused than upset with her son.

"Boy, have you lost your mind?" She looked at Gosland. "Did you switch up his meds without telling me?"

Gosland reached one hand up and gently rubbed the area behind her right ear. She suddenly felt like a boa constrictor had engulfed her head.

"L'Tanya, it's been a long night," she said.

Cameron offered an alternative explanation. "No, Mom, I'm perfectly sane. But I'm not *at all* about to have this or any other conversation with you right now. It's late, I'm tired. Everyone here is tired. Ground me or whatever in the morning." He shifted his attention to Taylor and Zack. "You ready?"

As the teens turned to leave, L'Tanya turned to her father and expelled a half-laugh, half-snort of incredulity.

"He's lost his mind. Steals my car like it's nothing, thinks he can do it again—"

Cameron paused midstep and rounded on his mother. "Mom, stop! Just *stop*. How do you not *get it* yet?" He pointed a finger at the door to Nova's room and said, with rising irritation:

"This, right now, that in there? It's bigger than you. Bigger than me, bigger than me *borrowing the car*. We already *did* this with Taylor, remember? We did the thing where I helped one of my friends and it was dangerous and you got pissed, but just like last time it's *over* now and I'm *fine*, okay?"

"No, little boy, it's *not* okay!" L'Tanya hissed the words *little boy* through teeth that were clenched to the point of shattering. "I don't know what this is, do you—do you need to puff out your little chest a bit? What, you think just because you're with your *boss* and your little *friends* that you can disrespect me like this? Do you have any idea how *close* you are to a major ass whooping?"

Gosland winced. While she agreed that Cameron had stepped way out of line, she also knew that L'Tanya felt zero qualms about weaponizing emasculation against any member of the opposite sex whom she deemed her enemy. Including her own son.

Perry tried to interject, but L'Tanya would have none of it. "No, Daddy. You can't spare him from this. Not this time. Clearly, he's forgotten who puts a *roof* over his head and *food* in his mouth and *shoes* on his feet. He's a spoiled, rude little *bastard*. And right now, his mouth's writing a check that his butt can't cash!"

From the corner of one eye, Gosland saw the same look of discomfort and embarrassment on the faces of Taylor and Zack.

Cameron did not share their sentiment. If anything, he looked like he could take and return another fifteen rounds of the verbal and emotional abuse.

"Okay, Mom. You're my everything, I'm your nothing. Thanks for clarifying that. Out loud. Feel better?"

"Cameron," L'Tanya began.

"Nah, keep going. *Keep going.* Tell my *boss* and my little *friends* what happens next. Take the bedroom door off the hinges, cut off my server plan. *Ooh*, how about you force me write your obituary, *again*? And please oh please . . . *Try* to lay another hand on me."

Cameron's eyes suddenly flashed with a cold, dark energy that had nothing to do with his Enhanthroid abilities. It was an energy that Gosland could only describe to herself as . . . otherworldly.

L'Tanya's own fiery eyes widened, but nearly imperceptibly. Gosland was astonished to recognize the expression as the closest L'Tanya had come to emoting genuine *fear*.

"You can't control me anymore, Mom. Really, none of You can even *hope* to control any of Us. So *stop trying.*"

With that, Cameron turned his back to his mother and his grandfather and stormed off down the hallway. Taylor followed suit a deliberate half-step behind him, but Zack missed his cue to leave and stayed rooted to his spot. As Cameron passed by, he pointed at the tiny teen and called out:

"And give Jas a job!" It was not a request.

Awkward Silence.

The three adults stared at Zack, waiting for an explanation.

Zack cleared a throat that was suddenly void of all traces of moisture. Then he cleared it again. "My sister, Jasmine Haynes," he said as he backed away slowly. "Licensed RN/LVN, current but soon-to-be *former* employee of your former son-in-law—*ahem,* I mean, *your* former husband . . ." Zack was tripping painfully over his words and was about to trip over his large feet, so he hastily concluded with: "Resume and references available upon request. Good night, sir. Ma'am."

Zack turned and ran to catch up with the other teens at the elevator, joining them right before a blend of authoritative and frantic footsteps announced the arrival of a pair of DHS-EX agents and Nova's father.

*   *   *   *   *

Two more hours elapsed before Randall Stevens and the feds left the lab. During that time, Gosland supervised Nova's transfer to a new room adjacent to the basement lab that boasted a more aesthetically calming ambience. She assured Nova that the collar around her neck was only a temporary inconvenience. It would be removed as soon as the Biogen scientists finished synthesizing a throat spray that mimicked the collar's ability to incapacitate the destructive capabilities of her vocal cords while allowing her to resume normal speech. But the throat spray wouldn't be ready until tomorrow afternoon at the earliest, so, for now, Nova still couldn't talk.

Gosland also swapped out Nova's pair of medical mittens for a new ion bracelet. The girl insisted that her device be strapped to an ankle rather than a wrist, and, after some additional research, Gosland acquiesced. With Nova's bracelet activated and safely regulating the level of EX ions in her body, the protective wall was no longer a necessary restraint. Nova was allowed to roam freely about her room and interact with visitors without fear of causing herself or anyone else any harm.

Now it was well past one in the morning. The lights in Nova's room were dimmed and, although her adrenal suppressants were supposed to last for a full twelve hours, sleep was nowhere to be found. After a while, Nova stopped trying to force herself to nod off and instead began wading through the pile of her unprocessed emotions and the implications of her new existence.

She was lying on her bed, midway through her introspective deep dive, when Allie came into the room to check on her. The silent nurse had a warm, inviting face that always looked on the verge of emitting a giant smile. Nova's sense of self-loathing was momentarily replaced with irrational jealousy, and her own face twisted in a scowl. That scowl turned into a look of bewilderment when Allie opened her mouth and said, in a clear, casual, and *audible* voice: "Was it worth losing him?"

Nova sat up sharply, blinking rapidly. She was unable to form words in her head, much less attempt to speak.

Allie repeated herself, adding context for Nova's benefit.

"Whatever it was you stole, was it worth losing him?"

That snapped Nova out of her stupor, and her scowl returned with a vengeance.

You know you suck *at being deaf, right?* she mouthed.

Allie nodded, apparently unoffended. "Sometimes. Mostly I'm great at it. Bacterial meningitis when I was four. I have a cochlear implant that helps with this ear—" she pulled back one brunette side bang to expose her left ear. In the low light, Nova could just make out the dull sheen of a small device the size of a hearing aid.

"Without it, I get absolutely nothing out of either one," Allie continued. "But I'm an excellent lip reader, and . . . sweetie, your face has been giving me a migraine all night."

Mind your own damn business and spare me the 'I'd trade places with you in a heartbeat' speech, okay? Nova spat. She had no desire to learn this girl's entire life story, no matter how poignant and ironic it sounded.

Allie gave Nova one of those sickly sweet smiles. "I guess it *wasn't* worth it," she said. "Don't worry, he's not gone forever. At your age, no one is." She paused to consider. "Unless his helmet's for a *motorcycle* instead of a *moped*. That cuts his chances in half."

Allie watched the color drain from Nova's already pale face and couldn't resist a laugh of combined guilt and sympathy.

"Oh, no! *Oh*, I'm sorry, sweetie, I didn't mean to scare you . . ." She narrowed her eyes in a conspiratorial manner. "Please tell me you got to ride it."

Nova looked at her blankly. *No*, she said. *Just him.*

It took the nurse a few seconds to decipher that. When the realization finally came, she winced in disgust.

"*Ooh*, okay. Did *not* need to know that."

You chose to listen, Nova mouthed.

Allie nodded again. "You're right. I did . . . From now on, you should, too."

You know I can't do that, Nova said.

Allie's pale blue eyes flashed with sudden passion. Pointing at Nova's collar, she said: "That's not the *only* thing I know! I also know that you can't *talk* right now because *that* thing won't let you. And thank God for that, because without it or your anklet, your voice and hands are an uncontrollable hazard to me, you, and every other person in this building. Who knows what'll happen when you start flying—"

Flying? As in flying?! Nova thought.

"—but none of that has anything to do with your ability to *hear*. Or *listen*."

Nova opened her mouth to respond, but Allie wasn't finished. "According to your chart, you've just developed the most powerful set of ears in the city, maybe in the entire world. But don't think for a second that *I* envy *you*. Quite the opposite. I feel sorry for you. *You're* the one stuck hearing the Best and Worst of everything humanity has to utter for the rest of your life; which, unlike that of your ex, is probably going to be *long*. That means you're gonna get every syllable of trash talk spoken behind your back. Every screaming child at every grocery store. Every teardrop you cry the next time you get dumped."

Nova threw up her arms in surrender.

So what the hell am I supposed to do for the rest of my long life, pretend like I don't *have the most powerful set of ears in the city, maybe in the entire world?*

"No way!" Allie exclaimed. The warmth slowly returned to her face, but any traces of the earlier sympathy in her tone were gone. In its place, Nova could detect a faint tone of . . . determination, almost empowerment.

"You just need some time to learn how to use them the right way . . ." Allie indicated her cochlear implant again and mimicked the act of lowering a dial before she added, in a soft, almost silent whisper:

And when to turn them off.

INTERLUDE

**Center for Enhanthrax
Research & Treatment
Keaton Layer—1:25 am**

THE AIR INSIDE THE WARMLY LIT CONFERENCE ROOM had long ago staled with exhaustion from the sixteen adults and four adolescents. Over the course of the night's interrogation, the casual atmosphere had inevitably turned harsh and overbearing. Neither Anderson, the teens, nor their parents wanted to spend a single unnecessary instant longer inside this room.

Anderson reached forward to pause the recording again when Zack's voice broke out like the crack of a whip:

"Nope! No way . . . sir. *No.* We ain't doing that anymore. We're all stuck here together until the end of this, and *this* isn't it."

Defeated, Anderson leaned back in his seat, crossed his arms, and continued to listen.

CHAPTER 8

Gordon Biogenetics Laboratory
Keaton Layer—8:48 pm

ZACK HAYNES HATED MONTAGES.

In animation, they were narrative devices used primarily to reduce the amount of time and manpower required to illustrate or digitally render costly yet nonessential expository sequences. In television and film, a montage (or its acoustic cousin, the *voiceover narration*) was often relied upon by writers as a narrative crutch to salvage an inadequate story, enhance an uninspired plot, or to accelerate character development.

Zack respected filmmakers' ability to manipulate the passage of time on screen while truncating key story events into a set of visually digestible images, all set to a catchy tune. Especially while balancing the impossible-to-satisfy demands from studio heads who, Zack was convinced, knew less than *zilch* about generating quality entertainment. Fiction was supposed to give audiences an escape from the burden of their mostly failed and useless lives. Or to hold up a mirror to humanity, exposing its good, bad, and ugly elements in a vain attempt to inspire positive change. (Zack often confused the two objectives.)

In Zack's armchair expert opinion, the trope of employing a montage to teleport viewers from one point in a character's life to another, more significant point was beginning to lose steam and emotional impact. Zack had long ago vowed that, should he ever make the leap from casual voyeur to full-fledged videographer, he'd be sure to leave that tool *out* of his arsenal.

Nonetheless, despite his personal feelings about its limited artistic value, Zack had to acknowledge the fact that most human memories took the form of . . . *sigh* . . . a montage.

Even now, Zack was replaying the day's events in his mind as a series of highlights rather than individual moments. And those highlights were totally worthy of a catchy tune . . .

It all went down at the gym. Not just any gym. And not quite a *gym* in the traditional sense. It was a medium-sized commercial aircraft hangar located down on Lowery that had been closed for a decade or more following Keaton International's latest expansion. After years of being passed back and forth between an assortment of private hands and public trusts, the building was eventually purchased by Gordon Industries and spared from demolition during the early planning stages of the company's massive fiftieth anniversary celebration.

Perry Gordon's original idea for the old hangar (whatever *that* was) never came to fruition. However, after the initial outbreak of EX, the business magnate had the good sense to convert this place into an E-roid research facility, the same as he had with the entire portfolio of Gordon Industries-owned buildings. In this case, he also had the foresight to outfit the hanger with a combination of conventional exercise equipment and special machinery designed to accommodate people manifesting an ever-increasing variety of EX abilities. Perry affectionately named this new training facility Gordon F.L.E.X., an acronym with no actual meaning (despite one widespread rumor that it meant *F*or the *L*ove of *E*nhanthra*X*).

Summer vacation was in full swing throughout Silver City. So, this Friday, just as she had done every other day this week, Dr. Gosland dragged Cameron, Taylor, and Nova down to Gordon F.L.E.X. to hone and tone their powers. And, as he had done every day this week, Zack Haynes accompanied the teens to document their progress and provide moral support (read: insightful color commentary). The day provided ample hilarity. And peril.

Next to soccer, Zack felt that the most boring sport to spectate was *running*, so he didn't bother wasting his camera's precious storage memory on Taylor as she completed a series of time trials and stress tests on a modified treadmill and, later, the outdoor track. How fast she could run, the effects of her speed on her surroundings, and everything else related to her zippy powers meant less than nothing to Zack. Instead, he focused his efforts and lens on Cameron and Nova, both of whom were set up in private training rooms tailored to their specific abilities.

Cameron's room was set up like something between a defunct electronics store and a maze. The walls concealed a myriad of tech devices that were either lying dormant, waiting to be activated elekinetically by Cameron; or, the exact opposite: spring-loaded and programmed to fire at the teen with such force that he only had a split second to render the devices inert before suffering injury. As an additional challenge, the room was pitch black. And Cameron was blindfolded.

Conversely, Nova spent the day isolated in a long, narrow, and blindingly lit shooting gallery. Her targets ranged in size and took the form of various hard surfaces ranging from a trash can lid to a twenty-nani coin. Her objective was to destroy the objects with little to no collateral damage.

From his seat next to Gosland in the control room, Zack held his camera's viewfinder dead steady on Nova as the girl assumed a crouching stance, took a deep breath, reared her head back, and expelled a measured blast of aural energy from her mouth.

The faintly visible sound waves whistled through the air and across the room like arrows on a direct course to the center of the largest target. The sound waves bounced harmlessly off the target, shot back across the room as quickly as they'd been fired, and smacked Nova in the face with the force of a brick.

Nova crashed to the ground, Zack laughed like an idiot, and Gosland scribbled in her digital notepad.

In the darkness, Cameron took his steps carefully to avoid stumbling into any concealed traps along his path. He trusted Dr. Gosland implicitly and knew that this was all just for practice, but there was just *something* about moving around in the dark that was unsettling on a primal level.

He was so focused on his own movements that he completely missed the electric *buzz* of the four rotors coming to life directly behind him.

Nova lowered the transparent shield over her rapidly bruising face. The shield was made of the same composite material as the barrier in her first hospital room a few weeks back. It wasn't nearly as thick, but Gosland had assured her that it was just as durable. (Something about more density per square inch?)

Two targets awaited Nova. This time, she employed a more focused approach and used one hand to shoot a smaller gust of concussive sound waves to the far end of the room. This time, she managed to arc her shot and successfully dispatched both targets without any measurable reduction in speed or kinetic energy. *This time*, she was prepared for the blowback and easily dodged the returning sound waves.

Those same waves ricocheted off the wall behind Nova and smacked her in the back of the head with the force of a baseball bat.

Nova crashed to the ground, Zack laughed like an idiot, and Gosland scribbled in her digital notepad.

Cameron reached out into the darkness with a tentative right hand to ascertain whether the obstruction in front of him was a standard wall, a doubly dangerous corner wall, or the worst: a dreaded dead end. All his senses were on full alert.

Suddenly, Cameron whipped an elekinetically charged left fist up and backward, smashing the camera drone hovering quietly behind him into smithereens.

"Really, dude?!" Zack cried from his seat next to Gosland in the control room. Cameron switched the lights on and grinned up at the booth. He saw Zack let out an exacerbated groan and toss the remote control into the trash bin.

Nova secured the straps of the bulky ice hockey goaltender's helmet completely enshrouding her head from the neck up. Then she verified that the target across the room was positioned in a padded corner to ensure the absolute minimum of reverberation. Finally, she checked one last time to confirm that the rest of her extremities were protected.

Nova was encased head to toe in an ungodly amalgam of heavy-duty defensive sports equipment that was on temporary loan from Douglas Andrews' store down on Clooney. The gear was unsightly, it was constricting. It was necessary.

Slowly—*very* slowly—Nova reached out a trembling, sweaty hand toward the target. Her middle finger crept gingerly toward her thumb until she felt the slightest pressure of both digits' embrace. She heard the saliva slide down her padded throat as she gulped in fearful anticipation. Then she snapped her fingers.

A sharp burst of auralkinetic energy shot across the room and destroyed the narrow target . . .

And that was it. Nothing else. No blowback, no crossfire.

Silence.

Nova shot a glance sideways to the control room. Behind the reinforced glass, Gosland wore a mask of neutrality while Zack slowly lowered his camera to offer Nova a reluctant thumbs up.

I did it, Nova thought. *I DID IT!*

Ecstatic, the girl snatched off her helmet, reared her head upward and expelled a quick, high-pitched *"whoo!"* in triumph.

She realized the gravity of her mistake a few moments after the chunk of broken acoustic ceiling tile fell two stories and smacked her on the top of her now *very* exposed head.

Nova crashed to the ground, Zack laughed like an idiot, and Gosland scribbled in her digital notepad.

*   *   *   *   *

Later that evening, Zack dropped by Gordon Biogen, where the other teens had regrouped to lick their wounds and assess the results of their day's training. Mostly the former.

Cameron busied himself reviewing the hours of raw footage from Zack's camera on the new jumbo-sized television monitor in the lounge. The lounge that, over the past few weeks, and, despite Gosland's objections, had been transformed into an adolescent flophouse.

A slew of empty pizza boxes and discarded snack wrappers sat among stacks of fashion magazines and medical journals on the corner of one file cabinet-turned-coffee table. Scratched-up movie discs and video game cartridges were piled haphazardly atop the small specimen fridge, which now held a continually replenished supply of sports drinks for everyone and disgusting non-alcoholic malt beverages reserved for Nova.

Zack was sprawled across the small, uncomfortable armchair in the center of the lounge when Taylor walked into the room and reached for the Pulse Charter track team hoodie slung over the back of the adjacent loveseat. As always, Zack allowed his eyes to wander lazily up the girl's body, from her sneakered feet and absurdly long legs all the way up to—

"Yo, what even *is* that?" Zack exclaimed.

The blonde—who, judging from the wisps of lingering steam emanating from her damp hair, had just exited the shower—was

142

wearing a grey sports bra and a matching pair of athletic trunks that left little to the imagination. The outfit itself was nothing out of the ordinary; after all, Taylor *was* once an aspiring athlete.

Tonight, however, the girl's outer garments were concealed under some kind of a thin, high cut mesh bodysuit. The mesh was sheer black and featured long sleeves that terminated in fingerless gloves. The entire getup reminded Zack of the sort of leotard a dancer might wear. An *exotic* dancer.

At Zack's outburst, Cameron snapped his head around to take a gander at his best friend. The struggle to keep his reaction neutral was a delicious sight to Zack's eyes.

"What do you care?" Cameron finally said. "It's . . . *airy* . . . but it still covers all the naughty bits." He paused before adding: "Not bad, Tay."

Poor putz, Zack said to himself.

Taylor slipped the hoodie over her head and straightened her hair, not the slightest bit disturbed by being the subject of such a frenzy of juvenile masculinity.

"Thank you for the defense, Cameron, but I assure you that it's unwarranted." She turned to look down at Zack and continued, in an even, factual tone: "Today, I burned through three full sets of spandex clothing. In total, unobstructed view of approximately two dozen people."

"Any children or nuns? Zack asked. Taylor ignored him.

"I finally determined that a mesh weave affords me enough airflow to prevent the total disintegration of external fabric during my rapid acceleration. Anything I wear beneath it is safe. Anything on top . . . no guarantees."

Zack and Cameron nodded slowly in understanding.

"Okay, so your Other Her is a tawdry whore," Zack concluded.

"*Zack!*" Dr. Gosland's voice rang out from the lounge kitchen a dozen feet away.

Zack winced. "Sorry . . . I meant a whore with tawdry *taste*," he clarified.

Gosland ignored the boy. "Thinking long-term," she said to Taylor, "we should explore a full twalium mesh bodysuit with a . . . hmm . . . a neoprenium lining. It'll be a bit form-fitting, but still breathable."

"Exactly *how* form-fitting are we talking about, Doc?" Zack asked lasciviously. He'd sat bolt upright in his chair and was now holding a stylus poised over his own digital notepad like an ace reporter awaiting the scoop of the century.

"*We* aren't talking at all, Zack," Gosland said simply.

"*We aren't talking at all, Zack*," the teen repeated mockingly before mumbling the words *twalium-reinforced neoprenium* under his breath as he scribbled them onto the tablet.

"That sounds like a viable solution," Taylor said to Gosland.

"Hold up, Doc—you haven't said how it's gonna handle all her split ends," Zack pointed out.

Taylor's face melted into a frown. "Leave it *alone*, already!"

"*Snip-snip, Tay . . .*" the boy persisted in a singsong voice.

"You first!" Taylor countered sharply, her cheeks suddenly red with embarrassment. More than anyone else in the room, she was painfully aware of the visibly negative toll her abilities had been taking on her long blonde locks over the past several weeks. There was one obvious albeit *drastic* solution, but Taylor couldn't bring herself to even *think* about it for longer than an instant.

Fortunately, she didn't have to. Cameron jumped back into the fray and changed the subject.

"Hey," he said to Zack. "You might wanna kill the 'no footage' thing for good. Your transition edits are seamless, and you can't even tell when you had to swap out batteries."

Zack brushed off the compliment. "Yeah, *no*. Trust me, don't nobody wanna see any evidence of you writhing about in a gym ever again." He mimed a sick kangaroo flailing its short forelimbs. "Besides, I didn't swap out anything!"

"Really, Zack? I know you shot in high-def for, like, seven hours of my apparent . . ." Cameron mimicked Zack's mimicry of a sick kangaroo flailing its short forelimbs.

"Yeah, and my battery died, like, twenty-five minutes after breakfast. That was all *you*, dude."

Cameron furrowed his brow. "What?"

Taylor's eyes brightened with the realization. "Of course!"

"Of course *what*?" Cameron asked.

Gosland entered the lounge, holding a bamboo serving tray containing a steaming bowl of her homemade kung pao. She took a seat directly next to Cameron and let the heavenly scent invade his nostrils before it quickly expanded to engulf the rest of the room.

"Your body must've generated an elekinetic field all day as you progressed through your drills," Gosland said. "That field apparently provided a perpetual energy source for any electronic device in the immediate vicinity." She took a healthy bite with her chopsticks and spent a few moments savoring the experience before adding: "Of course, it was unintentional."

Cameron rolled his eyes. "Of *course*." He moved away from his tortuous boss and started for the kitchen when an image on Zack's tablet caught his eye.

Amidst the scattered bits of text, Cameron could distinguish several sketches of abstract objects, including one he thought was a failed attempt at highlighting negative space. This particular object was a misshaped oval enshrouding the frontal perspective of some sort of . . . *being* . . . with giant, fierce eyes. The being held out a defensive open palm and a closed fist that was reared back, ready to throw a punch. The white ovular outline of the being, its scowling eyes, open palm, and closed fist stood in stark contrast to the image's black background. Cameron briefly envisioned how the object might look with different colored outlines.

"What's all that?" he asked.

"Marketing," Zack replied. The doc's obviously got a plan for your uniforms but y'all need a group logo. And *you* need a name."

Cameron snorted. "Zack, none of us are planning to save the world *or* go out on tour anytime soon. We just need protection when we use our powers—" He saw the frown on Gosland's face and added hastily: "—and only when doing so is *absolutely essential* to preserve our safety or the safety of those in our immediate vicinity. See, Doc? I remember!"

Gosland's expression softened.

"So there's absolutely no need to brand ourselves," Cameron concluded. There was a brief pause before he added, with a touch of irritation: "And why am *I* the only one who needs a name?!"

"Hey! I didn't say *brand*, I said *marketing*," Zack snapped. "I was very particular in my use of the word *marketing*. I hate the word *brand*."

Cameron rolled his eyes. "Whatever, there's no need to *market* ourselves—"

"Even more important, *you're* the only wheel on this gimpy tricycle without a cute, pre-existing alias. Tay came prepackaged with *babyBlaze* (which I *still* think is a little clunky, but I can work with it) and I already gave Nova the absolute *gem* that is Sonica."

Nova walked into the lounge and selected this exact moment to respond to what she'd obviously overheard from her room.

"I'm not going to answer to that, you little tumor."

Zack was not to be deterred. "Well, *duh*. Not when you're not *in uniform*, you won't," he said matter-of-factly. "Moving on," he continued, "What color do y'all want? Tay, I already got you down for baby blue. You know, 'cause—"

"We all know, Zack," Taylor said.

"The question is wholly irrelevant," Gosland chimed in. She set down her tray and wiped at one corner of her mouth with a fabric napkin. "Neoprenium only comes in black, and adding too many nonessential aesthetic elements can compromise the overall durability of the fabric."

Now it was time for some fast backtracking. "I know that, we all know that," Zack said in one breath. "I meant 'what color *trim* do y'all want?'"

Gosland and Tay exchanged smiles.

Inside the kitchen, Cameron lifted his head out of the fridge and said: "Canary or cobalt for me."

"I'll go with fern . . . no, wait. Emerald," Nova said.

Zack rapidly scribbled some words onto his tablet. "So, yellow or dark blue and green, gotcha," he said unenthusiastically.

"No, I said *emerald*," Nova persisted. "I was very particular in my use of the word *emerald*. And throw in some magenta."

"How come *you* get two colors?" Taylor asked.

"You sure you don't mean *fuchsia*, Princess?" Zack asked with not-so-subtle sarcasm.

"I'm sure I don't mean *fuchsia*," Nova answered with simple yet unmistakable conviction.

"Yeah, howco *you* ge twooo colorsth?" Cameron repeated through a mouthful of cold pizza.

Instead of waiting for Nova to justify her answer, Tay shifted her attention from form to function. "Ooh, Dr. Gosland! When you design the footwear, be sure to *skip* the heels."

"Who said *I* was designing the footwear?" Gosland said.

"Definitely no heels," Nova agreed. "The last thing I need is to drop a stiletto on someone's head from a hundred feet in the air."

Taylor looked pointedly at the other girl and remarked, with what sounded to Zack like a shade of jealousy: "You can't fly yet."

Nova's response was as deft as it was irrefutable: "And you never will."

Silence.

Gosland sighed wearily. "No heels. Zack, make a note."

Zack dutifully obeyed just as Cameron passed by and stole another glance down at the digital notepad. "No *way*, Zack!" he exclaimed with genuine annoyance. "I'm supposed to pick one of *these* rejects?" He snatched the tablet out of the small teen's hands and rattled off a sampling of the names that Zack had clearly pulled out of his ass.

"Shock Jock? Taser Wave? You've gotta be kidding me, dude. You've gotta be *kidding* me—Shockwave? That's kinda really lazy,

Zack. Especially when you consider the fact that my powers have absolutely *nothing* to do with electricity *or* the speed of sound—"

"Well, what the crap are we *supposed* to call you, huh?" Zack snapped back as he reached up to retrieve his tablet. "Not Quite Black Lightning? The Elekine Teen Dream? Shock and *Aww*?"

Taylor smiled. Nova covered her mouth to restrain a chuckle. Cameron rolled his eyes.

"Wait, hang on, I got two, maybe three more in me!" Zack said excitedly before Gosland cut him short.

"Those were plenty, Zack, thank you. Now it's almost time for bed." She rose from her seat and motioned for Zack and Cameron to do the same.

Cameron elekinetically reached out to the nearest electronic device with a timepiece.

"It's not even nine!" he said petulantly.

Gosland looked at her watch. "You're right. But it is 'get out of the lab' time," she said firmly. "Go home now, all of you. You too, Nova."

With extreme reluctance, Cameron, Zack, and Taylor shuffled to gather their belongings. Nova hesitated, her face a case study in apprehension.

"Doc . . . My dad is still . . ."

Randall Stevens was vocally reluctant to allow Nova to return to their home on Kilmer for fear that she might endanger his life, the lives of their pets, or any of the many additional residents of the Corsican Towers. His fears, however valid, only served to increase the rate of erosion of his relationship with his only child.

Gosland understood the argument and sympathized with both father and daughter.

"I know, but it has to happen at some point, and tonight is as good as any. If you want to, you can come back tomorrow night. Your room here is still *your room*," she said.

Nova's anxiety relaxed a fraction.

Gosland directed her next words to everyone, including Zack: "Don't set foot inside this lab before seven p.m. I need at least one full day to update your files and plan the next phase of treatment."

As the teens boarded the elevator to exit the lab, Cameron mumbled: "You mean you need a day to *recover* from us."

"I mean I need a day to *recover* from you," Gosland affirmed. "Now get out of here, go get some rest. Big day tomorrow, right?"

Zack saw a wave of despair washed over the faces of the other three teens. In the excitement of the day's activities, they had completely forgotten what awaited them in the morning.

"Yes," Cam and Tay responded unenthusiastically.

Nova sighed. "Ah, f—"

"*Farewell*, Dr. Gosland." Zack finished for her.

Gosland took one last look at the departing adolescents. In a very real way, they were her progeny: three hormonal, irrational, *dangerous* genetic aberrations. And their blabbermouth mascot.

Gosland smiled. "Farewell, kids."

*   *   *   *   *

Later that night, when the screaming and convulsions finally came to an end, Zack's eyelids fluttered wearily open and he gradually registered the familiar visage of maternal concern on Jasmine Haynes' face.

Zack was curled up in a tiny fetal ball on the floor of his room, entangled in a sweaty mess of bedclothes. His head and shoulders were cradled between his sister's loving arms. In the soft light emanating from the hallway, her face was ghostly yet comforting.

"*Shh shh shh*, you're okay, Little Man. It's *okay*. Little Man, you're *okay*. It's okay. *Shh shh*," she repeated soothingly.

"I didn't *do* it, Jas. I didn't do it, I swear to God. I *never* do it. It's not my fault," Zack mumbled incoherently. His heart was rattling like a Thompson submachine gun.

Jas locked eyes with him. "I *know* you didn't, Little Man. I know. I *know* you didn't."

"Then who *did*, huh? And how come they're after *me*?" Zack asked for the hundredth time, although he had little faith that Jas could or *would* give him a satisfactory answer. After all, *he* was the one having the same horrific nightmare for the last three years, not she. *He* was the one always being chased down the endless, claustrophobic corridor; *he* was the one who was always captured by the giant, looming figures with no faces; *he* was the one being strapped to the icy metallic table; *he* was the one being jabbed with the large—

Jas took a calming breath and rose to her feet. "Let's go," she said simply.

Zack followed suit and trudged behind her into the kitchen of their darkened, modest two-bedroom apartment. He flicked the overhead range light on, opened the refrigerator, and filled a small glass with water from the filtered pitcher. The digital clock on the stove read *2:14.* The clock on the microwave was apparently one minute too fast. Or too slow.

Jasmine joined her brother a moment later and set a single, tiny pill on the granite countertop next to his glass.

Zack stared at the pill, then looked at Jas blankly.

"Go on," she said.

Zack stared at the pill, then looked at Jas blankly.

"Come *on* already. I gotta be up early to call in a refill."

"This the last one?" Zack asked.

"Yeah. For now."

"So maybe you tell me what's going on?"

Jas gave her head a faint shake. "Nope."

Zack's face twisted in a blend of fury and desperation. "Jas, I can't *take* this anymore! Three weeks in a row—"

"Zack, please!" she interjected with equal intensity. Then she saw the genuine despair in her brother's eyes and took a beat to regain her composure before starting over.

"Please, just—just take it and go back to sleep. We'll talk about it next week."

Zack's expression hardened.

This *sucked*. Jas, his sister, his Closest and Only Family in the Universe, was keeping something from him. Something *epic*. And, once again, rather than divulge that Something, she wanted to shut him up and medicate him with . . . Zack wasn't sure *what*, but it packed one hell of a fast wallop.

"Whatever," he said sourly. "Drugs over hugs, right?"

He snatched up the pill and swallowed it with a single gulp of water, slamming the glass down on the granite before exiting the kitchen.

Jas intercepted him. "No! That's not it at all!" she insisted as she clenched him tightly again.

Zack looked up and saw tears forming in the corners of her eyes, he felt the warmth of her embrace, and some of his anger that was really just sublimated fear began to dissipate.

"Drugs *before* hugs, Zack," Jas said. "Drugs *before* hugs."

She held onto Zack for what seemed like forever, and, as the unidentified pharmaceutical started to take effect, all of the awful imagery from the boy's nightmares faded from his memory just like the morning mist.

Zack was already half-asleep when his sister redeposited him into his bed and covered him with a fresh duvet.

"Sweet dreams, Little Man," Jasmine said softly. "It was never *your* fault."

She closed the door and stared absently down the hallway, her eyes narrowed in a rage born of deep-seated guilt.

It's all on Her, she thought.

PHASE 3/5:
ASSEMBLY

CHAPTER 9

Keaton Beach Boardwalk
Keaton Layer—11:42 am

THE SOUND OF THE BREAKING WAVES POUNDED IN HER ears like the roar of a jet turbine, and the hundreds of rattling footsteps were an aural massacre rivaling St. Valentine's Day.

Yes, there were smiling faces streaked with unevenly applied sunscreen and *yes*, volleyballs were whistling through the air and *yes*, excitement permeated the ocean airwaves. And *yes*, there were churros.

But today, Nova Stevens couldn't care less.

She didn't care that she no longer needed to worry about negative fallout from her disastrous performance. Nobody who actually mattered could agree on what they saw transpire that night, so details surrounding the incident were scarce. Injuries besides her own had been minimal, and there had been no casualties. Anyway, Pulse Charter was slated to get a new theater sometime before the end of the next school year, courtesy of its inexhaustibly wealthy founder.

But, instead of possessing a healthy and overwhelming sense of gratitude, Nova didn't care that she was not currently strapped to a table inside some putridly-lit laboratory. Or bouncing off the walls of a padded cell. Quite the contrary. From the moment she arrived at Gordon Biogen, Dr. Gosland had encouraged her to personalize her room without restraint; and, of course, DHS-EX backed off once her ion bracelet went live. As long as she kept up with her treatments and cut back on the libations—acid reflux from alcohol was total *murder* on vocal cords that were suddenly capable of generating enough force to shatter masonry—Nova was free to resume her normal life. Free to attempt to, anyway.

But today, Nova Stevens couldn't care less.

She couldn't be bothered with the fact that today was one of the most beautiful days she'd ever experienced, ever. She didn't care that she was at the best beach on Keaton. Or that every few minutes, another male head would turn and shoot a longing glance in her direction. Or that every one of those glances was followed up with a jealous scowl from an accompanying jealous female. No, none of that information could assuage her current mood.

It was the headphones.

They were supposed to help her adjust to the onslaught of ambient noises bombarding her newly enhanced eardrums. From the moment of her manifestation, Nova had been suffering from crippling migraines and lost nearly an entire week's worth of sleep due to her ability to hear everything, always.

When Dr. Gosland presented Nova with the headphones, she explained that they were not *noise-canceling* in the strictest sense. They did *not* create an inverse pressure wave to lower unwanted sounds or do the other thing like a car muffler, *blah blah blah.* Instead, they were designed to absorb, filter and redistribute any unwanted sounds in Nova's vicinity to a part of her brain that was reserved for . . . something else.

All Nova knew was that the headphones "tricked" her natural ability to perceive any sounds that she wasn't actively focusing on at any given moment. In essence, when Nova wore them, she could actually choose *what* she heard and *how much* of it she wanted to hear. The technology was the product of a scientific revolution waged on behalf of an individual, and Nova should have been thrilled that her transition into a functioning auralkine was now an all but guaranteed smooth one.

But the headphones were a huge eyesore, and the headband pinched into her temples and got tangled in her hair and *Seriously, why couldn't they be earbuds?!*

So Nova wasn't wearing them right now. They were just a pair of bulky ornaments slung around the base of her neck. And, consequently, every sound she registered triggered another jolt of pain in her eardrums. That pain, in turn, vibrated down through her molars and resonated in the nerves connected to her jawbone. A frown had been plastered on her face all day, starkly contrasting her surroundings.

At this moment, Nova was standing next to Cameron and Taylor behind a Gordon Biogen information/snow cone booth on the massive boardwalk adjacent to the pier on Keaton Beach. The three teens were stuck attending yet *another* company-sponsored

EX awareness event. In response to the well-orchestrated media campaign, the usually large crowd of summer beachgoers had swollen to almost unwieldy proportions. Supposedly, there was plenty of food, freebies, and fun to go around. According to Cameron's grandfather, the aim of this event was to "unite [our] citizens, beach vendors, and public service workers in an effort to spread the word about community responsibility in the midst of our growing population of enhanced individuals."

Blargh.

And, as if things couldn't get any worse, Zack Haynes was here, darting in and out of the booth and shoving his stupid little camera into everyone's faces.

Today, however, something about him was . . . off.

Nova could sense that the tiny whelp's heart wasn't as into the endeavor as it had been yesterday. *Literally.* Even without the aid of the headphones, Nova could easily detect the frequency of his resting beats per minute. They kept jumping around sporadically, almost like a nervous twitch. Something was wrong with him.

Nova dismissed the observation almost immediately. Zack Haynes' problems were as insignificant to Nova as Zack was.

"Here you go. And please ask your parents to check out our website, **www.gordonex.org.** Enjoy!"

Cameron reached across the counter and handed a perfectly crafted snow cone to a little girl, who smiled her appreciation before disappearing into the sea of bodies walking past the booth. She was instantly replaced by a sunburned middle aged man with a sunburned wife and three sunburned children in tow. The family, in turn, was followed by a single man who looked to be in his early thirties, and on and on it went. An endless amount of open hands and, Cameron hoped, open minds about the plight of the E-roid community.

As quickly as Cameron could call out quantities and flavors, Taylor would scoop and deliver. She took pains not to be *too* quick in fulfilling her task, lest the display of her abilities cause widespread alarm and draw exactly the kind of attention she and Cameron were doing their best to avoid.

Taylor understood the mechanics of her inverse inertia much better than before and possessed enough confidence when using her powers to accomplish basic tasks more efficiently. But it was still a mild challenge to direct the Other Her in a clear and straightforward path, and some actions requiring precision and dexterity were still hit and miss. The last thing she wanted to do was to hand over a snow cone to some unsuspecting elderly man with enough force to fracture his carpals.

Instead, Taylor focused on the innocuous rhythm of her duties: one scoop of ice, one pump of syrup, and one smile on her face as she passed the completed confection to Cameron.

Scoop, syrup, smile, she repeated in her head. *Scoop, syrup, smile. Scoop, syrup . . .*

"I'm warning you, pest—"

"*Smile!*"

Taylor heard a growl of annoyance from Nova, a sudden *crash,* and an accompanying burst of laughter from some passersby. The blonde didn't hyper-run, normal run, walk, or so much as set foot out of the booth to inspect the commotion. She knew exactly what had transpired and was only mildly surprised that it had taken so long to occur.

Out on the boardwalk, Zack was sitting on his butt with his legs splayed out in front of him. Most of his crimson-flushed face was concealed behind hair that was dripping with lime-colored ice shavings. A crumpled paper cone sat crooked atop his head like a miniature dunce cap.

Nova towered over Zack, holding his beloved camera in one hand. Her eyes were ablaze with murder.

"Come near me with this thing again and I'll scream *it* and *you* off the pier!" Nova tossed the camera at Zack's crumpled form and stomped back to the booth.

Zack picked himself up with all the dignity he could muster and wrung the last bits of snow cone out his orange locks. He decided that Now was the perfect time to scout for some new talent. And perhaps another filming location.

*   *   *   *   *

Hours later, the miles of sand castles erected along the coast were abandoned and family barbecues turned into bonfires as the last sliver of the sun vanished below the Pacific horizon. A second glut of surfers dressed in all manner of fluorescent attire and neon accessories took to the waves, eager to capitalize on the break in congestion from the departing crowds. The ocean itself seemed to breathe a sigh of relief at the end of another long day.

Two thousand feet out from the shoreline, Zack stood near the end of the pier capturing random moments of normal, boring Life. Fishermen baiting their hooks, a couple of awkward-looking young adults obviously on their first date. That hideous pelican perched atop of one of the emergency fire hose boxes.

Behind his viewfinder, Zack snarled. He *hated* pelicans. Ever since that poorly CG rendered squawkbag stole the game board and nearly ruined everything . . . And *oh, how they stank!*

Zack panned over to the large, two-story diner situated by the edge of the pier. It was one of those nostalgia places, but done surprisingly well. Inside, he knew, Cameron and the girls were polishing off burgers and shakes in celebration of completing their Public Relations prison stint. Zack would join them shortly to review his work. Surprisingly to everyone, including himself, Zack had actually succeeded in documenting a legitimately *nice* compilation of the day's happenings. With some creative editing, maybe he could convince Cam's folks to use the footage in the official Gordon Industries press video about the EX awareness event. At worst, it could end up playing in a loop on one of the Gordon Biogen labs' lobby screens. Either option would be cool.

Several dozen feet below and away, Zack saw a midsize luxury motor yacht slice northward through the waves, no doubt on its way home to the marina. Zooming in on the passengers' faces, he noted a shared look of exhilaration that could only be the product of intoxication.

Zack took the opportunity to formulate the hypothesis for an improbable case study.

"Ladies and gentleman of the jury," he began, sweeping his camera back and forth among his fellow piermates, none of whom paid him any attention. "I present Exhibit A: One SwiftStream 2000 weekend cruiser. Approximately thirty-five feet in length and traveling at a speed of . . . *Whatever*, I dunno nothing about *knots*, but at least forty-five miles per hour. Vessel is currently helmed by a drunk WASP and—"

From off-camera, Zack heard someone offer: "A knot is equal to 1.5078 miles per hour, but you've gotta factor in the opposing wind current, drag, and—"

"*Uh huh*, so probably less than forty-five, but a lotta knots anyway, thanks," Zack said dismissively. "Anyway, beneath us is Exhibit B: One network of dilapidated wooden support pillars, each one at least a couple feet in diameter, all of them engineered to hold the weight of Exhibit C: One 1950's-themed diner."

He paused to allow his nonexistent audience to absorb and process the seemingly disparate pieces of evidence before setting up the challenge:

"I ask—nay, I *implore* you—what conflation of circumstances, what possible *contortion* of the laws of probability and physics would it take for Exhibit A to crash into Exhibit B, sending Exhibit C (and me!) into the . . . the . . ."

Zack's attention and his camera's focus were snatched away by a pair of passing girls in low-cut bathing suits and swim wraps. The girls were, in Zack's unbiased opinion, absurdly sexy.

"Your Honor, at this time the People request a brief recess to review some newly discovered evidence in the form of Exhibits Thirty-two and, um, Thirty-*four* double-D," Zack rattled off before scurrying after the girls.

Cameron took a clump of french fries, used it to scoop out the last bit of garlic aioli from the paper ramekin, and gulped it down with a swig of his peanut butter malt. His head was pounding, but it wasn't the result of a brain freeze.

For hours now, he'd been trying to understand the Sensation. That was how he described it to himself, since it wasn't exactly *pain;* rather, some intangible *force* invading the deepest part of his psyche. It felt like every individual around him was whispering his name a split second before he could identify who it was.

At first, he'd dismissed this phenomenon as exhaustion from a full day of interacting with hundreds of people. Cameron was no introvert, but he didn't care for large, unwieldy crowds, either. And this Sensation persisted so long after he was relieved of his duties that Cameron began to wonder if it was a result of his new EX maintenance regimen. In addition to the routine of physical exercises at Gordon F.L.E.X., Dr. Gosland had recently prescribed Cameron and the girls a new medication designed to calibrate and align their EX abilities with their natural circadian rhythms. The Doc explained that, in Cameron's case, the drugs eliminated the risk of him accidentally releasing elekinetic discharges during REM sleep.

So perhaps this constant sense of *Who's there? You there!* was a pharmacological side effect, one only Cameron was experiencing. He hoped not. Perhaps he was developing some secondary ability, like precognition or even telepathy. He hoped so. Why couldn't he? After all, Nova displayed almost *three* different gifts during her initial manifestation (a fact that Taylor seemed to resent more than a little bit).

Speaking of Tay, right now she was sitting across from Cameron with her head buried in her server. Even though she was less than two feet away, he could *feel* her presence more clearly than he saw it.

Without intentionally snooping for details, Cameron could elekinetically perceive that she was poring over media coverage of the day's festivities. As anticipated, all of the local and even a few national outlets deployed secret shoppers to sample all of the kiosks at the EX Awareness event. What was their final analysis, what would be the focus of tonight's and tomorrow's headlines?

"The latest poll indicates that public perception of E-roids has jumped from a low of fourteen percent three months ago to an all-time high of twenty-four percent," Tay said.

"Of course it jumped," Cameron responded as he polished off the last of his malt and pushed the empty goblet to the edge of the table. "We always knew that we're awesome, and today the crowds validated that fact."

"That's only because we didn't kill anyone," Nova clarified glumly from her seat beside Cameron.

Taylor lifted up her head to shoot Nova a glare but was suddenly distracted by the image of Zack on the other side of the window. In the light of several lampposts lining the pier, she saw that the boy was shamelessly photo-stalking a couple of girls who were irrefutably out of his league.

Nova craned her neck to follow Tay's glance and was about to comment on the inevitability of Zack's failure when a sound pricked her ears. It began as a shrill whine that rapidly became a steady *humm*, like an engine or something. Unconsciously, Nova wrinkled her face in confusion.

Cameron was beginning to recognize that particular look.

"What, what is it?" he asked.

Nova didn't answer. She was too busy trying to concentrate.

Whatever was making the noise sounded like it was far away but was moving closer to them. It was super big but super *fast*, almost like a giant jet ski—

The sound of the crash was deafening.

Nova fell to the ground and clutched her head in agony long milliseconds before the entire diner lurched as if seized by an earthquake.

Outside, the speeding motoryacht collided into several of the pier's corner support columns. On impact, the vessel's captain and his passengers were ejected violently into the churning waves.

Several people in the diner reacted with surprise, but most of the patrons kept their cool. A few pieces of silverware and some soda cups were knocked to the floor, but the latter were made from that indestructible 1950s red plastic and survived unscathed.

That *should* have been the extent of the damage. But this current iteration of the pier was over thirty years old, and its most recent remodeling date had been pushed back several times in recent years by a couple of city council members who favored the funding of a new high-rise development over renovating the historic seaside landmark.

So when the motoryacht's engine *exploded* a few minutes later, the force of the blast splintered the rickety surrounding columns and triggered a series of violent spasms across the edge of the pier. Inside the diner, dinnerware shattered, lightbulbs burst, and gas lines ruptured. Workers and patrons alike were tossed about like stringless marionettes. Outside the diner, a number of poor unfortunate souls standing near the pier's railing were jolted overboard and plunged over fifty feet into the mysterious fathoms below.

Zack Haynes was among that number.

Cameron and the girls rose slowly to their feet and took a few moments to assess themselves and each other for visible injuries.

Fortunately, they couldn't find anything serious beyond a few bumps and bruises where they'd bounced off the edge of the table. Nova finally slipped on her headphones to help calm her senses.

Then, even without the help of his new yet somewhat *glitchy* extrasensory perception, Cameron felt the stampede of a hundred diner occupants hastily evacuating both floors of the diner. In one frenzied mob, the people clawed their way out of the woefully inadequate single-doored exit and raced up the pier back to the mainland.

Well-toned muscle memory prevented Cameron and the girls from joining the crowd; the cacophony was unbearable *and* unsafe. The teens figured they could wait a few minutes before leaving. They figured wrong.

Surprisingly, it was Taylor who heard it first: a long, dull *moan* of creaking timber. Then came the successive rattle of *pop crunch pop crunch* as the remaining support columns buckled under the added stresses until they snapped like toothpicks. All of the lights inside the diner winked out, which only added to the confusion and chaos. Finally, all three teens heard and felt a bloodcurdling *CRACK* as the ancient diner floor split open between their feet and the roof followed suit above their heads. A heartbeat later, the entire rear of the building collapsed into the ocean.

*   *   *   *   *

As Cameron tumbled downward through the emptiness of space, he seemed to experience the ordeal in clear, unblinking slow motion. Through the gaping maw of the bisected building, he felt the warm breeze of the summer night air whipping across his cheeks. He could see Nova falling beside him and he watched, entranced, as the headphones slipped off her head and twirled balletically away from her. He spared a moment to think of Taylor, daring to hope that she was still inside the remaining half of the diner. If so, he knew she would find a safe way out.

And then, with horror, he saw a glimmer of light reflecting off the wall-length window beneath him. The window that he was about to crash through, headfirst.

Cameron remembered that he was only wearing boardshorts and a tank top and sandals. None of those were even remotely protective. If the blunt force trauma from hitting the glass didn't immediately kill him, the myriad of subsequent lacerations would *certainly* finish the job—

The screaming, flailing body of an anonymous diner employee shot past Cameron and Nova, crashing through the window and turning it into a million tinkling raindrops. A split second later, the two teens fell through the opening and out of the diner. They landed, hard, on knotted wooden planks and continued tumbling downward as the pier rapidly descended from a steep incline to a completely vertical orientation.

Cameron flung his arms out vainly in search of something, *anything* to grab onto. He felt a jolt of searing pain in the right side of his ribcage as he bounced off something hard and angular. Then he fell another few feet and finally slammed to a stop, the wind knocked out of him.

Cameron shook his head, momentarily dazed. Then he took a quick scan of his surroundings.

In the light of the moon, he was relieved to see that the back of the diner hadn't completely detached from the pier. If it had, at this moment he'd be inhaling saltwater. He felt something cold and metallic beneath his arms and registered that he'd fallen onto one of the coin-operated viewers mounted near the railing at the edge of the pier. Cameron looked up and saw Nova hanging precariously from one hand. She was dangling on the back edge of one of the numerous iron-clad wooden spectator benches bolted across the pier—almost certainly the source of Cameron's painful initial impact. Not surprisingly, Nova was screaming at the top of her lungs, but this time it was *strategic*: a series of focused vocal blasts targeted to deflect and disintegrate the debris showering down on them from the diner above. In between breaths, Nova was using her free hand to encapsulate bits of falling scrap in nearly invisible "bubbles" of aural energy before tossing them out of harm's way.

Cameron looked down and saw the flaming husk of some kind of sport yacht some twenty or more feet below him. It had finally dislodged from the web of demolished support columns but now the bulk of the boat was struggling to keep afloat in the churning ocean. It wouldn't be long before the luxury wreck was completely submerged beneath the dark waves.

With sudden, savage fury, the Sensation came rushing back to Cameron's head. It was so jarring that he almost lost his grip.

He could clearly sense the presence of at least a dozen people floundering in the water, including . . . *Oh, crap.*

"Hey, Nova!" he called out.

The screaming paused and the girl turned her head to look down at him. Cameron could see the exhaustion on her face. He sympathized with her, but this was *not* the time to rest. Not with lives at risk, including their own.

"How big can you make those things?" he asked, pointing to her hand to indicate the sound bubbles emanating from her fingertips.

"I don't know!" Nova answered.

"Is there any air in them?"

"I don't know!"

"Well, *figure it out*, and fast! I'm going to get Zack!"

Cameron swung his legs back and forth and from side to side in an attempt to gain a solid foothold somewhere on the mounted viewer. Eventually, he managed to raise himself up to a crouching position where he could look out over the ocean and select a safe point of entry. Then he took a deep breath and prepared to jump.

For the first time since she gained her powers, Nova couldn't believe her ears.

"What do you *mean*, 'get Zack?!'" she said incredulously.

Before Cameron could elaborate, a large shake goblet flew past Nova and struck Cameron on the base of his skull with a loud, metallic *THUNK*. The teen's head lolled, his body slipped off of the viewer, and he fell the remaining distance to the inky water.

"No!" Nova screamed, instinctively reaching out her free hand to try and catch him. She had no idea if she was even capable of creating an aural sphere large enough to catch and transport a full-sized person. And, in this instance, she didn't get to find out.

Instead of generating a bubble, Nova released a powerful gust of sonic energy from her open palm. The sound waves bounced harmlessly off the horizontally mounted viewer; but, rather than whistle back up to smack Nova in the face yet again, the returning energy actually *propelled* her entire body upward into the air.

Everything was a blur as she ascended thirty feet through the gaping hole of the diner window, past the now darkened booth she'd shared with Cameron and Taylor and out the giant orifice left where the building split. Her designer wetshoes finally found purchase on the edge of the surviving half of the diner. Nova immediately whipped her head back around and down to locate Cameron, but the action was too frenzied. She lost her balance, and for an instant she knew she was about fall to her death for the third time in less than a month, this time for *real*—

Nova caught a glimpse of a faint light blue streak and felt a hard yank on one arm, so hard she could've sworn it was being ripped out of the socket. But the discomfort only lasted a second, and then Nova was lying in a heap next to Taylor on the solid and surprisingly warm planks of the pier.

"That doesn't count as *flying*," the blonde said, forcing a smile.

Nova exhaled deeply and returned the smile. Then, reality kicked her in the face.

"Cameron!" she exclaimed.

*   *   *   *   *

This time, he fell hard and fast.

Cameron opened his eyes the moment before his body hit the surface of the icy water with a loud *smack* that was instantly drowned out by the pulsating waves. The goblet to his dome hadn't knocked him unconscious—it'd merely stunned him. But now, as he sank into the churning darkness, he formed the single, final thought that, given his affinity for water, this impending death by drowning would be as appropriate as it was macabre . . .

And suddenly, his senses went into hyperdrive.

Okay, maybe not *all* of his senses. In fact, none of the primary senses except *touch* and *sound* were of any use to him right now. And the only useful information they were transmitting was that it was freaking *cold* down here.

But now, the Sensation that'd been plaguing Cameron all day was fully active. And somehow, immersed in the vastness of the ocean, he could "see" everything and every*body* nearby: a group of displaced diner patrons and workers swimming furiously toward the shore; other survivors inching their way up the emergency ladders imbedded into the few remaining pier columns; several near-lifeless bodies drifting aimlessly among the waves near the wreckage of the collapsed pier.

Then Cameron registered that one of those bodies belonged to Zack, and, in the same moment, he recalled that *breathing* was not only a fun but essential activity for most living beings.

Cameron kicked hard to the surface and took a gulp of fresh night air. In the dim light from the burning yacht, he saw a small figure bobbing like a cork ten feet away. He swam vigorously over to the floating figure, which was indeed Zack. As he'd detected, the boy was still alive, but he wasn't conscious.

Cameron had no idea how to properly carry a potentially drowning person to safety, but he figured that lifting the victim's head out of the water was a good place to start. So he grabbed Zack, flipped him onto his back, and began paddling backwards toward the closest column with a ladder.

"Be glad you weigh nothing . . . This is super hard," Cameron muttered to Zack in between ragged breaths as he navigated the maze of shrapnel floating in the water around them while debris rained down from above.

Zack retched and let out a string of forceful coughs. Water poured out of his mouth. Then he flopped his head back and forth like a sopping dog. Long, wet tendrils of hair slapped across his face and doused Cameron with even more ocean spray. Eventually, Zack relaxed and began kicking his feet in the same direction as his rescuer.

"Well aren't *you* just super . . . hero," he said weakly.

They reached the support column, and Cameron summoned the last ounce of his strength to pull himself and the tiny teen up the first few rungs of the emergency ladder, taking special care to avoid the ring of razor-sharp barnacles encrusting the pillar just beneath the water line.

After a few moments, Cameron paused to look down at Zack. "Hey! You got this?" he asked, pointing to the top of the ladder and the safety of the undamaged part of the pier.

Zack nodded. "Yeah."

"Good, 'cause I gotta go get the captain."

Zack considered the probability that he swallowed too much seawater and was suffering a momentary bout of delirium.

"Excuse me, sir?" he asked.

"The *captain*," Cameron repeated impatiently. "He's stuck in the wreckage, he's not gonna last much longer and the Coast Guard is still a few miles out!"

Zack didn't exactly know how to process all of that, but he nodded again. "Okay, I totally understand, but this ain't on *you*, dude—"

Without another word, Cameron pushed off of the ladder and dove back into the water.

"What the crap?!" Zack cried out. *"Cam!"*

Then he heard a wispy, vaguely familiar sound, and the next instant he was enveloped in total silence.

Cameron powered his way across the waves back toward the scene of the motoryacht crash. His arms and calf muscles were screaming in agony, but the faint traces of the Sensation assured him that his efforts would soon be rewarded, so he took another deep breath and went under again.

Once again, he couldn't see a thing, but this time he didn't need to. His unidentified extrasensory perception immediately honed in on the body of the captain, who was also unconscious but floating several feet *beneath* the surface of the water, trapped by one foot in a viselike tangle of kelp. He wouldn't last much longer.

Cameron swam past the sinking bodies of two people he assumed were the yacht's passengers. He detected, with a pang of sadness, that they were already dead. Nevertheless, he powered on and eventually made contact with the third body, the captain. Cameron quickly removed the kelp, grabbed the man, and raced upward toward salvation.

Just as they broke the surface, the rear of the diner decided to finish collapsing into the ocean. Directly on top of them.

Cameron opened his mouth to offer one final scream . . .

. . And that's when a giant sphere of shimmering emerald silence completely engulfed him. The next thing Cameron knew, he was floating up and out of the roiling waves, far beyond the wreckage of the crash, and away from the ruins of the diner.

The mysterious ball of quiet, green energy deposited the dripping clump of Cameron onto a safe section of the pier. He sat up, glanced around, and finally let out a sigh of relief.

Twenty feet away, the captain had regained consciousness. He stood uneasily on one knee, hacking up a gallon of water and foamy bile from his lungs as the paramedics scrambled to render him aid. Further up the pier, emergency crews were tending to as many displaced patrons and workers as they could. Several SCPD beach cruisers had already formed a barricade to secure the area and control access to and from the boardwalk.

Cameron sensed the familiar and welcome presence of three individuals in his immediate vicinity. He looked up and saw a combination of relief, exhaustion, and bemusement on the faces of Taylor, Nova, and Zack. They were standing inconspicuously in the crowd that had gathered behind the yellow tape of the police cordon.

Then Cameron sensed and saw Dr. Gosland.

She looked . . . less than jubilant.

CHAPTER 10

Gordon Biogenetics Laboratory
Keaton Layer—8:45 pm

THE TRIP BACK TO GORDON BIOGEN WAS UNEVENTFUL, save for a brief recap of the evening's happenings as mumbled by Taylor and Nova.

As Gosland guided her car through the hustle and bustle of a typical Saturday evening, she took note of Zack's uncharacteristic silence and Cameron's lethargy, both of which she attributed to shock and exhaustion from the disaster at the diner. To her credit, Gosland took great pains to project an aura of calm in an effort to maintain a peaceful atmosphere for the teens after their chaotic ordeal. She was genuinely excited to hear about Nova's newest manifested ability, and she was positively *delighted* to learn of her rescue by the quick hands and even quicker reflexes of Taylor. By the time Gosland pulled into the Gordon Biogen garage, her mood had softened from *nervous wreck* to *cautiously relieved*.

Then she heard about Cameron, and her mood took a turn.

"What the hell did you think you were doing?" Gosland's scream echoed over the roar of the water. She was standing in front of the frosted opaque door to a smart glass shower enclosure inside what had recently become Nova's bathroom, tucked away in one corner of the basement lab.

Inside the shower, Cameron responded immediately, almost dismissively: "You're a *scientist*, you have a better vocabulary than that."

"Don't you *dare* try to minimize, Cameron!" Gosland snapped. "Not this time! Tonight you went too far."

"You're absolutely right."

The admission stopped Gosland cold.

"I should have been wearing a *suit*," the teen continued in a matter-of-fact tone. "What's the ETA on those, anyway?"

The question fired Gosland up again.

"ETA? The concept is less than twenty-four hours old! And what did I just *say* about minimizing?"

"I'm not minimizing, Doc. I'm *deflecting*," Cameron clarified. "I *get* it, I should've waited for some help before going back for the captain. But it's like I told Zack, the Coast Guard—"

"No, Cameron, you *don't* get it! You shouldn't have gone down there to begin with—not the first time, not the second time! *None* of the times!"

Behind the convex smart glass door, Cameron frowned.

"Oh yeah, Doc, that makes total sense. So . . . Zack *dies*, we all regroup here, and me and the girls warm up with a cup of hot cocoa while *you* look Jasmine Haynes in the face and explain why none of his *superpowered friends* tried to save him?! I mean, *okay*, Tay was legit preoccupied with not falling to her own death. But, even though Nova hates Zack more than second dates, she still tried to help him. Successfully!"

Again, Gosland was silent. She couldn't argue with the teen's reasoning.

"Exactly. So no more *'see here, young man,'* all right?" Cameron said. Now he was dripping with exuberance, confidence. After all, he was dealing from a position of clear logic and strength.

"Now, Doc, *I* have a question for *you*: What's that extra sense that sharks have, the one that helps them find prey without sight or smell? What's it called—electric radar? Electro*something*."

Gosland wrinkled her upper lip in irritation at the sudden and drastic change of subject. Then she closed her eyes in surrender and rubbed her supraorbital ridge with a thumb and forefinger.

"Electroreception," she sighed.

"Electroreception," Cameron repeated. "Yeah, that's the one. I'm pretty sure I—what do you want, Zack?"

Gosland opened her eyes and turned to see Zack standing beside her.

"Okay, dude, *that's* not creepy at all," the pint-sized teen said with wide eyes and thick sarcasm. "Also, pizza's here."

"I'm not hungry," Cameron said plainly.

"Good for you. But I've just made the fascinating discovery that drowning *really* kicks up the ol' appetite . . . When'd you get *electroreception?*"

"It's been blinking on and off all day, I guess it locked in fully just before the diner went under," Cameron explained. "It's how I knew you were in the water. It's how I know that, at this moment, Nova's trying to sleep in her room and Tay is in the lounge on her server hunting for any captured footage of us that might've leaked online." He paused to concentrate. "It's also how I know the Doc is maybe two seconds away from *exploding.*"

Through her clenched teeth, Gosland said: "*Less* than that."

"Cool," Zack said coolly. "So now you're a platypus."

"What?" Cameron asked.

"A platypus. They've got that extra Shark Sense too, y'know? Except that they're mammals. With duck bills. Who lay *eggs.* And they're poisonous . . ." Zack's voice trailed off as he contemplated the absurdity of that randomly assembled aquatic monotreme.

Now Gosland was deep in thought. She knew that, within the animal kingdom, only a handful of species of vertebrate fish—and a few mammals—possessed *electroreception,* a biological ability to perceive living creatures based on the innate electrical fields they emit. The ability ranged from *passive,* like the one belonging to sharks, echidnas, and platypi, to *active,* most common to rays and eels. But, in nearly every occurrence, the animal's ability could be traced back to specific organs or cells situated along their lateral line—

"This doesn't make sense," Gosland said to Cameron. "None of your recent exams yielded *any* evidence of the development of Ampullae of Lorenzini or any other external electroreceptors."

Cameron's chuckle reverberated throughout the bathroom. "Well, I'm definitely *not* leaking any cranial jelly, Doc. So I guess we can chalk this new sense up to a funky batch of EX ions?" He paused and then added: "Zack, I need a name for it. Preferably one that *doesn't* suck."

Zack bit his lower lip as he searched the depths of his creative well.

"Elekine awareness," he shrugged.

Gosland said nothing, ashamed to admit to herself that the moniker truly *didn't* suck.

"I'll take it." Cameron turned off the faucet and, a moment later, the shower door slid open with a gust of steam.

"Aw, *come on*, dude!" Zack exclaimed in disgust, whipping his head around faster than Taylor ever could in an attempt to avoid the horrid sight of the other teen's naked body. He threw up one arm for extra protection as he grabbed a nearby towel and hurled it in the direction of the steam cloud.

Cameron stepped out and easily caught the towel in midair. He was fully clothed in his beach attire, and there were zero visible signs that he'd been anywhere near water, save for a few straggling drops on his face. Those drops were rapidly absorbed into his skin and ever-so-slightly lengthened the tips of his hair.

Gosland turned around and exited the bathroom, exhausted and unimpressed.

And, as Cameron casually replaced the towel on its hook and walked past Zack, the tiny teen slowly opened his eyes and finally unclenched.

"Disgusted reaction retracted," he said.

*   *   *   *   *

In the lounge, the television was turned to a twenty-four-hour streaming news feed. Footage of the damaged pier, the hollow remnants of the diner, and the wreck of the motoryacht cycled across the screen. Cameron elekinetically unmuted the monitor's speakers, and the three teens and Gosland heard the voice of an anonymous reporter:

"Engineering experts agree that, given the extent of the structural damage to the pier, it was certainly fortuitous that the entire restaurant didn't sink into the ocean sooner. If it had, the likelihood of recovering any survivors would have been drastically lowered. Preliminary damage estimates are in the tens of millions of nanos—"

"See that, Doc?" Cameron said. "It was only a ton of *money*, not *lives*. This could've gone so much worse."

Gosland slowly uncrossed her arms. Her face finally softened.

"Well done, kids . . . Cameron," she said reluctantly.

Just then, Nova slogged into the room past everyone, heading straight for the mini fridge. She was wearing a set of lightweight cotton pajamas with matching fuzzy slippers and a sleep mask strapped tightly over her eyes. It occurred to Gosland and the others that she was using her amplified hearing to navigate her steps. Clearly, her desire to preserve the sleepytime atmosphere of her darkened room was greater than any concern for potentially bumping into objects.

"Yeah, sure," Nova yawned. "Good job, you crazy bastard."

She generated a thin aural wave with one hand and gently lassoed the door to the mini fridge open before creating a small green sound bubble to retrieve a bottle of sparkling water. And then, as if suddenly bored with this flagrant display of her newest ability, Nova walked over the fridge, stretched out a leg, and lazily closed the door with the tip of one fuzzy foot.

Taylor's face twisted into a glare.

"You too, Sound Babe. Really saved my bacon, y'know?" Zack was saying from the armchair. He suddenly remembered the open pizza box on the coffee table and reached for a slice. "Ooh! Extra bacon!"

Taylor resisted the urge to zipheel out of her seat and snatch the pizza out of Zack's mouth before it made contact with his teeth. Instead, the girl took a deep breath and calmly reached into the gym bag at her feet. She extracted a pair of unsolved Rubik's Speed Cubes and took one in each hand.

Nova froze in midstep, whipped her head around, and lifted one corner of her mask. "No no *no*, Taylor, not *two* of them, don't you *dare*—"

The loud *HISS* of plastic rattlesnakes suddenly drowned out the sound of the television and everything else in the lounge as Taylor started to solve, shuffle, and resolve both 3D combination puzzles. Simultaneously. At superspeed.

Conceived by Dr. Gosland, this mentally and mechanically dexterous activity with one cube afforded Taylor the same healthy release of stress hormones that traditional hand grippers offered the average Neutral. She only resorted to using both cubes at once to suppress a nuclear-level meltdown. Or to satiate the occasional compulsion to deliberately annoy the *crap* out of Nova.

"You suck you suck you suck you SUCK!" Nova wailed.

"I'm sure I don't know *what* you mean by that, Nova," Taylor said with the innocence of a newborn fawn. Her hands were a whirling, multicolored blur as the snakes kept hissing.

"Zack got extra bacon, you got extra powers . . . What's wrong with an extra cube?" she asked sweetly.

"Taylor," Gosland began, but Zack's voice cut her off sharply.

"Oh, get *over* it already, *babyBlaze!*" The tiny teen swallowed a mouthful of pizza and wiped sauce from the corner of his mouth.

"Last I checked, *you* got to save someone's life tonight too," Zack continued, pointing to Nova.

Taylor attempted to mask a sullen pout.

"Was it as flashy? *Nope.* Was the rescuee as relevant as Yours Truly? *Eh.* That's debatable."

Nova peeled off her mask and raised an eyebrow. "Eh?" she repeated with obvious irritation. Zack pretended not to hear her.

"My point is, three out of the five people in this room can do things most humans only dream of, and *I* ain't one of them, but *you* are, and right now you're bitching about some missing extra credit points!"

"That's enough, Zack," Cameron said.

"Almost done, dude," Zack replied. Then, to Taylor:

"I'm just saying—you *all* took a risk tonight and it played out great. *Stop* selling yourself short, Tay. That's *my* gig."

Taylor gradually slowed her speedcubing down to a normal pace. Eventually, she stopped altogether and replaced the cubes in her bag. With the noise abated, they could once again hear the television:

"*—saddened to report that thirty-eight-year-old Grant Mizumi, captain and owner of the disabled motoryacht, has died.*"

"No!" Cameron exclaimed in astonishment.

"*It was originally reported that Mizumi suffered a sudden medical emergency attributed to a previously undiagnosed heart defect, one that directly contributed to his losing of control of the vessel—*"

"Like I said in the water—that *wasn't* on you, dude." Zack said reassuringly. Cameron responded with a simple, violent "*Shh!*"

"*—despite initial resuscitative efforts from an anonymous citizen, officials at Silver Grace Hospital have since confirmed that Mizumi's cause of death was an acute stroke triggered by electrocution—*"

Silence spread across the lounge, a silence thicker than winter molasses in Connecticut.

Four heads refused to turn in Cameron's direction. Four pairs of eyes avoided his gaze.

"*—a beloved husband and devoted father of two—*" the television continued, indifferent to the tension in the room.

Cameron finally mustered enough moisture in his throat to form words, but the result was a paltry stammer: "But I—he—he was al—*alive*, I could *tell*, I didn't . . . he was alive . . ."

"Cameron," Gosland said softly.

"Alive," Cameron repeated. "He was *alive* . . . ALIVE!"

A sudden flash of elekinetic energy surged outward from the teen and directly into the television. The device exploded, leaving a faint odor of melted plastic and electrical components lingering in the air.

More Silence.

Nova walked decisively back over to the mini fridge, opened the door, and returned the unopened bottle of water to its place. Then she lifted the cover to the concealed butter tray and grabbed a glass pint of Scotch whisky before closing the fridge and leaving the room again. Nobody acknowledged or objected to the action.

In the safety of her room, Nova unscrewed the cap and took a long, solid pull of the liquor. It was the only thing she could do. Despite her efforts to heed the advice from Nurse Allie, Nova just *couldn't* turn off the sound of Cameron's body as it convulsed with his sobs.

"*Alive . . . I—I didn't kill him . . . I saved his life . . .*" she heard him blubbering.

Nova remembered the moment she snatched Cameron out of the ocean. The overwhelming sense of pride she'd felt when she deposited the captain onto the pier, still very much *alive*.

Not 'the captain,' Nova corrected herself harshly. *Grant Mizumi. His name was Grant Mizumi.*

She took another long pull from her bottle. Then she gave way to her own tears.

Zack finally lifted his head from where it'd been buried in his hands. He rose silently to his feet and headed for the elevator, but not before giving Cameron a light yet reassuring pat on the back. It was the least he could do . . . after all, the teen did save *his* life tonight. That was undeniable.

As the elevator doors closed, Taylor and Gosland approached Cameron to offer him a consoling embrace, refusing to allow the small embers of doubt in the back of their minds to combust into suspicion.

Both the student and the scientist knew that Cameron and Actual Electricity were as estranged as sun*rise* and sun*set*. Grant Mizumi could have been accidentally electrocuted by any number of devices at any time from the moment paramedics first attached leads to him in the ambulance. The phenomenon was rare, but it happened.

Grant Mizumi's death was *not* on Cameron's hands.

Right?

CHAPTER 11

526 Grant St
Clooney Layer—6:45 am

NOBODY IN THE CRADLE EVER SEES THE LIGHT OF DAY. Or the glow of the moon at night. There are seldom April showers or May flowers. No June gloom. None of the other meteorological occurrences are routinely visited upon Silver City's beleaguered lowest layer.

Not unless someone flips the right switch.

Situated nearly a quarter mile beneath sea level, Clooney is the beneficiary of some of the most advanced civil infrastructural developments and cutting-edge climate control technology in the world. Unfortunately, with the exception of a handful of new engineering grad students who make the mandatory pilgrimage to the Cradle each year, the rest of the world doesn't care.

Visitors to Silver City make it a point to skip their visit to Clooney's dilapidated downtown, which has become home to an ever-growing collection of strip malls, seedy clubs, and seedy strip clubs. The Cradle's historic Old Town plaza was relocated to the Keaton layer so long ago that most native Silver Citizens above Lowery grow up without ever learning about their subterranean heritage. Naturally, local tax revenue is always in short supply for the residents of Clooney; and, as a result, the deficit is almost always reflected in the quality (or lack thereof) of care for that layer's artificial ecosystem.

Blizzards in July. Lagoons on Labor Day. An overhead blanket of constellations blinking on and off, embarrassingly low on juice. It is a miracle that the skeleton crew of round-the-clock operators housed in the Lowery-Clooney sublayer can wrangle the ancient weather-generating equipment to turn the sun on at the right *time* each day.

On the other hand, residents of Clooney also experience all four seasons, a phenomenon utterly foreign to most Californians outside of Lake County. And since the summer lasts half the year across the entire state, it's easy enough for the operators to set the blue sky on autopilot each morning and leave without worrying about having to render a pesky marine layer or a sudden heat wave. A heat wave that occasionally triggers a wildfire . . . and the subsequent hike in utility rates.

After all, an overlit and overcooked Cradle is also an *expensive* Cradle.

Joe Lindsey opened his front door and rolled lazily down the porch ramp to the mailbox some twenty feet away at the end of the broken concrete path. He paused halfway and leaned forward to scoop up the morning edition of the *Nascent*, musing briefly that the paperboy's aim was improving.

Yesterday's mail got delivered well past dark, again, but Joe was pleased to see that the mailbox hadn't been vandalized (also, *again*). He extracted its contents and sorted through assorted fliers and envelopes, ignoring the obvious junk adverts and bills.

A small, nondescript parcel caught Joe's eye. It was a simple bubble mailer the size of an overstuffed greeting card, addressed in handwritten script to *Maximus SylVester*. There was no return address, save for an anonymous PO box. No clear indication of the sender's identity beyond the odd combination of upper and lower case letters in the teen's surname.

Joe smiled. Anyone else would've missed the subtle clue. Joe didn't.

In six years, only one person had ever sent bubble mailers to the Lindsey home addressed to Joe's son. The only person who dared to refer to Max by his full name.

A shadow suddenly darkened Joe's view, and for an instant he thought that Clooney's overhead Midnight Cloud Cover program had accidentally been tripped. But the shadow was quickly joined by several others, and Joe looked up to see that he was surrounded by a group of young men, teenagers, all of them with nasty expressions on their faces. Before Joe could utter a sound, they were on him.

Denise Lindsey came out onto the porch to scold her husband for leaving the front door open so long, just like she did every morning that didn't start with coffee.

She blinked several times in the unusually bright morning light and her eyes finally rested on a motionless blob on the sidewalk beside the mailbox. The image sharpened to reveal an upturned wheelchair and Denise recognized with horror that the blob on the ground was her *husband*, and her scream echoed down the block.

Max rarely enjoyed a full night's rest. While he wasn't exactly prone to nightmares, it was extremely difficult to fully cede control of his consciousness long enough to enter the dream state without some unknown impulse jarring him, at regular intervals, back to the valley between light and deep sleep.

So, when the sound of his foster mother's howl of terror reached his ears, Max was not jolted awake. Still, he bolted out of bed, through the rear basement exit, and up to the front of the house. In the glaring morning sunlight, Max saw and heard the *SLAM* of an unfamiliar car door just before it tore off down the street.

*   *   *   *   *

The average response time for local emergency services on Clooney ranges anywhere between thirty-five minutes to an hour plus. This time, the difference was split sixty/forty, and the medics were nearly finished with their preliminary analysis of Joe by the time the SCPD officers arrived to investigate the attack.

Joe had been pummeled within several inches of his life. His injuries were quickly and brutally inflicted, but they'd also been targeted to the non-vital areas of his body.

"It's a miracle that they didn't hit anything vital," confirmed Ignacio, the lead paramedic. He slung the stethoscope around his neck and rose from the queen-sized bed in Joe and Denise's room.

"Okay, Mr. Lindsey. You seem coherent and alert, no slurred speech or any additional external signs of brain trauma," Ignacio continued. "But you really *should* let us take you in for a CT scan."

Joe used both arms to lift himself up and leaned against the headboard. Beneath the bandage around his head and one swollen eye, he looked exhausted but unbowed. "No," he said dismissively. "Again, that won't be necessary, thanks. I appreciate the concern, but I'm not about to put you through the trouble over a few love taps."

"Love taps?" exclaimed William, Ignacio's twin brother and the junior EMT. He looked over at the wife, Denise, who was sitting in a reading chair in one corner of the small room. The son, Max, stood leaning against the wall beside her with his arms crossed and a look of annoyance plastered on his face.

"Mrs. Lindsey, help us out here?" William pleaded.

Denise paused from dictating the last of her statement to one of the officers and held up a hand in objection.

"My husband is perfectly capable of speaking for himself, you just confirmed that. I'll keep an eye on him over the next few days, and if the situation gets worse, we'll consider scheduling an appointment with Urgent Care. Thank you both."

Her response flabbergasted William enough to briefly shatter his veneer of professionalism. "A few days—Are you crazy?" He turned to face Joe. "Mr. Lindsey, we're less than five miles from the hospital, and we're willing and eager to transport you—"

Denise cut in sharply: "Don't you speak to me like that!"

"Now hold on, everyone," Joe started to say with the faintest hint of irritation, "There's no need to raise our voices, so—"

"I didn't raise my voice," William said defensively.

"Hey!" Max's deep voice silenced everyone in the room.

"You idiots *know* what zip code we're in. The ambulance ride isn't happening. Or the scan."

Unobserved by Max, Joe, the medics, or the police, Denise's countenance was slowly taking on a pale, sickly pallor. To Denise, it felt like her discomfort was rising with the intensity of Max's tone.

"Max," she began, but the name felt mushy coming out of her mouth, and she couldn't quite finish the phrase *these men are here to help us.*

To her blessed relief, Joe stepped in to quell the maelstrom. "That's enough, son."

Max let out a sigh through his nostrils that could easily have been mistaken for a snort. "You're right," he said. He turned his head to face the cops and, with sufficient sourness, asked: "Are we done here?"

Unger, the officer closest to Denise, said: "Not so fast, kid. We still need to take your statement."

"Kiss my ass, I'm going to school. That's my statement," Max responded. He started for the doorway.

"Max!" Denise said disapprovingly.

"No, it's fine, it's fine. Let him go," said Crivello, the other officer standing near the door. He smiled with false amiability.

"Kid should be in class. Maybe he'll learn not to piss off the wrong crew again, eh?"

Max recognized the scorn and insinuation in the cop's words. "Really?" he scoffed. "You saying this hit was my fault? Pathetic."

Crivello stepped into the doorway, blocking Max's exit. "Care to run that by me again?"

"Move," the teen said simply.

"You better put some *respect* on that ask," Crivello responded through clenched teeth. The corner of his upper lip was curled in a barely restrained sneer.

Max had no problem looking the officer directly in the eye. *Literally*; they were the same height, though Max probably carried a good fifteen extra pounds of muscle over Crivello.

"Don't pretend your piece is in your hand right now," the teen said coolly.

Crivello exploded. "Oh yeah, smartass? How 'bout I rap my piece across your *face*, huh? How 'bout *that*, eh, tough guy?"

Denise jumped to her feet, terrified that one or both officers were about to subject her son to one of those infamous Cradle SCPD "pacification" beatings.

Unger seemed to materialize from across the room to restrain his partner with a calming hand. "Hey! Come on, come *on*. He's a kid with a mouth, that's all," he said.

"That's en . . . that's *enough*," Denise offered weakly. Then she felt a sudden, intense head rush, and she swooned for a moment before collapsing back down into her chair.

"Denise!" Joe said in alarm. Max and both medics rushed to her side.

"Everyone out," Ignacio said forcefully. "Out! *Now*."

"It's fine, we're gone, we're done here," Unger said. To Joe, he added: "We'll be in touch."

Joe nodded absently, his attention focused on his wife.

William got up and ushered the officers out of the bedroom.

"You too," Ignacio said to Max.

Max looked at Denise again. Then at Joe, who gave a slight nod of his head in agreement. Without another word, Max got up and stomped bodily out of the room. As he passed by the cops, Max met Crivello's eyes and glared at him.

In the tension of the moment, no one noticed that the officer's right thumb was now quivering above the retention strap of his service holster.

As the muted roar of a hybrid motorcycle engine announced Max's departure, the twin medics carried Denise to the oversized living room couch. The Lindsey matriarch stubbornly resisted, insisting that she was perfectly fine, that her dizzy spell was only a passing, minor (albeit embarrassing) inconvenience that was not worthy of all the fuss.

"That might be true, Mrs. Lindsey, but there's no extra charge for us to make sure," William said amicably. He knelt by Denise's side, grabbed a blood pressure cuff from his jump bag and slipped it onto her arm before attaching the tube to a small digital meter. A few moments of silence elapsed, broken only by the low *hum* emitted from the device.

"Pulse rate is steady, BP is 123/72," William called out to his brother, who entered the figures into his server.

"See? I *told* you everything's fine," Denise said moodlily. "And you can drop the formality. 'Denise' will do just nicely."

"Okay, *Denise*. I'm done, and you did great." William detached the cuff from her arm and disassembled the meter. He opened his bag and was about to replace the items when a peculiar sound stopped him cold. It was a low, repetitive electronic chirp. And it was coming from inside the bag.

William's eyes widened. He looked up at Ignacio, who was slightly better at concealing his surprise. Academically, both of them knew what the sound was, but neither of them had actually heard it in *real life* before.

"What's that? What's that noise?" Denise asked.

Ignacio gave his brother a serious, *knowing* look, and William reluctantly reached into the bag to retrieve his EX ion reader. He looked at it, then at his brother again, then back at the device.

"What is that thing?" Denise asked.

Ignacio cleared his throat. "Mrs. Lindsey, how long ago did you contract Enhanthrax?"

The question came so far from left field that Denise felt as if she'd been slapped across the face.

"What? Never. I didn't . . . I *don't*. I don't have—"

"Stop," William interjected severely. His entire demeanor had shifted to one of serious concern. "Just stop. You did, and you *do*. And, in the last ten minutes, your ion count dropped to near-fatal levels and then somehow rebounded like nothing ever happened. *That's* why you almost passed out, the drop was too sudden."

Denise opened her mouth, but nothing came out. She was too stunned to form words. An E-roid? But *how*? She hadn't recently developed any new abilities, super or otherwise. And what was all this about ion levels dropping? Denise was not your typical Cradle yokel, but she *was* accustomed to living a simple, unobtrusive life. In fact, she prided herself on her vigilant efforts to avoid exposure to Enhanthrax for so long, going so far as to self-quarantine for an entire month. Her family had survived the epidemic completely unscathed, save for Joe's brief scare back in April that turned out to be a bad sinus infection.

"I don't know what any of that means, but I assure you I haven't displayed any symptoms that could be mistaken for signs of infection," she finally said.

"We're inclined to believe you," William offered with just the slightest bit of condescension, "but that's irrelevant. Right now, I need you to think carefully—*very* carefully before you answer my next question: Has anyone else in the house tested positive for EX?"

Another slap. This time Denise turned her head to avoid both pairs of eyes.

Absolutely not. There was no way. Joe worked full-time from home, and though it pained Denise to acknowledge the fact, she knew that her son had few, if any, close friends. Certainly not a *girlfriend*, from whom he could have unknowingly caught the dreaded virus and subsequently brought it home . . .

"Denise? Denise!" Ignacio's sharp tone snapped her back to the present.

"Denise, the law clearly states that anyone who tests positive for EX has to properly identify themselves within—"

"I *know* the law, okay? And keep your voice down!" Denise hissed. She struggled to keep her own voice to a harsh whisper. "I'm the only one here with it," she said emphatically. "No one else. And I'll go to a lab later today, I promise."

From inside the bedroom, they heard Joe's voice, groggy through a high dose of sedatives: "Is everything all right?

"I'm fine, honey. We're all fine. The paramedics are leaving," Denise called back in a loud and reassuring manner. Then she turned back to the twin medics. Her face was stony.

"*Now*," she said with finality.

William hastily finished repacking his bag and rose from the floor to join his brother, who was already at the front door.

"Registration and bracelet in twenty-four hours," William said. "No later. Understand?"

"Get out," was all Denise said.

From his seat next to Unger in their squad car, Crivello watched as the medics boarded the ambulance and pulled away from the Lindsey home. Then Crivello took out his personal server and sent a concise, encoded message:

All clear

*　　　*　　　*　　　*　　　*

Pulse University
Faculty Parking Garage
Keaton Layer—12:52 pm

Max Sylvester exited the stairwell onto the fourth floor of the parking garage and walked determinedly to his bike. Even though his head no longer pounded and his hands had finally ceased throbbing, he was beyond *done* with this day and eager to get home.

During summer school, Max always parked on this level in between the two giant support columns in one rear corner of the garage. He chose this spot because the columns were situated far away from the other well-lit parking spaces; thus, the columns and his vehicle were perfectly concealed in shadows broken only by the dull light of one perpetually malfunctioning overhead bulb. Fortunately, Max feared very little, least of all the dark.

Even before he reached his motorcycle, Max knew that it had been sabotaged. In the dim light, he registered that the bike was resting awkwardly against one of the columns, still upright but not where he had stationed it earlier that morning. Plus, both tires were punctured flat.

Furious yet focused, Max crouched to his knees to inspect for additional signs of damage. He methodically scanned every part of the machine, from its front fender all the way back to the muffler. He was so absorbed in his task that he failed to observe that his helmet, which he'd secured to one of the handlebars rather than opting to carry it with him all day, was also missing.

THWAP!

The helmet suddenly reappeared, whipped viciously across the back of Max's head. Stars exploded in front of Max's eyes as he lurched forward, slamming his face into one side of the mercifully cool engine before his body crumpled to the harsh concrete of the garage floor.

Through the dense fog of pain, Max struggled to pick himself up. His head was on fire again and his legs were spaghetti. As he rose slowly to his feet, Max had the fleeting thought that his assailant was deliberately allowing him time to regain his senses before launching the next attack. Someone was *toying* with him.

That idea sent another surge of anger through Max's veins, but he was bizarrely satisfied to lock eyes with John Porter an instant before the thug swung the helmet again. This time it caught Max in the left cheekbone, knocking him down a second time and scrambling his thoughts back to the first time he saw Porter that day . . .

The Pulse Charter summer school courses were conducted in a handful of modular trailers located on the far end of the Pulse University campus near the dance studio, but direct access to the area was still blocked due to some landscaping project that was several weeks over schedule.

Max's head had been aching long before he left Joe and Denise's bedroom that morning, and throughout his ride to Pulse, his hands felt like they were being alternately dipped in molten lava and liquid nitrogen. Somehow, Max arrived on campus right on time for his first class. But by the time he parked and traversed the thirty-yard detour to Prof. Langen's English Lit classroom, Max had exactly Zero remaining tolerance for anything or any*one* extraneous today.

So when he saw John Porter perched at the top of the ramp outside the entrance to the trailer, flanked by several of Aiden Marcell's known flunkies, Max's mood was doubly ruined.

In the wake of Marcell's sudden vanishing act, Porter had purportedly been promoted to the top of the gang food chain. He now enjoyed all the perks of leadership while exuding none of his predecessor's subtle menace. Max tried his best to ignore Porter as he walked up the ramp toward the hoard.

"'So close I could reach out to hold you,'" Porter said between snickers as he read aloud from something that resembled an opened greeting card. The prose sounded to Max like someone's awful first draft of an even more awful love letter. Or Porter's attempt at last week's homework assignment.

Max refused to make eye contact with any of the thugs but couldn't help but notice the derisive glances they and Porter kept shooting in his direction.

"'. . . you are thrice the man'—Yo, he ain't *twice* the man, he's *twice plus one!*" Porter exclaimed to a chorus of jeers as Max walked past him and into the classroom.

Porter and his boys followed him inside, relentless. Porter darted a few steps ahead, circling in front of Max to cut him off.

"Porter, today is *not* the day," Max offered in a low, exhausted voice. Then he saw that the punk no longer held the card in his hand. In its place was a small, black object that Porter dangled enticingly in front of Max's face.

It was an object made of what looked like tightly braided black leather with a magnetic screw clasp. An object that featured a familiar brushed nickel dog tag.

Max's eyes narrowed.

"'. . . not with you, *I'll always be around,*'" Porter finished with a sneer. At his point, he was obviously reciting from memory.

"Sincerely, Em Ess . . ." Porter glanced behind Max to one of his boys for clarification. "What was it, *Em Ess Vee*? Miss—"

With lightning speed and savagery, Max snatched Porter by the front of his shirt and shoved him into the nearby blackboard with enough force to raise a small cloud of chalk dust. The *SLAM* of Porter's body startled a few still-groggy students fully awake a moment before Prof. Langen's authoritative *"Hey!"* echoed across the classroom.

Ignoring the searing pain radiating through his fingers, Max tightened his grip on Porter, digging his knuckles into the thug's carotid arteries. Then he leaned forward, slowly.

"You come near my home again, I'll put you in the *ground*," Max growled through his teeth.

Instead of yelling, trying to break free, or passing out, Porter's body and face remained eerily calm. He cocked his head and shot a quick glance behind Max's head to deliver the signal for his boys to *not* interfere. Then he looked back at the teen.

"You already missed your shot, *Maximus*." Porter spat out the name like it was a vulgar ethnic slur.

"Ain't gon' be another," he added in a low tone.

With a roar, Max reached back with his right fist and swung with all his might.

*   *   *   *   *

In the garage, the impact of Max's fist into John Porter's jaw spun the thug around a full one hundred eighty degrees before he dropped to the ground like a sack of potatoes.

Max turned his head away for an instant to spit a mouthful of blood from the shreds of his inner left cheek and wipe his mouth with the back of one hand. When he turned back, Porter was already to his feet, the matte black switchblade already in hand and sweeping out in a wide arc. Max felt a slashing jolt of cold penetrate his leather jacket and the shirt beneath, running across his right pectoral all the way up to the top of his left shoulder. Before his brain had time to register the pain, another blow from behind sent him sprawling to his knees.

Took them long enough, Max thought.

Unlike Marcell, Porter would only ever be a *beta*, and betas always brought backup—

Before he could finish the thought, the rest of Porter's gang emerged from the shadows of the garage and pounced on him.

*   *   *   *   *

Owing to his nature as a sympathetic educator, Professor Kenneth Langen did *not* immediately place an emergency call to have university campus police come and haul Max off in chains. The fist-sized hole in the chalkboard and underlying vinyl-coated gypsum was compelling evidence, but Langen knew full well that John Porter was an incurable asshole who must have provoked Max beyond his limits. Langen *did*, however, expel Max from the class with a threat to fail him for the semester if he so much as set foot in any of his other classrooms before the beginning of tomorrow. And so, Max spent the rest of the morning rotting in On-Campus Suspension, or OCS—also known as "detention on steroids."

He didn't harbor resentment toward Langen or Porter, didn't feel any lingering anger. In fact, for the next few hours, Max Sylvester didn't really feel much of anything, except *inert*. Sure, his hands still stung from the encounter with Porter, and there was a constant, dull ache in his head that was situated directly behind his eyes. But those were only distant sensations that paled in comparison to the leaden realization that had slowly formed in Max's mind as he sat in a putty-colored student chair/desk combo in the drab, poorly ventilated OCS trailer:

It was all MsV's fault.

Joe's attack. Porter's preschool antics. Max's removal from class. None of those events would have occurred if that incessant, mysterious Presence hadn't suddenly decided to step out of the darkness of Max's fantasies and into the light of reality.

Max was still pissed with Nova Stevens for ruining his meet-and-greet with his unknown benefactor, but it had suddenly occurred to him that the underlying problem was the fact that MsV (whomever she, he, or *it* was) had led him on an emotional wild goose chase for more than a decade.

Nova was right, Max conceded bitterly. MsV was nothing more than a random *voice,* words on a screen. Psychological mist.

Max concluded that, even if he would've been able to read MsV's letter—which Porter conveniently ripped to shreds and blew in Max's face like confetti with a wicked smirk before tossing him the bracelet—it still wouldn't make up for all the years of intentional anonymity.

And, just like that, Max Sylvester was *over* MsV.

The bell finally rang to dismiss everyone for lunch, and Max rose from his desk to join the throng of juvenile delinquents exiting the OCS classroom. But, instead of following the crowd to the Pulse University Student Center, which housed a vaunted four-star cafeteria, Max cut left at the clock tower and kept on going until he reached the northeastern edge of the campus.

At the entrance to the parking garage, Max ripped off his necklace and tossed both it and the new bracelet unceremoniously into a trash can before climbing the stairwell that would take him to the fourth floor where his bike was parked.

*　　*　　*　　*　　*

Max's body slammed into his motorcycle, hard. He felt the wet *snap* and accompanying pain of a rib cracking against one of the foot pegs, but he had the wherewithal to roll away an instant before the vehicle tipped over and crashed to the ground.

So far it'd been a fair fight. There were only four of Them against one of Him, and one of Them was lying motionless several feet away, incredibly unconscious. Another thug was on his knees beside him, trying desperately to revive his fallen companion, which left Porter and one more, a freckled babyface named Mike Miller.

Porter advanced slowly, closing his switchblade and stowing it in a back pocket. For a moment, Max considered that the game had finally come to an end.

He was partially correct, since Porter replaced the knife with a semiautomatic pistol. Porter thumbed off the safety and pointed the gun at Max's head.

Max crawled weakly to his feet, every breath an exercise in agony. If he was about to be killed by a coward, he'd make damn sure he wasn't a snivering puddle when it happened . . .

Suddenly, Miller's eyes glazed over. He moaned and clutched his abdomen as if he was being eviscerated from within by some otherworldly parasite.

Porter shot him a sideways look. "The hell's *your* problem?"

"I dunno, but his—" Before Miller could finish, he lurched forward and retched violently, ejecting a stream of dark green vomit onto the concrete floor of the garage.

"*Oh, yo!*" Porter and the remaining conscious thug exclaimed in disgust. Both of them scrambled to put some distance between themselves and the pathetically puking Miller, and so they failed to observe the cause of his gastrointestinal disruption.

Unbeknownst to everyone else, including Max, the big teen's naturally black eyes were suddenly glowing bright *crimson*.

Miller lifted one weak hand to point out the phenomenon, but before he could speak he was seized by another wave of nausea that brought him to his knees and triggered another bout of vomiting.

Porter sneered, reached out with one foot and shoved Miller out of his way. He turned back to his target and that's when he *saw them*, he saw the twin glowing red orbs in the center of Max's face. They were brighter than arterial blood and more penetrating than a sniper's laser.

Porter felt terror race up his spine, but his grip on his gun never wavered.

Instinctively, Max held out both hands in front of his body in a vain attempt to shield himself from what was about to come.

Porter let out an animalistic snarl and fired.

Inside the Pulse University Campus Police office, two officers split their attention between the live camera feed of the parking garage on the wall of monitors in front of them and the crossword puzzle in this morning's *Nascent*.

Then one of them saw a bright red flash in the bottom corner of one of the monitors. It came from the camera nearest the blind spot by the darkened corner of the fourth floor.

By the time the first officer finished the call for backup, his partner was already out of her seat and at the door, strapping on her gun.

John Porter opened his eyes, dazed. He felt his body peeling loose from something cold, hard, and metallic. He realized with astonishment that he'd been *embedded in the side of a parked car* a good dozen or more feet away from Sylvester and his busted bike.

Porter got to his feet quickly, shaking his head to regain his senses. He looked around the garage, but Miller and his other boys had vanished. The last thing Porter remembered was Miller lying in a puddle of his own throwup while Sylvester and his weird-ass glowing eyes were—

Porter caught sight of the fading red glow in Max's eyes and noted that the glow had somehow extended downward to his hands. But the gun was still in *Porter's* hand.

Without further hesitation, Porter fired. And fired. And kept on firing until he'd emptied all sixteen remaining rounds from the Smith & Wesson into Maximus Sylvester. The sound of his last shot was drowned out by the echoing screams of police sirens rapidly approaching from several levels below.

Porter lowered his gun and was astounded to behold Max still in one piece. The teen's eyes and hands were still emitting a dull red glow, and there were no obvious signs of perforation about his body, which meant one of two things. Either Porter had a lousy aim—which he *didn't*—or, Max was one of those . . .

Porter leapt out of the way a split second before a second blast of bright red concussive energy shot forth from Max's hands. The energy whistled through the air and punctured a hole the diameter of a large pizza in the car behind Porter, hitting the fuel tank. The car exploded in a shitake mushroom cloud of flames and smoke.

Before either teen had time to consider what happened, the same nondescript car from earlier this morning screeched to a stop in front of Porter. Miller opened a rear passenger door, beckoning for Porter to jump in.

With a head full of cotton, both ears ringing and adrenaline pumping through his veins, John Porter took one last look at Max and tossed his now empty and, apparently, *useless* weapon in the teen's direction. Then he dove into the car, which sped away toward the rear exit just as the Pulse University campus police cruiser screeched to a stop in front of Max. There were more sirens and bright lights, and the officers were soon joined by SCPD and DHX-EX.

Six uniformed men and women poured out of their vehicles with tasers, tranquilizers, and traditional handguns at the ready. Their shouts were muffled by the sound of blaring sirens. One of the uniforms was Crivello.

Max blinked several times in ironic disbelief but instinctively dropped to his knees, placing his glowing red hands behind his head.

Crivello and the others opened fire.

CHAPTER 12

Silver City Police Department
DHS-EX Annex
Keaton Layer—6:00 pm

THE COMMUNITY SERVICES OFFICER DIDN'T BOTHER looking up from his server at the lone woman who nervously approached the X-ray and body scanners stationed at the entrance of the federal wing of the Silver City Police Department complex. Instead, the overpaid and underachieving non-sworn civil servant pointed to a sign posted next to a stack of dull plastic trays near the small conveyor belt. The sign read:

IN COMPLIANCE WITH FEDERAL CRIMINAL LAW, ALL VISITORS TO THIS FACILITY MUST SUBJECT THEMSELVES AND ALL PERSONAL EFFECTS TO AN X-RAY EXAMINATION. EFFECTS INCLUDE BUT ARE NOT LIMITED TO: BACKPACKS, BRIEFCASES, PURSES, WALLETS, SERVERS, EYEWEAR, JEWELRY.

FAILURE TO SUBMIT TO THE EXAMINATION MAY RESULT IN ARREST AND FEDERAL PROSECUTION.

The woman immediately grabbed a tray and emptied the contents of her navy blue blazer pockets before setting the tray on the conveyor belt. Finally, she unclipped the identification badge from her lapel and tossed it into the tray just as the officer flipped a switch. The machine came to life with a faint *hum*.

Next, the woman stepped gingerly through the body scanner, anxiously awaiting any indication—an alarm, an authoritative shout from the officer, perhaps—that she'd made a grave error, one that could only be rectified with more shouts from more officers, *armed* ones this time.

Part of her felt foolish. This was hardly, after all, the first time she had entered this secure facility under similar circumstances. In fact, over the past several months, she'd visited dozens of patients in lockup and undergone multiple similar scans.

But this time was different. This place was so much more *ominous*, so much more imposing. And *this* patient . . . This one meant more to her than all the others.

The CSO motioned her forward without ever looking up from his device. After what felt like an eternity, the woman shrugged off any lingering paranoid thoughts and joined her possessions at the opposite end of the X-ray scanner, located five feet and thirty miles away. She grabbed her things and scurried across the lobby, past the vacant reception desk and toward the bank of elevators in one corner. The clatter of her Tuesday Noir Collection buckle strap pumps echoed hollowly off the grimy wide-tiled floor. Five floors above, the woman exited the elevator and was immediately subjected to three additional, progressively more invasive, body scans. Each scan was conducted by a pair of silent plainclothes DHS-EX agents. Each agent stared at her with more scrutiny than the last.

Eventually, two agents escorted her to a dark room that was clearly some law enforcer-slash-failed interior designer's hybrid of a hospital room and an interrogation cell. The woman took her seat in an uncomfortable chair at one narrow end of a six foot long, half-inch thick ceramic-coated stainless steel table mounted to the floor.

Max Sylvester sat at the other end of the table. Both his wrists were encased in a double set of twalium handcuffs chained to a doubly reinforced cuff bar in front of him. In place of the sole thin yellow ion bracelet affixed to one wrist, the woman observed a thick, wide black band strapped around each of Max's biceps directly above the elbow. A quick visual analysis suggested that the bands were designed to deliver a massive and perhaps fatal EX ion override if necessary.

The room was cold and sterile. Conversely, the teen looked alert and mildly intrigued at having been summoned on account of a visitor.

After confirming the security of the room and its occupants, the agents left, locking Max and the woman in on their way out.

Silence.

Dr. Vivian Gosland inhaled deeply, savoring the breath before releasing it slowly through her lips. Then she reached into one blazer pocket, extracted two objects, and leaned forward to set them gently on the tabletop a few feet in front of Max.

"You dropped these," Gosland said in a low yet clear voice.

Max spared a momentary glance down at his old necklace and the new bracelet from MsV, both of which had obviously been retrieved from the Pulse University garbage. Then he looked plaintively at the woman sitting at the other end of the table, the reality washing over him like a tsunami.

This was MsV. *She* was MsV.

Gosland could see the torrent of emotions sumo wrestling in the teen's mind. As a result, all Max could do was stare silently at the woman. Fortunately, Gosland had anticipated such a response.

"It's amusing to consider that, this time around, the postage to Clooney actually cost more than the tracking chip," she said with toneless irony.

Now Max's silent stare was a piercing, glowing red glare. Gosland recognized it as a permanent side effect of the teen's new abilities; most likely, it was an autonomic reflex triggered by any change in mood. It was fascinating, but it was still *unsettling*, and Gosland scrambled to clarify her statement.

"Please understand—I haven't been using the necklace to spy on you. I couldn't, since that first chip shorted out years ago. It only lasted for a few weeks after I sent it to you—I think you took it on a field trip to the beach?"

Max suddenly recalled the stench of chlorine and the sounds of juvenile ridicule.

"Community pool," he said flatly.

"Community pool," Gosland repeated with only *slightly* more enthusiasm.

Silence.

"You know, each time I ran this scenario in my head, you were a bit more inquisitive," Gosland said. "And loud. And cussy."

The silence and Max's glare increased in intensity. A bead of sweat formed above Gosland's eyebrows.

Adopting an air of nonchalance, she finally asked: "I assume you read my card before disposing of it and the enclosed gift?"

Max closed his eyes and turned his head to one side. "Porter and his boys destroyed it before they jumped me."

"Oh!" Gosland couldn't conceal her surprise, but she kept the satisfaction out of her voice. This simplified things exponentially. If Max never laid eyes on her most recent message, it meant that Gosland *and* MsV had been granted a rare opportunity to start over without the toxic cloud of her explanation hovering over them.

Gosland cleared her throat and straightened in her chair. "My name is Vivian Gosland. We . . . *met* . . . a couple months ago. On the night Nova Stevens—"

"I remember," Max interrupted. "Did I kill anyone today?"

Gosland felt momentarily deflated. Then she sighed again and shook her head. "No."

Max nodded slowly in what Gosland presumed was *relief.*

"One of the cops shot first, the guy from—"

Now it was Gosland's turn to interrupt: "If that's the case, I'm sure he only did it to protect himself and his fellow peace officers from the perceived threat of imminent bodily injury." The words were delivered with a subtle inflection that meant *I wholeheartedly believe you, but here and now are not the place or time to make such an accusation. Not when every move and breath taken in this room is being monitored and recorded for future use against you.*

Gosland waited for Max to lock eyes with her in receipt of the warning. Instead, the teen opted for a change of subject.

"Where's my bike?"

"In vehicle evidence impound. Under quarantine, like you."

Max lowered his head and contemplated the heavy duty bands on his arms as if seeing them for the first time. Then Gosland saw a shift in his posture and countenance as he finally asked her The Question:

"What's wrong with me?"

Gosland's heart was breaking into a million pieces, but she forced herself to maintain a neutral demeanor. Unfortunately, in the process, her words came across as harsh and clinical.

"Nothing—look at me—*nothing* is wrong with you, Maximus." She pretended not to notice the subtle wince Max gave upon hearing the sound of his full name coming live out of her lips. "But, your newly manifested EX abilities do present a significant and . . . *unique* hazard to everyone around you."

Max rolled his eyes. "Please, no more science shit."

"Oh, there's *definitely* more science shit," Gosland said with a sardonic chuckle. "The sooner you listen without talking back, the sooner we can leave this place." Before the teen could respond, Gosland gave Max a condensed version of his diagnosis:

"Simply put, Max, you're living death. Radioactive. Poisonous to everyone around you. E-roid or Neutral, it doesn't matter. From what I can tell, it's some form of ion avulsion."

Max gave her a look that sneered *That's your 'simple?'*

Gosland took a deep breath and tried again. "Your cells emit an energy wave that accelerates the replication of EX ions in an E-roid's body. That energy eventually absorbs and destroys them. The same phenomenon occurs, albeit inversely, when authorities use their crude little override device. Normally, EX ions are so plentiful and regenerate so quickly that the average E-roid doesn't experience any lasting harm. But the radiation *you* put out is different. It's so intense that it leaves the person clinging to life."

Max was silent, contemplative. For a moment, Gosland was convinced that she'd have to resort to even smaller words in her explanation. But then she caught a flash of realization in Max's eyes and the teen asked:

"So Denise and Miller are . . .?"

"Yes, though I doubt either of them knew it before today. Their individual ion counts must have been resting just below the manifestation threshold, and their exposure to you today tipped them over the edge."

Rather than satisfying Max, her response led to a maelstrom of follow-up questions: "So what put *me* over the edge? What's up with the hand lasers and me being *bulletproof*? Even if Porter isn't an E-roid, since when is radiation *concussive* instead of corrosive? And . . . if I'm as dangerous as you say, then how are *you*, right now, this second, still breathing?"

Gosland was equally stunned and impressed. Eventually, she recovered and responded with: "Those are all excellent questions that I'm eager to answer. Unfortunately, they'll have to wait until we get back to the lab."

Max looked at her with renewed suspicion. "You keep saying 'We' like it refers to You And Me. From where I sit, there's you and there's me."

Gosland leaned forward on the table, pointing to the giant one-way mirror behind Max to indicate the hoard of DHS-EX agents that were less than a heartbeat away from them. "*We* don't have that many options, Max. I saw the footage from earlier. You destroyed several police vehicles and almost killed four people, and you did all of that without so much as balling a fist. It took all six officers and agents to finally bring you down. *Believe me* when I tell you that every badge in this building is *terrified* of you. It's only because I work for a very important, very *wealthy* family that you're still alive. At this point, the feds are either going to release you into my custody . . . or let me take possession of your *remains.*"

Max glared at her, and his eyes went red again, but this time Gosland didn't flinch. She had to maintain her ground, had to let him know who was in charge.

Eventually, Max blinked. The glow faded.

"I needed you a lifetime ago," he said. "Why now?"

Gosland heard the sound of her heart breaking again. The first signs of dry rot began to form in her resolve, and she couldn't help but flounder.

"I'm so sorry, Max . . . It-it wasn't supposed to be this way—"

"Not the time and *not* an answer."

Gosland's face hardened and she settled back in her chair.

"You're right. But why now? Because right now, I'm all you've got."

Gosland watched the expression on the teen's face transmute from one of confusion to anger, then from anger to acceptance. In that moment, Vivan Gosland hated herself for having to voice her next words, even though she and Max both knew damn well what they were.

"Joe and Denise, they're both . . . they're both dead. Somebody killed them, Max."

"When did it happen?" Max asked. The words sounded like gravel in an industrial garbage disposal.

"Max, it wasn't your—"

"*WHEN?!*" The teen pounded his glowing red fists on the tabletop with a terrible *thud* that startled Gosland into nearly falling backward out of her chair. She recovered quickly and looked up at the security mirror, offering a subtle shake of her head to communicate to the agents that she was not in danger.

"Less than an hour after you left for school this morning," Gosland answered softly.

Max's facial muscles strained with rage, and he uttered a deep *groan* from inside his marrow. Then Gosland could only watch, helpless, as he finally expressed that most fundamental of human emotions associated with the cruelties of everyday life: grief.

Max Sylvester valiantly fought back a wave of tears and lost. His body rocked with silent sobs and he surrendered a few tears.

Gosland waited respectfully for several long minutes before attempting to speak. When she did, she was astonished to hear something foreign in her voice. Something faintly maternal in her words.

"Max, this is *not* on you. I can't possibly understand the depth of your loss, but I *absolutely* know the guilt coursing through your veins at this moment."

Not surprisingly, Max remained silent.

"I know I can never make up for the lost lifetime I owe you," Gosland continued. "But I'm here *now*. And I've got the rest of our lives to do whatever it takes to be there for you. If you'll let me."

Max sniffed and finally met her eyes. "Trust is expensive, and you're already at a deficit."

Gosland nodded. "Agreed. But, like I said—this time I'm not just around. I am *right here. With you.*"

Max brushed aside the familiar closing line from MsV's—*No,* he thought, *Dr. Gosland's*—letters with a quick and unemotional "We'll see. How do I get out of here?"

Gosland breathed half a sigh of relief and signaled to the agents behind the glass.

"First, you go to sleep for a while, then—"

One of the unseen agents hit a button. Max's heavy duty ion bands glowed faintly and the teen collapsed, facefirst, onto the ceramic tabletop.

*   *   *   *   *

Gordon Biogenetics Laboratory
Keaton Layer—7:42 pm

Max regained consciousness amidst a dull chorus of vaguely familiar voices.

". . . like a black and red panda," said Cameron Gordon.

"More like some kinda wild *boar,*" corrected the short and annoying kid—Zack Haynes or Hayes or whatever.

The blonde girl, Taylor Something, said: "Or a ladybug. With mutated striations instead of spots."

There was a bit more mumbled banter before Zack said, in an overly exaggerated whisper: "And now for the obligatory *'Shh! He's waking up!'*"

Max opened his eyes to the blinding haze of a half dozen fluorescent lights. He immediately ascertained that the lighting emanated from the ceiling and that he was lying on his back. He jerked his body forward and sat up straight, blinking rapidly to recover his senses more fully.

In stark contrast to the rich darkness and discomfort of the DHS-EX holding facility, Max was resting on some kind of plush hospital bed in a room similar to the one Nova was in when he'd visited her all those weeks ago.

He looked around the room and confirmed the presence of the three teens he'd previously identified—Cameron, Taylor, and Zack.

Then he saw *her*.

Nova Stevens stood in one corner. She was adjacent to the others but not too close, almost like she was attempting to remain inconspicuous. It was a futile endeavor. Even if Nova had been stripped of all ability to utter sounds like the last time they'd seen each other, there was no way Max could mistake her for anyone else on the planet.

"What the hell are you wearing?" Max asked, which was a perfectly rational place to start, considering that Nova, Cameron, and Taylor looked as though they'd jumped out of the pages of a *Super Sentai* manga.

Form-fitting black material encased the teens' bodies from their necks down to their toes. The outfit resembled a full-length jumpsuit comprised of what looked like a combination of glossy and matte *liquid*. If there were any seams, they were invisible to Max's eyes, concealed behind lengths of black trim strategically placed at major anatomic locations.

In no uncertain terms, the three of them looked *ridiculous*.

Max allowed his eyes to wander up and down Nova's body a few times . . . and decided that only Cameron and Taylor looked ridiculous. Especially wearing those serious expressions on their faces. Nova, at least, had the dignity to project *embarrassment*.

"Protection. From you," Cameron answered coolly, pointing a black gloved finger in Max's direction. "And vice versa. How's it feel?"

Max looked down and saw that he was encased in the same inky, skin-tight jumpsuit. The only distinction between his and the other teens' outfits was that the trim lines surrounding Max's major muscle groups were blood red instead of black.

"You're lucky the palette swap worked," Zack commented. "*These* fools got basic black rush jobs."

Max's nostrils flared as he considered the situation. Setting aside Porter's attack, Max's manifestation and subsequent arrest, his incarceration, the simultaneous revelation of Dr. Gosland as MsV *and* the loss of the only two people who'd ever truly cared for him his entire life . . . setting all that aside, right now, there was only one concern pressing on Max Sylvester's mind.

"*Who* put me in this thing?" he demanded.

Zack responded immediately: "We all did. *Duh.*"

Before Max could explode, Cameron jumped in with: "What Zack *meant* to say is 'we all helped,' which . . . hearing those words out loud, they sound *way* less comforting than originally intended, but . . . Anyway, Zack and Tay and I helped Dr. Gosland carry you from her car down here. But when it came time to undress you, we all agreed it was best for Nova to handle that."

Max stared blankly at Cameron. Then at Taylor. Then at Zack. Then, finally, at Nova.

"You know, 'cause *she* was the one who—*well*, since you two are already, um . . . *familiar* with each other," Cameron stammered painfully. He searched desperately among his colleagues, hoping that one of them would rescue him from the pit of awkwardness. No one did.

Max stared blankly at Cameron. Then at Taylor. Then at Zack. Then, finally, at Nova.

Zack allowed Cameron to twist in the wind for a bit longer before rejoining the fray. "That's his butchered euphemism for *'you two have already had lots of* sex. *Also, she gave you EX,'*" he said in another feigned whisper.

"*Zack,*" Cameron groaned.

"Zack!" Taylor exclaimed.

"*Ass!*" Nova hissed.

Zack was genuinely surprised at the reprisals. "What?! They *have,* and she *did.* I didn't make up the rules of viral transmission!"

"*You did this to me, bi—?*" The insult was not even halfway out of Max's mouth when Nova held up a hand to interject.

"I know, I know. I'm *sorry,* Max. I'm sorry." She sighed briefly but audibly to communicate that her moment of contrition had elapsed. Then, she manufactured a smile and said, "Glad you're not dead. Welcome to our depressing little club—"

Wordlessly, Max leapt off the bed and lunged for Nova, both of his glowing red gloved hands grasping for her throat. Cameron dove to intercept him, and the two boys crashed to the floor in a ball of adolescent anger and attempted restraint.

Bursts of crimson ionic energy sprayed across the room like wayward fireworks. Nova instinctively threw up an aural shield to protect herself but was shocked to see Max's radiation start to eat away at her sound barrier, almost as if it'd been splashed with acid. As Max's uncontrolled fury ricocheted haphazardly around the room, Taylor's Other Her finally made the executive decision to seek refuge somewhere else. The baby blue streak zipped past Max, Cameron, and Nova to crouch behind a bank of diagnostic equipment in one corner of the room. A few seconds later, the streak and Taylor returned to retrieve Zack just before a molten blast of radiation hit the spot where they'd both been previously standing.

"Max . . . Max!" Cameron's voice was lost in the cacophony as he wrestled frantically to subdue the burly teen. He felt the impact of a thousand small needle pricks everywhere across his body and knew that his suit was attempting to absorb, neutralize, and redirect Max's new and devastating abilities. That was fine; that was what the suit had been designed to do.

But Cameron's suit wasn't performing any of those functions fast enough, and he entertained a horrifying thought that maybe, just *maybe*, Taylor and Dr. Gosland had grossly overestimated the effectiveness of this twalium-coated neoprenium onesie. Either that or they'd grossly *underestimated* the scope and intensity of Max's powers. It was probably both.

Cameron took a concentrated blast of Max's energy to the chest and his own elekinetic abilities went haywire. One of the diagnostic machines exploded. All the lights in the room blinked out.

There were a few lingering sounds of surprise from the teens and then . . . Silence.

One by one, the overhead lights came back online. The final light illuminated a weary but determined Cameron standing over an equally exhausted Max. One of Cameron's hands was balled tightly into a sparkling, crackling fist; the other hand was open but ready to deliver a savage volley of cobalt elekinetic blasts at the slightest provocation.

"MAX!" Cameron's voice finally pierced through the air like a gunshot, sending literal shockwaves throughout the room.

"These outfits don't just *stabilize* our powers! They *amplify* them. So calm the hell down before I *make* you!" he said with an irrefutable tone of authority.

Max said nothing.

A few tense moments passed before Cameron discharged and unclenched his fist, extending the hand down to help Max to his feet.

Taylor, Nova, and even Zack looked at Cameron with a feeling of newfound respect.

Max stood up slowly from the dull linoleum floor, ignoring Cameron's offered hand. None of the other teens were so gullible as to anticipate hearing the words *I'm sorry* issue forth from Max's lips; therefore, no one was surprised when the burly teen simply brushed himself off and asked:

"How am I supposed to take a piss in this?"

Dr. Gosland's footsteps announced her arrival a split second before her voice echoed sonorously: "The same way anyone over the age of two takes a piss while wearing any piece of clothing . . . You *don't*."

"Hey hey, the Doc's got jokes now," Zack chuckled nervously. "Well, *joke*, anyway."

"Thank you, Zack," Gosland said passively. She surveyed the room archly, taking in the portrait of the four uniformed teens and Zack. All of them were either standing or crouching amidst a waning backdrop of chaos and destruction.

"Everything okay here?" she asked wryly.

Cameron, Taylor, Nova, and Zack all uttered sounds in the affirmative. Then Gosland focused her attention on Max.

"I trust you're playing nice with everyone?" she asked in a simple yet penetrating voice.

Cameron and the three remaining teens saw a dark cloud roll over Max's face. "Yeah," was all he said.

Gosland nodded slowly. "That's a relief, because they're also a part of the deal." She cocked her chin sideways to indicate Nova and added, in a tone that left absolutely no room for debate:

"Even her."

Taylor, Nova, Cameron, and Zack watched Max's jaw tighten and the ensuing staring contest between him and Dr. Gosland.

Silence.

The contest finally ended, and Max was the apparent loser. Or rather, he *conceded victory*. He stormed past Gosland, out of the room and down the hallway.

"The zipper's in the back, like a wetsuit," Cameron called out. "And you want the last door on the—"

A door slammed, and Cameron looked at the other teens and Gosland. "He found the door. He—he found it."

Gosland sighed in profound exhaustion. To Nova, it sounded like a parade balloon had just been punctured.

"So, Doc . . . Maybe you move the zipper to the front?" Zack remarked.

"Thank you, Zack. I'll take it under advisement," Gosland said wryly. "Okay, kids, that's enough excitement for today. Off you go. Keep the suits on until you get home. And, from here on out, they have to be worn at all times whenever you're inside this building."

The three uniformed teens groaned in mutual displeasure, but apparently Nova's was the only audible reaction because Gosland added irritably:

"I *mean* it, Nova! Don't give me any crap about *aesthetics*. Be glad I'm only enforcing *ninety* percent coverage!"

Nova shuddered at the mental image of herself in the suit's accompanying full face mask, which concealed every part of the wearer's head except for the eyes and mouth.

"Summer's almost over," Gosland was saying. "If you wanna start a *trend*, figure out how to pair long sleeves with cargo pants!"

Nova nodded sulkily.

"Same goes for you, Taylor," Gosland continued. "No more bare legs. Now that Max is here, the mesh won't be enough."

"Right, Dr. Gosland," Taylor said resignedly. "Full suit."

Nova looked at the other girl. "But—Can you at least fastrack syncing these up with our Synth bands?" she asked pleadingly.

Zack shot Nova a look of profound disappointment. "A speed pun? Really?"

"You can discuss that elsewhere," Gosland said firmly. "Right now, *off you go!*"

Without another word, the teens left.

*　　*　　*　　*　　*

Cameron and the others exited the lab via a rear emergency exit and marched up and out of the Gordon Biogen underground parking garage. The soles of the three uniformed teens' boots and Zack's oversized skate shoes padded silently past an enclosed area containing the twisted fragments of Max's motorcycle. The sight of the machine brought the same thought to the forefront of each teen's mind, but none of them dared to give it voice.

Eventually, inevitably, Zack spoke. "So . . . we're gonna talk about the *thing*, right?"

"What thing, the thing between Doc and Max?" Cameron asked with feigned ignorance.

"The 'deal' thing?" Nova asked in a similar manner.

"No, he means the *weird* thing," Taylor clarified.

"Oh, *that* thing," Nova said.

They reached the car, another innocuous Gordon Industries loaner sedan. Cameron unlocked the doors and everyone piled in. This time, Taylor sat up front while Nova tried to place as much distance between herself and Zack in the back seat.

"Yeah, *that* thing," Zack said.

Cameron started the car, backed out of the parking space, and drove out of the garage.

"Nope," he said to Zack as he merged into the evening traffic.

They passed through several green lights before Cameron glanced into the rearview mirror and added, with finality:

"Whatever it is . . . It's *their* thing."

Zack nodded slowly, but he wasn't truly listening. Right now, he was focused on his *own* thing.

Specifically, he was fighting to suppress the mild nausea and lightheadedness he'd been battling ever since the moment Max woke up in the lab.

The mild nausea and lightheadedness that refused to subside, even though Zack was several miles away from Gordon Biogen and its newest, most dangerous resident.

That thing.

CHAPTER 13

Transcript of SCBN Interview [DRAFT]
Interviewer: Randall Stevens
Guests: Perry & L'Tanya Gordon

L'Tanya [L]: *(faint)* This chair?

Randall [R]: Yeah, that one. Wait—no, the other one.

Perry [P]: *(faint)* Too late, sweetie.

[L]: *(clearer)* Daddy! *(pause)* Whatever, okay. This one's fine.

[R]: Yeah, that one's fine.

[L]: Okay. All right.

[R]: Everybody good? Everybody comfortable?

[P]: *(faint)* Absolutely.

[L]: I'll get there. *(pause, chuckles)* Oh, that's *good*, Randall. Do you make your guests stare at your Arlees the whole time?

[R]: Only when they're in your seat.

[L]: *(smirks)* And, of course, this is the main seat.

[P]: *(faint)* Now, now, Tanya, don't begrudge the man his accolades. Hard-earned, both of them!

[**R**]: Thank you, Perry—wait, hold on. Pull that closer . . . Yeah, go ahead and get right up on the mic. If you're gonna compliment my achievements, I need to make sure everyone can hear you.

[**L**]: Oh, are we going? Did we start already?

[**R**]: Sure, why not.

[**P**]: *(faint, getting louder)* Oh, okay. Let me put these on. *(slips on headphones)* Ooh, okay. Yeah, that's much better.

[**R**]: It certainly is. *(clears throat)* All right! This is Randall Stevens from SCBN, and I'm *delighted* to welcome the face and mouth of Silver City's largest employer and philanthropic entity. Ladies and gentlemen, Gordon Industries' ultra powerhouse daddy-daughter duo that is . . . Perry and L'Tanya Gordon. Thank you both for joining me.

[**L**]: Thanks for having us.

[**P**]: A pleasure.

[**R**]: Excellent. Right. Our lawyers went back and forth for weeks before greenlighting this interview, so I'm contractually obligated to kick things off with a softball: *SkinEX*. Skin-Ex? Skinex? The bracelet thing. What is it, and how do—how am I supposed to pronounce it?

[**L**]: You wanna take this one, Face?

[**P**]: Be my guest, Mouth.

[**L**]: For starters, any way you say it is correct. We wanted the name to be instantly identifiable as something connected with Enhanthrax, but we also wanted it to roll off the tongue. The choice is unique to *you*, just like the enhanced abilities.

[**R**]: And what exactly is it?

[**P**]: It's a silicone band with a host of built-in features designed to fit snugly over the EX ion bracelet.

[**L**]: Think of it as a cross between a server screen protector and a friendship bracelet. And it comes in an endless variety of colors and designs available from more retailers than I can count.

[**R**]: I don't remember any of my friends holding me down at gunpoint to put on a friendship bracelet. *(softer)* Then again, I don't remember having any friends . . .

[**P**]: Well, you might have made some if you were wearing one of these. *(Reaches into inside pocket, pulls out a SkinEX band and hands it to Randall)*

[**R**]: Ohh, *okay*, here it is, folks! I'm holding it in my hand. Is this mine?

[**P**]: That's yours.

[**R**]: Cool. Hang on— *(voice muffled a bit as he moves away from the mic to strap on the band)* Hmm . . . okay. Not a bad color . . . Snug fit. It's thicker than a hospital band but thinner than something from Livestrong. And, even though I'm not a registered E-roid with an ion bracelet, I can barely feel it on my naked skin.

[**L**]: Well, the term *ex* can also mean *formerly* or *without*, so—

[**R**]: I see what you did there, yeah. *Oof.* On a scale of 'marketing genius' to 'low-hanging fruit,' where would you—

[**L**]: I'd say it's somewhere in the middle, and I can live with that. Can you live with that, Daddy?

[**P**]: *(acting distracted)* Huh? Sorry, I stopped listening after 'genius.' *(The three of them chuckle douchebaggedly)*

[**R**]: *(holds up wrist)* Hopefully this'll slow down the rising number of self-inflicted EX Noxion cases.

[**P**]: *(seriously)* We certainly hope so. Deliberately taking one's life to avoid the consequences of abusing Enhanthroid abilities is a heinous, cowardly crime. But simply contracting the condition is *not.* This device is designed to both instill confidence in people with EX and foster acceptance of them in the larger community. We see it as a right of passage, like when you pass your driving test for the first time and get your license.

[**R**]: That's a lovely sentiment. But let's not overlook the obvious: Drivers' licenses and passports—in fact, *every* government-issued identification card—all look the same. Horrible picture, official watermark, DOB, expiration date, all the rest. The differences are minimal and may vary according to state, but there is a definite template everyone has to follow. In contrast, since you're offering this to the general public without federal approval or support, aren't you worried that your new Swatch line will only make it more difficult for local police and DHS-EX agents to identify EX offenders?

[**L**]: *(irritated)* Oh, come *on*, Randall—

[**P**]: In point of fact, just the opposite. Using your Swatch analogy, we see the bands as a simple means of personal expression, not a tool of anarchy.

[**R**]: Easy to say when you're being sponsored by the authority—

[**L**]: Nope! That's Strike Three, Randall.

[**P**]: Tanya . . .

[**R**]: Wait, already? How'd I miss Strike Two?

[**L**]: *(to Perry)* No, Daddy, don't 'Tanya' me. You know I *hate* Swatch references and he *knows* we've been outta the defense game for months now. He's just being an [CENSORED] on purpose—

[**P**]: Tanya!

[**L**]: —should ask his *daughter* if *she* sees the bracelet as a 'tool of anarchy' or whatever—

[**R**]: *(hisses)* Hey [CENSORED], you know our kids are *off-limits!*

(L'Tanya and Perry stare blankly at Randall)

[**R**]: *(clears throat)* Sorry. I apologize. Sincerely.

(Perry looks at L'Tanya, then at Randall, then nods.)

(L'Tanya inhales deeply, exhales and nods.)

(Awkward silence)

[**R**]: All right . . . *(clears throat)* L'Tanya. Another softball: the new research lab. How's it coming along, and when will it be open for business?

[**L**]: *(seems relieved, but rolls eyes)* That's one for Daddy to answer. It's his new favorite child.

[**P**]: That's only mostly true. *(pause)* To answer that question, you have to retrace the root of the problem. Let's face it: since the outbreak of Enhanthrax, Gordon Biogen has been nothing more than a genetic urgent care clinic. *Lifesaving* and revolutionary, to be certain, but *adequate* at best. After the springtime surge in EX manifestation events, everyone at Gordon Industries agreed that we needed a larger, permanent intake and long-term treatment facility. Our analysts and engineers squabbled back and forth for a while—too long, if I'm being honest—on the idea of a new build versus a revamp of one of our existing facilities. Eventually, they settled on the latter. Contractors have spent the last several months working around the clock to renovate our central Keaton office from the studs to the ceiling, rebuilding it into something wonderful. So, Randall, this evening, Gordon Industries is thrilled to announce—

[**L**]: *(harsh, nervous whisper)* Daddy, we're making announcements? Last I checked, *I'm* the only one who makes announcements, and right now I *don't* have any announcements to make—

[**R**]: Sure sounds like you're making announcements—

[**P**]: —Gordon Industries is *thrilled* to announce that the Center for Enhanthrax Research and Treatment will be up and running Saturday night this coming Labor Day weekend! *(pause, whispers)* Do you want me to pause for a moment so you can add some reaction sound effects in post?

[**R**]: *(snorts, whispers)* Sure, if you want to. But I leave all the sound magic up to my editor. *(clears throat, returns to normal volume)* Congrats on the new facility! And is that the official name for it? The Center for Enhanthrax Something Whatever Treatment?

[**L**]: Just call it the Center, that's what we've been calling it.

[**R**]: *Whew!* Much better, thank you—

[**End of Transcript**]

INTERVIEWER'S NOTE: *Sorry, Stan, we lost the last three minutes of the interview due to some freak technical glitch. Nothing on my end, I swear. My home studio gear is totally fine, no signs of tampering.*

Part of me wants to believe that L. Gordon's kid did it remotely—I think he can manipulate wall sockets or something. Or maybe it's that other one [REDACTED] talks about, the blonde. She's supposed to be some sort of felon-level hacker. Nevermind. The recording cut off and there's no way to recover the end of it. Sorry, Stan.

Don't worry, we didn't lose anything of value. P. Gordon repeated the date and time of the Center's opening, tried to make a joke about the event being bigger than some pop star who's performing down on the Cradle that same night. I feel like [REDACTED] mentioned it a while ago, but my plate's been so full the last few months that I forgot. (Does Jodie in Local Entertainment know anything about this?)

Anyway, L. Gordon lost interest in the interview long before I could ask about the "suspected" data breach in the GI mainframe. I'm curious how P. Gordon would've spun it, but a vita dolce hè merda, amiright?

I'm sure that accelerating the Center's opening is a smoke screen to buy their IT guys enough time for damage control. I also highly doubt that I'm on the guestlist for the gala event. No big loss. I'm taking the entire Labor Day weekend off. Be back first thing Tuesday morning.

Yes, Stan, I already put in the PTO request.

Randall

CHAPTER 14

Ford Solutions
Conroy Layer—8:45 pm

SEATED COMFORTABLY INSIDE HIS EIGHTEENTH-FLOOR office, Alberton "Butch" Fordsworth Jr. stared absently at the engraved invitation resting on one edge of his massive U-shaped desk. It was a personalized yet *perfunctory* invitation from L'Tanya Gordon to the gala opening of the newly renovated and rebranded Center for Enhanthrax Research and Treatment. In fanciful gilded script, the words *SATURDAY, THE THIRTY-FIRST OF AUGUST* shone brighter in Fordsworth's mind than an Atlantic lighthouse beacon. To him, it was much more than a date on the calendar.

Historians would mark that night as a seismic paradigm shift for every inhabitant of Silver City, perhaps the entire world. It would also signify the end of a punitive sentence Fordsworth had been serving consecutively for the last six months. It was a small price to pay for committing a biogenetic genocidal mistake. And, to be honest, the timing couldn't be better.

Silver City was a national hotbed of controversy following a recent announcement from DHS-EX regarding all registered Enhanthroids; specifically, their ion bracelets. The announcement centered around a mandatory software update from the feds that would enable any bracelet wearer to be located anywhere within city limits. *In real time.* The E-roid community was in an uproar, even though DHS-EX officials were quick to point out that the update was merely a *proactive* measure and that there was no foreseeable rollout date for the actual tracking feature. "How could there be," they argued, "when such technology does not yet exist?"

Gordon Industries was back in the spotlight again, this time for publicly denying requests from DHS-EX to add the mandatory update to the forthcoming second wave of SkinEX bands. Perry Gordon was on record in multiple media outlets emphatically asserting that he had been approached by DHS-EX to assist with the development of the tracking technology but that he flatly refused.

"Gordon Industries got out of the defense game long before EX and we're *not* going back," Perry said proudly. "Besides, under the custodianship of the authorities, it's a very short flight of steps from 'simple tracking' to 'mass overrides,' and Gordon Industries will have nothing *whatever* to do with the intentional harming of anyone, E-roid or Neutral."

Critical reactions from Silver City's business and political elite were divided between two schools of thought. One one side, there was an outpouring of support of the company leaders who applauded Perry's conviction to remain, no pun intended, *neutral* on the issue. On the other, more than a few cynics were spreading rumors that the issue came down to the parties' inability to agree on the amount of money involved. Just like *every* issue.

Butch knew better. Ever since his team's successful breach of the GI network, Fordsworth had spent countless hours personally sifting through every iota of data related to the tracking tech that he could locate. His efforts proved fruitful, to say the least.

Perry's virtuous soundbites were undeniably founded in truth: multiple confidential memos from DHS-EX to Perry early in the software's development stage confirmed a formal request for GI to integrate the tracking software into their newest line of SkinEX bands. And Perry's subsequent refusals corresponded with an immediate company-wide termination of all research related to the matter, including any current or pending projects.

Except one.

Perry was a congenital muser. Long on vision, short on proof of concept, and notorious for documenting everything his mind conceived. Despite his objection to assisting the government in creating a tool he knew would be converted into a weapon, Perry couldn't help but devise something that could isolate and identify the unique frequency emitted from a single EX ion bracelet.

In short, Perry Gordon cooked up his own personal EX ion tracking device. Just to see if it would work.

After reviewing several crudely drawn plans and a handful of incomplete notes, Fordsworth was delighted to learn that Perry's imaginary contraption *did* work . . . or at least it *would* just as soon as those drones in Fordsworth's manufacturing division finished assembling the prototype! Time and Fordsworth's patience were waning, and, over the past few weeks, the device had undergone several major adjustments. By applying his encyclopedic medical expertise to Perry's *whimsical* designs, Fordsworth easily married the practical components of the tracker to the basic function of an EX ion override.

The resulting creation was equally crude in its design, but its immediate effects would be indiscriminate. And devastating. And permanent. Best of all, Gordon Industries—specifically Perry and his ex-cow of a wife L'Tanya Gordon—would shoulder the blame entirely. All that remained was for Fordsworth to clone the new device's override feature onto Perry's server, which necessitated obtaining it from him. A relatively simple task that only required Fordsworth to make a phone call sometime before *SATURDAY, THE THIRTY-FIRST OF AUGUST.*

*   *   *   *   *

"No, no, he's out of the loop on this one. I mean it, no calls, no briefings, absolutely Nothing between now and the opening. The same goes for his team." Fordsworth paused to ignore the objection from the official on the other end of his call before adding: "No, this time he's more useful in the dark."

Fordsworth turned around in his chair and fought to hide his surprise. A tall, broad-shouldered man wearing a rumpled blazer and a white construction hard hat was standing on the other side of the desk. His normally soft and kind face was hard and lined with tension, almost fear.

"Butch, we've got a situation," the man said in a clear and firm tone.

Without an explanation or a farewell, Fordsworth killed his call. "We're going to have a *problem* if you roll up on me like that again, understand," he replied, still mildly flustered. The last part was *not* a question.

The visitor's tone was equal parts unfazed and urgent. "I found some items that shouldn't be here."

Fordsworth gave the man a look of extreme indifference. "Nothing in that building—including the *building*—exists, John."

John Brodene was currently overseeing the decommissioning of one of Ford Solutions' blacklisted facilities, a random building somewhere in Silver City that was scheduled for demolition sometime next month. For the last two months, clandestine labor crews had been identifying and packaging assorted off-the-books items and equipment for removal. Most of the offices in the building were already empty, while some floors still retained unmarked containers of—

"Of course, Butch," Brodene acknowledged. He indicated the electronic tablet in his hand. "But, according to this inventory log that also *doesn't exist*, these particular items were supposed to have been scrapped months ago. *Scrapped*, not stored."

Brodene saw impatience growing on Fordsworth's face, so he skipped to the point: "Two crates labeled *L.L.* Both are stamped with the GI logo."

Panic seized Fordsworth, but he took pains to keep it out of his voice. He failed. "Those crates were supposed to be scrapped months ago, not stored!"

"Most of them were. These weren't."

"Handle it," Fordsworth barked. "Now."

"On it, Butch," Brodene said before vanishing in a mist of pixels. Fordsworth turned around in his chair and took a calming breath. Then he wiped away a bead of sweat from his brow.

Brodene was a competent and reliable man. Fordsworth had no qualms that the matter would be resolved in as much time as it took to consider.

Thus reassured, Fordsworth took out his personal server and placed another call.

Alone inside the blacklisted facility, John Brodene pocketed his server and composed a few notes in his tablet before preparing to leave. He'd been here since five this morning and worked a full day *plus* two hours of overtime. Now he was starving, and his wife Mary was waiting for him at home with a fresh pot roast and smashed potatoes.

John took one last look at the two crates that had been stored, for whatever reason, inside a maintenance closet near the service elevator. They were enormous, almost the size of refrigerators. John didn't fully grasp the significance of the initials *L.L.* on the crates, nor did he particularly care what they contained. But he *absolutely* knew where they had originated. He also knew that if Butch Fordsworth was found to be in possession of even a single piece of letterhead from Gordon Industries, either by accident or intentionally, the consequences would be devastating for everyone at Ford Solutions, Brodene included. So, the first thing tomorrow morning, John would ensure that the crates in question were destroyed. Even though this floor was scheduled to be emptied in two weeks, John would make a note to expedite the process.

John killed the light in the maintenance closet and turned to leave. Suddenly, he felt a wrenching pain in the center of his chest and saw a burst of blinding white sparks behind his eyes. Then he collapsed to the ground with a loud *plop,* like a pile of wet laundry.

The attack might have been attributed to a long life of good living and bad eating. Or, perhaps, the family history of coronary artery disease combined with the rigors of a stressful job.

But none of that mattered.

Because John Brodene was dead.

*　　*　　*　　*　　*

Gordon Biogenetics Laboratory
Keaton Layer—7:45 pm

Several nights later, the late summer sun sank reluctantly at the edge of the Pacific Ocean off the coast of Silver City. As it dipped beneath the horizon in the final moments of its death throes, the super luminary emitted a flash of tungsten-hued green light that brightened the sky like a distress flare.

At Gordon Biogen, Cameron Gordon finally caught up with Max Sylvester. It wasn't difficult; the burly teen was holed up in the private section of the subterranean garage, completely engrossed in repairing his motorcycle. A pungent scent of engine grease hung in the air.

Over the past few weeks, the headstrong hermit had literally set up shop beneath the lab, refusing to come upstairs for meals, pleasant conversation, or air. Cameron was still attempting, with great difficulty, to bury his growing resentment, trying to temper the irritation by reminding himself that Max was a victim, just like he was. Just like Taylor, just like Nova. *Yes,* Max had also been genetically screwed over without consent, and *yes,* he had a right to cope in whatever way he saw fit. As long as that didn't involve breaking any laws or acting like a total jerk. Unfortunately, ever since his arrival, that was exactly what he'd been—an unmitigated ass more concerned with reassembling the scraps of his ego than those of his derelict bike.

Tonight, the familiar metallic chorus of engine repair was muffled by the rhythmic beats, mildly sensual choreography, and saccharin nonsensical lyrics of the most popular girl group from across the pond. The music flowed in a steady stream from Max's server, which was resting horizontally in its charging cradle on top of a grease-stained foldable table littered with spare parts and tools. The server was connected by a long auxiliary cable to a portable media speaker the size of a basketball resting beneath the table.

Cameron's first and strongest impulse was to kill the music video, permanently, with an elekinetic charge. He toyed with that notion for almost as long as it took for him to tap the side of the server and lower the volume several notches, just enough to hear himself call out: "Max."

Max paused in his work and looked up at Cameron, the familiar scowl not yet formed on his face. "Yeah?"

"We're leaving in about a half hour. Granddad's treat. Pesto rotini with garlic bread and a spinach and kale salad. Tiramisu for dessert," Cameron said, trying desperately to keep his enthusiasm to a minimum. In truth, his mouth was watering in anticipation of the meal. But Max was possessed of an innate, if not unconscious, talent for making a person feel dumb for having a thought and feel even *dumber* for voicing it in his presence. Whether Max cared about this trait was, like everything else about him, a mystery.

"No thank you." Max rose to his feet, walked over to the table, and tapped his server to restore the music video to its original volume.

Cameron muted the music again; this time, elekinetically. His frustration was rising. "You know you've only got a few more valid *No's* left in the tank. And you're seriously gonna burn one tonight? You telling me that's what you want?"

Max flashed a rare mischievous grin as he calmly unmuted his server again and returned to his work.

"It's what I really, really want," he said dryly.

Cameron sighed and rolled his eyes. "What about *playing nice* with us, huh?" he asked pointedly.

Max was silent.

"Come *on*, man," Cameron continued, insistent. "You know this isn't just another dinner. We're already a sideshow to the rest of the city; this is a chance to show a bit of cohesion in public. What matters more? You? Or everything else?"

"Do you hear yourself?" Max asked scornfully. "You just used the words *sideshow* and *cohesion* in the same breath. You're not a publicist and you're *not* the golden heir to some fantasy empire. You're the face of a *disease*. You *are* a disease. And one day, very soon, everyone in this city who's Not You is gonna rise up against you. You and the girls . . . even the pest. All because you put on your tux and did your little tap dance again and shoved your *sideshow* down their throats while trying to convince them it's just as good as their main event."

Cameron clenched his fists, attempting to contain his anger. He closed his eyes to take a calming breath. Finally, he looked at Max with fresh eyes and flared nostrils.

"Okay, point taken. But what about your middle finger to my grandfather? *Again?*"

Max remained silent.

"Max?" Now Cameron was pissed.

"I'm not going to bring him into this," Max responded.

"Why not?"

"Because you don't want that."

"I *said* why not?!" Cameron demanded. "If it wasn't for him, you wouldn't even be here right now!"

Slowly, Max craned his head upward to meet Cameron dead in his almond-shaped brown eyes.

"You're right," was all he said.

The implication stung Cameron like a slap to the face. "Oh, you *suck*, Max, you know that? *You. Suck.*" He emphasized the last two words with a stabbing finger. "Why do you always gotta act like an emo twelve-year-old girl?"

To Cameron's surprise, Max snickered at the insult. "Come on. If I was, I'd just kick you in the nuts and tell everyone you're *gay.*" He rose again and advanced slowly yet deliberately toward Cameron, his deep crimson eyes glowing brighter with each step.

"But I'm not. I'm *living death, remember*? A walking, breathing hazard to everyone and everything around me. A cancer that *kills* cancer. So, once again—*No*, I don't want to join you or your Granddad or anyone goddamn *else* for dinner tonight!"

Cameron felt the weight of Max's presence looming over him and swallowed in apprehension. But he stood his ground.

"You don't scare me," he said in a steady voice.

"Yes I do," Max replied. "You're just too far up your own ass to realize it." He reached over to restore the volume of the music playback one final time before returning his attention to repairing his bike.

Cameron knew he'd struck out and that there was no easy or clean way to salvage his offer. So he sought refuge in an arbitrary change of topic, a tactic he'd picked up from Zack.

"Okay . . . What about fun? You remember what *fun* is, right?" he asked with as much nonchalance as he could muster.

"Food is *food*. It's never fun," Max replied just as carelessly.

Cameron held both hands up in an exaggerated gesture of surrender. "I *got* it, tonight's out. I'm not talking about tonight; I'm talking about *actual* fun. Like my party was?"

Max paused, and Cameron sensed that the teen was genuinely puzzled, if only momentarily.

"Are you sure *you* remember what fun is?" Max asked in a low tone.

Cameron sighed in exasperation. "No, I mean the *first* part, before the cops and the breakup and the . . . The first part."

The brief silence between the last music video and Max's next playlist option stretched into an eternity.

"Max, I'm talking about **t.Æ.k.2.**," Cameron said. The words began pouring out of his mouth like a broken faucet: "In concert, here in Silver City. One night only. This Saturday. I've already got a private box at Club Delerium. Just you, me, the girls . . . even the *pest*. No grownups. All you gotta do is show up and walk through the doors. The arm bands have to stay on, of course, but the club owners are enforcing mandatory EX suppression for all attendees, so none of us have to suit up . . . well, me and the others won't have to suit up."

The subtle shift in Max's posture beneath his bike was all Cameron needed to discern that he'd hooked his marlin.

t.Æ.k.2. was the glittering, glamorous, and globetrotting mother-daughter duo composed of the Russian Israelis Mira and Amanda Arroyo. **t.Æ.k.2.** was universally regarded as a pair of velvet-voiced vixens gifted with the uncanny ability to bend any instrument, any microphone, and any libido—male or female—to their will. And, perhaps most inspiringly to a certain burgeoning segment of the population, **t.Æ.k.2.** was an unrivaled phenom that continued to dominate the international charts long *after* the two announced their EX diagnoses last month.

Simply put, in every conceivable sense of the term, **t.Æ.k.2.** was the hottest pop rock duo on the planet.

Cameron could sense Max's reluctance to make eye contact. "Think about it, Max. Zero risk of cancer equals zero body guilt," he offered encouragingly.

More Silence.

Finally, Max responded: "Why don't you just blow your nose with some more cash and get them to do a private show for us *here*, like last time?"

Cameron was ready for that argument. "I know, right? That was totally my first thought. But guess what? Scoring Moloko that night cost Granddad more than my freshman year of college will, and I got absolutely *nothing* to show for it except an eight-year-old crush destroyed in an instant, and . . ." His voice trailed off as the memory played out to its bitter end.

". . . And a lifetime best friendship that mutated into a bland, hollow '*Let's not talk about it anymore,*'" he finished softly.

Max looked at him contemplatively.

"Whatever," Cameron said with a quick, dismissive wave of one hand. "I thought about asking again for this. Turns out that **t.Æ.k.2.** loves putting on private concerts for newly manifested E-roids even more than regular cancer kids. Unfortunately—for us—Dr. Gosland hates Mira Arroyo. Like, the actual word *hates* her."

"Would I care why?" Max asked absently.

Cameron shook his head. "Probably not. The Doc and Mira were undergrad roommates forever ago, and *something something* about a scholarship turned them into enemies. At least, that's the way the Doc tells it." Cameron recalled that time last year when he asked Gosland to reach out to Dr. Arroyo to record a surprise shoutout to Taylor when she won some biology award. Gosland responded by viciously biting Cameron's head nearly clean off his shoulders. Ever since that incident, the teen suspected that his mentor's animosity was extremely, if not *completely,* one-sided.

"My point is: Even if I *could* get the money, there's no way the Doc would allow Mira or Amanda to play anywhere *near* her lab. Virtually or otherwise." Cameron conceded a shrug of honorable defeat.

Max snapped his fingers and pointed to a torque wrench on the table. Cameron grabbed it and held it out to the burly teen.

"Okay," Max said.

Cameron snatched the tool away, dangling it above him like it was a coveted treat.

"*Okay* meaning you'll join us?"

Max glared at him again, but this time with his naturally intense black eyes.

"*Okay* meaning *Let's not talk about it anymore,*" he growled.

Cameron persisted. "Nope, not good enough this time. Either I get a definitive *Yes* from you or I switch from bribery to good ol' fashioned blackmail."

Max's eyes began to glow the familiar eerie claret when both his and Cameron's attention was seized by, of all things, an ad break on Max's server. Cameron instantly recognized his mother's distinct Public Relations (read: *carny barker*) voice as it bellowed through the media speaker:

"*—for Enhanthrax Research and Treatment, this Saturday evening. Black-tie event . . . Press, city officials, and internal personnel invited to tour the new facilities . . . Dinner, drinks, and a bonus demonstration. Visit* **www.gordonexcenter.org** *for more details!*"

Max looked ironically at Cameron. They both knew that, at least in the eyes of L'Tanya, the young Gordon squire and his two EX maidens were considered *indentured internal personnel*. So much for **t.Æ.k.2.**

"Have fun," was all Max said.

Cameron extended the tool to Max again. His face was stony, resolute.

"The offer's still open," he said.

Max took a moment to absorb the implication of those words.

"I'm impressed," he said simply before snatching the wrench from Cameron's hand with ease.

"Don't be," Cameron said with a touch of juvenile defiance. "I told Mom about this concert forever ago. Long before EX, long before the Center. She'll understand."

"No, she won't," Max said.

"No, she won't," Cameron agreed, shaking his head. "But she'll get over it. Eventually." He sniffed. "Like you said, it's just another tux and tap dance for the cameras, right?" Suddenly, his eyes went cold.

"Besides, me missing one of these isn't gonna kill her. Or Granddad."

Silence.

"Are we done?" Max asked.

Cameron knew by his tone that there was only one acceptable answer to that question. He sent one final elekinetic charge into Max's server to raise the music video's volume, just in time to hear Justin, Chris, Joey, Lance(ton), and J.C. bid him a harmonious, if somewhat *overt*, farewell.

Max looked at him expectantly.

Cameron rolled his eyes again and left the garage.

CHAPTER 15

Gordon Biogenetics Laboratory
Keaton Layer—7:30 pm

"WE'RE ALMOST DONE . . . THERE."

The kindly old man sitting upright in the hospital bed winced in pain at the sudden pinch. Sweat formed above his brow. He inhaled deeply, savoring the breath for a moment before releasing it slowly through his thin lips.

Seated beside the bed, Dr. Vivian Gosland smiled brightly as she made a few minor adjustments to ensure that the ion bracelet was bonded securely to her patient's wrist. Then she activated the device and waited patiently for it to cycle through the flood of new data as it went live. She took the opportunity to wipe away the perspiration from the old man's face with a soft towel. Finally, she dictated a few rapid-fire followup notes to Nurse Allie, who transcribed them just as quickly in shorthand on her tablet.

"You did *great*, Dr. Haas," Gosland said to the gentleman. "No change in vitals and your pallor is virtually the same. I'm serious, this should've been recorded! Your reaction to the install should be mandatory viewing for all newly manifested E-roids from here on out."

Michael Haas was a beloved member of the family behavioral health community. With an undergraduate degree in music from Julliard and a Master's in medical science from Harvard, Hass was that rare hybrid of artistic academic who brought a sense of whimsy to his sessions continuously for more than twenty-five years. Gosland had been an avid follower of Haas' career since her early days in college. She even benefited personally from his services during that brief dark period after the tragic loss of her younger sister all those years ago.

So it had come to Gosland as a bittersweet (mostly sweet) surprise to learn that her beloved Dr. Haas had both contracted EX and immediately manifested his abilities within a week of flying into Silver City to celebrate the opening of the Center. Gosland was as eager to express her gratitude to her mentor as she was to show off her own skills as a practitioner.

"I called your wife again and told her she can visit you in the morning," Gosland said warmly. "She said that your daughter and the kids are flying in tomorrow evening."

"That doesn't suck," Dr. Haas said.

"No, that definitely doesn't suck," Gosland agreed as she rose and removed her gloves, disposing of them in a nearby hazardous waste container. "Allie will show you some options for your complimentary SkinEX band. And . . . that's all I've got for you tonight. Barring any unexpected mayhem, you should be ready for release Monday morning. Too bad you couldn't break in one of the new beds at the Center," Gosland winked.

"Maybe next time," Hass smiled with an answering wink. "You'll do great tonight, Vivian," he added with conviction.

Gosland turned away to hide her flushed cheeks. She quickly regained her composure and gave Allie some instructions before excusing herself from the room. As the door closed, a sensor built into the door jam reactivated the privacy smart glass, rendering both the door and the adjoining wall opaque.

Jasmine Haynes was waiting for Gosland in the hallway. Clad in a set of navy-blue scrubs with her long, wavy hair twisted up in an intricate yet sensible bun, she could've passed for Allie's twin. The stern expression on her face, however, suggested anything but goodwill.

"I called the police," Jasmine said.

Gosland walked past her without a word or even a look. As she did, the bottom hem of her simple yet elegant black evening dress peeked out from beneath her lab coat, flaring slightly.

"Jasmine, I don't have any more time for you tonight," she said in a simple but firm tone.

Jasmine matched Gosland's stride with ease and renewed vigor as the two of them crossed the hallway toward the elevators. "The *real* police," she continued, "not those federal goose steppers you call a 'containment crew.'"

Gosland ran her fingers slowly through her hair, sensing the emergence of premature grey amidst the brunette waves. She tried to hide her growing impatience.

"And I'm sure the SCPD gave you the same three pieces of information that DHS-EX did." She pushed the *DOWN* arrow on the elevator panel. "First, they reminded you that they're busy investigating the *alleged incident* that brought your brother to me in the first place. Next, they kindly divulged that the only reason why Zack hasn't been hauled in as a 'subject of interest' is that he's exempt from any legal fallout from this incident for the next twenty-four hours pending *my* diagnosis. Finally, they informed you that, due to Zack's status as a fully manifested Enhanthroid, they are unable to disclose any additional information relating to him *or* the incident."

Jasmine's response was intercepted by the arrival of the elevator. The doors slid open and both women got into the empty car.

"But we both know that all of that was just fancy talk for *Go away*," Gosland concluded.

Jasmine frowned as the elevator doors shut.

"I'm taking Zack away from this place," Jasmine finally said with zero trace of ambiguity in her intonation. "He has special needs that require specific treatment and medication from his own doctors at Silver Grace—"

And now came the moment where Gosland fell victim to her corrosive thoughts. "What do you think I am, some half-assed med school dropout? I'm a *physician* as much as I am a scientist, and I can assure you that my team is the only one capable of accommodating Zack's *special needs.*"

That first remark was gonna leave a burn, and Gosland knew it. She had already contacted Zack Haynes' team over at Silver Grace Memorial and reviewed every detail surrounding his rather *colorful* family history—including the part where Jasmine abruptly left CSU Northridge at the beginning of her second semester of pre-med studies despite achieving Dean's List grades during her first term. According to the sparse and heavily redacted file, Jasmine decided to shift her focus to her younger brother on a more full-time basis. Gosland could not fully ascertain *why*, but she had her suspicions.

As the elevator came to a stop and the doors yawned open, Jasmine clenched her teeth and swallowed the load of bile rising in her throat.

"Listen, lady—I don't care if you single-handedly pulled him out of a five-alarm fire yesterday, you need to understand that I am *not* leaving here without my brother."

Instead of exiting the car, Gosland took a long, hard look at the other woman. She suddenly grabbed the badge dangling from the lanyard slung around her neck and waved it in front of an access panel next to the EMERGENCY STOP button. The doors immediately slid shut and the elevator ascended rapidly to an unidentified floor.

"I've always hoped to avoid theatrics at the expense of my patients," Gosland sighed, "but it's painfully obvious that Zack's stubbornness is *also* genetic, so . . ." She let the answer hang in the air as the elevator came to a stop. Gosland stepped out with a confused but determined Jasmine hot on her heels.

The elder Haynes sibling instantly noticed a subtle difference in the atmosphere between this ward and the one they'd just left. Sure, the layout was identical and equally aesthetically pleasing, but this floor somehow emitted an air of . . . *despair*, was the only word Jasmine could think of.

Gosland paused at the entrance to a random room. But instead of opening the door, she entered a sequence of numbers into the digital keypad mounted on one smart glass wall to turn it transparent.

Jasmine Haynes, someone who was never swayed by cheap melodramatic surprises, was completely unprepared for the sight that met her.

A girl of about ten years of age lay outstretched on her back, her slender arms and legs straining mightily against the glowing electronic shackles around her tiny wrists and ankles. Her room must have been soundproofed—a feature for which Jasmine was grateful—because her mouth was wide open in what seemed a clear, continuous scream of otherworldly agony. But it wasn't in response to her bonds.

Every ten seconds or so, a random patch of skin on the little girl's body would turn green, then brown, and finally *black* as it withered and dissolved before regenerating a new patch of skin as fresh as before. Jasmine fought to restrain a wave of nausea as she watched the girl's left cheek shrivel inward and disappear as if doused with acid. It was followed by the palm of her right hand. Then her left patella.

Gosland watched the scene with what seemed to Jasmine like extreme dispassion.

"This is Hannah Fanning. Nine years old, a fifth grade GATE student," Gosland began. "Level Two Enhanthroid with as-of-yet unidentified psychofloral manipulation abilities. Hannah is a sweetheart who loves to make flower wreaths for her friends and play handball at recess—but only with a slightly overinflated volleyball, because '*duh*, that's the best way to get the biggest bounce!' After contracting Enhanthrax from a classmate, Hannah developed the ability to mentally control the properties of all known plant life. She can even generate plants and flowers from her body. Unfortunately, for some unknown reason, her epidermis can't tolerate chlorophyll; it's eating her alive."

Jasmine frowned uneasily. "Why is she strapped down like that?"

"For her own protection. Hannah was already living with hypermobile Ehlers-Danlos syndrome, so every move she makes puts an enormous strain on her joints. The last time she tried to sit upright in bed by herself, her hip flexors gave out and she nearly shattered her pelvis. And if you're wondering why she's by herself, her mother and father are currently in federal lockup on charges of attempted murder." Gosland took a moment to wrangle her emotions—and her voice—as she formed her next words.

"Instead of giving Hannah her after-school chocolate milk, they poured her a glass of industrial *herbicide*."

Without another word, Gosland re-concealed the smart glass wall to Hannah's room and walked off down the corridor, leaving Jasmine speechless.

Gosland stopped at two additional rooms on her way back to the elevator. In the first room, Jasmine was introduced to a young man who couldn't control his ability to enlarge certain parts of his anatomy. His lovely fiance was under sedation in the next room over. Neither she nor her future husband would ever be able to reconcile her new gift of elasticity and shapeshifting, primarily because it came at the price of an emergency hysterectomy and any dreams of motherhood.

"These people and thousands more across all five layers have little to no hope of regaining anything close to a normal life," Gosland concluded severely. "Many of them are only a heartbeat away from suffering a premature and *painful* death. With all due respect to the doctors at Silver Grace, traditional hospitals are simply ill-equipped to treat this growing population, a population that now includes Zack."

Gosland looked Jasmine directly in the eyes and spoke in a clear tone that was void of hyperbole.

"Without this facility or the one I'm currently running late to help inaugurate, your brother will—not *can*, not *might*—*will* end up like little Hannah. Or worse."

Jasmine nodded slowly as the reality settled in.

"Take me to him," she said. "Now."

They entered the elevator again. This one was full of Biogen personnel, all of whom could sense the tension between the two new occupants.

"For the sake of clarity, I didn't pull him out *single-handedly*. SCPD Hazmat Response did," Gosland remarked.

"And it was only a *two*-alarm fire."

The doors slid shut just as Jasmine's expletive-laden scream echoed down the ward.

*   *   *   *   *

Five interminable minutes later, the door to Zack's temporary living quarters slid open and Jasmine rushed in. Half of her expected to see the charred and bandaged remnants of her baby brother's corpse scattered about the hospital bed. If the boy was still in one piece, the other half of Jasmine was ready to strangle him into permanent anesthesia the moment he opened his mouth.

(Un)fortunately, neither of those impulses was rewarded.

Jasmine was hardly prepared for the sight of Zack's tiny body, naked except for a pair of tighty whities, as he struggled furiously to put on some kind of matte black wetsuit.

"Yowza!" Zack shrieked, understandably startled.

"Zack!" Jasmine shrieked, understandably confused.

"Jas," Zack said with regained calmness.

"Zack?" Jasmine said with fresh confusion. "You . . . you're—"

"The same ruggedly handsome scamp you've come to know and tolerate, I know, but—more to the point—getting dressed!"

Gosland rushed in a second later. "What, what happened? Oh, *jeez*," she exclaimed in disgust, quickly averting her eyes. "I'll give you two a moment." She turned to leave the room.

Zack held up one semi-gloved hand. "No, no, Doc. You stay. I need some help with this thing. *You—*" he pointed to his sister. "You go. We'll pow and/or wow later."

Jasmine exploded. "We'll pow and/or wow *now*, Zack. Don't play with me, I'm not in the mood. The cops've been stonewalling me for the last twenty-eight hours and your Nightclub Nurse here just gave me a guided tour through this hellhole-turned-'hospital.' Now, tell me using actual *words*: What exactly happened to you yesterday, and—*more to the point—why* haven't you called me?!"

"You think I wanted to deal with y—wanted you to deal with this?" Zack asked with a failed attempt at sincerity. He paused to regroup and tried again.

"Truth be told, I was out cold for most of the episode. Then I got hot . . . really, *really* hot. The details are a bit fuzzy, but, at some point, my server got torched. Literally and completely, get it? *No more server. Bye-bye server.* But I'm good now. And check out my new gear!" He held up his other arm to show off the SkinEX band around his wrist. It was black, just like the suit covering the lower half of his body, but it was also decorated with small red and orange designs shaped like tongues of fire.

Jasmine was incredibly unimpressed. "Quit dancing around this, Zachary. What happened?"

"Fine! *Fine.*" Zack took a calming breath. "I was kinda held hostage in a bank heist—"

"WHAT?!"

"Attempted! *Attempted* bank heist. Well, *failed* is actually the best descriptor. There were some bad guys, they had guns. One of them grabbed Nova, which was super dumb. *(You know, because preexisting childhood hostage trauma and superpowers make a gnarly cocktail, amiright? Yeah, I'm right.)* Anyway, some robber douche snapped my deck and that's all I can remember. No more server, no more deck."

To her credit, Jasmine processed all of that rather quickly. Then a sudden thought ravaged her mind, obliterating all others.

"What about the fire? Did you start it?" she asked.

"I *was* it," Zack replied matter-of-factly.

Jasmine burst into laughter, which somehow added to the awkwardness in the room. "Wrong verb, Little Man," she said.

Zack's serious expression did not change.

Jasmine looked over at Dr. Gosland, who shared Zack's face. Slowly, Jasmine's smile faded.

"How—?" she began before Zack cut her off.

"Doc, I'm serious. Help me out with this. And *her* with *that.*"

"Cover up your bum first," Gosland demanded before moving closer to help the teen wriggle the rest of the way into his new twalium-reinforced neoprenium jumpsuit. As she fumbled with the zipper, Gosland tried her best to explain the situation to Jasmine, who looked one step away from passing out from mental and emotional overstimulation.

"Zack has somehow jumped from a Neutral to a Level Three E-roid with partially manifested pyrosinesis," Gosland said.

"That means I can totally fart out *fire*, Jas!" Zack chimed in gleefully. "And probably a bunch of flamey shapes too. Like *balls* and *blasts* and . . . other words that start with *B*—"

"Emphasis on *partially*, Zack," the scientist continued. "You haven't generated a single spark since yesterday afternoon, which is both comforting and worrisome. Quit squirming."

"Ooh, *bursts* is another one!" Zack commented.

"Besides, your powers seem to be triggered by an increase in your adrenaline and norepinephrine levels, so—"

"So he can't control them, either," Jasmine interjected. "That's just *great*." She well knew how unpredictably the average person's endocrine system tended to fluctuate. Especially when that person was a male on the cusp of puberty.

"Not *yet*," Zack corrected, his pride wounded.

"*I said quit moving!*" Gosland snapped.

"No, you said quit *squirming*. Was I squirming, Jas?"

Jasmine ignored her brother and pointed to his getup. "And this is some sort of power-regulating containment suit?"

Gosland looked up at her sharply, surprised that she'd put everything together with such ease.

"You betcha," Zack replied. "How do you like my colors? I know, the orange trim is a bit *obvious*, but you gotta love the visceral imagery it immediately evokes. Not as blatant as Blaze's choice—I mean, come *on*, her Other Broad is actually *blue*—but not nearly as esoteric as Sonica's, either. I mean, does sound even *have* a color? And don't worry, the Doc's working on an upgrade that'll put the zipper in the *front*, aren't you, Doc?"

The look on Jasmine's face confirmed that she comprehended none of that. Gosland's expression suggested that she hadn't fared much better.

Zack sighed again. He slipped two gloved fingers inside the high collar around his scrawny neck to make an adjustment. "I meant to say 'thanks for coming, Jas, but now you gotta go.' Doc here is scheduled to show off the new Center in about an hour, and there's a VIP seat waiting for me."

Jasmine turned to Gosland. "You're letting him out around other people? But you just said he—"

"I know, I did. Don't listen to him, he's only eighty percent accurate," Gosland said quickly.

"That's a lotta percent accurate," Zack remarked.

Gosland ignored him. "In compliance with federal guidelines, Zack is confined to this building until Monday morning at the earliest. The only VIP seat waiting for him is in the basement lab that he and his friends have turned into the inside of a soiled gym bag."

Jasmine winced at the mental image. And scent.

Zack's mouth parted in a wide, toothy, diabolical grin. "Oh, I *promise* you, Jas—It's *much* worse." He motioned for his sister to leave. "Bye now."

"I . . . I guess I'm going," Jasmine said reluctantly. "What can I bring you tomorrow?"

"Michelangelo," Zack answered immediately. To Gosland, he said: "Stuffed Ninja Turtle." Then, back to his sister: "And a big ol' box of Otter Pops. Feels like an oven in here!" He waved a hand to indicate his entire body encased in the suit.

Jasmine and Gosland stared at him.

"Lookit that, I *engulfed* you both in *scathing* humor in the face of *scorching* uncertainty!"

Jasmine and Gosland stared at each other.

"I should've mentioned at the outset that he's on some heavy beta blockers. He'll run out of fuel soon enough," Gosland offered. Then she realized her own awful pun and cringed. "Sorry."

"Ha *ha*, the Doc made an 'I-hate-myself' joke," Zack laughed mockingly.

Jasmine rolled her eyes. "No, I'm certain he *won't*," she said to Gosland before holding out both her arms.

"Hugs, mutant," she said to Zack. "Get over here."

Reluctantly, Zack walked over and submitted to his sister's suffocating embrace. "As far as copyright laws are concerned, I'm more of a *mutate*," he said in a muffled voice.

"What?" Gosland asked.

"I said 'you and I are running out of time, Doc, but Jas here is *already late*.' For work, that is."

Jasmine was finishing her last week of twelve-hour ER shifts prior to the start of a new gig with Gordon Industries. The details of said gig had yet to be fully ironed out, but the offer letter featured Perry Gordon's personal signature, so Jasmine had zero doubts about its verisimilitude.

Jasmine glanced at the small gold watch around her left wrist. "Nice try, but I gave myself a large window," she said with a hint of smugness.

"Okay, so go jump out of it," Zack said.

"Zack!" Gosland exclaimed scoldingly.

"I'm leaving, I'm leaving," Jasmine said. She released her little brother and turned to leave.

"Love you, Little Man," she added in farewell.

"How could you not?" Zack asked rhetorically.

"I'll walk you out," Gosland said.

The two women left and closed the door, reactivating the privacy wall.

Silence, save for the faint sound of running water coming from the small en suite bathroom at the far end of the hospital room. A moment later, the water was abruptly cut off.

Then there was Real Silence.

Zack waited a couple seconds, then he walked briskly over to the bathroom and pulled open the door.

A cloud of steam poured outward, followed immediately by the sodden and sullen forms of Taylor and Nova. Both girls were wearing dark cocktail dresses complemented by a thin layer of moisture covering every inch of their exposed skin. Their outfits were accessorized with a pissed expression on each of their faces.

Cameron was a half step behind them, dressed in his second favorite shawl collar tuxedo. He was dry as a bone but looked equally irritated.

"Otter Pops?" Cameron said scornfully.

"'Other Broad?'" Taylor said incredulously.

"Esoteric?" Nova said confusedly.

*　　*　　*　　*　　*

Five stories below, a dark luxury SUV glided to a stop at the entrance to Gordon Biogen. Perry Gordon exited the vehicle and ascended the stairs to the building.

Inside the lobby, he was greeted by Dr. Gosland, who exuded that rare and intensely attractive combination of *exhaustion* and *determination*.

"Well well, don't *you* look lovely!" Perry said, his trademark wide smile already set in place. He crossed his legs and leaned his weight on an ebony formal walking stick capped with a gleaming tungsten carbide bulb handle. "The lab coat is a perfect accessory, Vivian. Don't change a thing!"

Gosland chuckled goodnaturedly and extended her hand for a shake. Perry grasped it with his free hand, brought it to his lips and planted a tender yet paternal kiss on the back of it.

"Thank you, Perry," Gosland said. "You look rather dapper yourself. Most men can't pull off a walking stick. You are a rare exception."

"Nonsense! I'm just an old *dog* here to pick up my grandson and his friends for a party." He glanced behind Gosland's shoulder and saw Cameron, Taylor, and the Stevens girl approaching at an accelerated pace as if they were in a hurry.

"And here they are!" Perry added.

"Hey, Granddad. Nice tux," Cameron said. The girls offered similar greetings.

Cameron turned to Gosland. "Bye, Doc."

"Later!" Nova added.

"You'll do great, Dr. Gosland," Taylor said sincerely.

"Thank you, Taylor," Gosland responded. "Where's Max?

Cameron pointed to the floor, indicating the basement garage beneath them. "Where else? You know he ain't going anywhere anytime soon. No biggie. Zack's been aching to give him some unwanted company."

"Poor kid," Gosland muttered.

"Which one?" Nova asked wryly.

Cameron gave Perry a pat on the shoulder. "Okay, Granddad, change of plans. We're gonna meet you there," he said.

"Meet me there? Why? I'm here now and you're all ready to go," Perry said with understandable surprise. Gosland shared the sentiment.

Cameron let out an exaggerated sigh. "The demo's gonna last *forever* and we want to get some food first—some *real* food, not the boring Fancy Party Spread Mom always gets."

"The car is waiting for us in the garage," Perry replied.

"I get it, Granddad, but *burritos*."

"Well, I can't argue with *burritos*," Perry conceded with mock seriousness. He pulled out a few fifty thousand nano bills from his billfold and handed them to his grandson, who quickly pocketed them.

"There you are, dinner's on me," Perry said. "Now, please do me a favor: On your way out, tell Emerson I'll need another ten minutes or so. Just need to run up to my office and grab my spare glasses."

"Will do. Thank you, love you, see you both later!" Cameron rattled off as he and the girls left the lobby as quickly as they'd entered it.

"Love you too, son!" Perry returned, but Cameron was already gone.

As the sun set peacefully along the western coast, the teens found the SUV in the garage and hopped inside.

Emerson Henley was waiting patiently in the driver's seat. She was one of Perry's youngest yet most reliable drivers whose services were usually called upon for corporate functions and special occasions. Tonight counted as both.

"Hey kids," Emerson said. In return, she received a collective grunt that almost resembled *Hey*.

Cameron wasted no time; he extracted the cash from his inside jacket pocket and dangled the bills enticingly in front of the driver's eyes.

"Okay, Emmy. You got ten minutes to get us to the O'Donnell 'Rail station before my grandfather discovers that you helped us ditch the most important night of his life."

Emerson's face and neck flushed beet red. "But I didn't—I haven't—I won't!" she stammered.

"Yes, you will," Cameron said.

Just then, one of the back passenger doors opened and Zack darted inside. He wore a pair of jeans and his skate shoes over the bottom half of his new suit. A small backpack hung from one shoulder.

"We're still here?" Zack asked impatiently.

Cameron looked at Emerson. "I dunno, are we?"

Through her rearview mirror, Emerson looked at each of the teens in the backseat. Their expressions were firm, their resolve completely locked in. Finally, the driver looked back at Cameron. And the money.

"Come *on*, Cam! My job!" she pleaded.

"I'll make sure you keep it," Cameron said with honey in his voice. His tone went suddenly cold, ruthless.

"Or . . . I won't."

Emerson sighed in defeat and accepted the offered money. Then she started the vehicle and drove off.

Zack rifled through his bag and produced his favorite hoodie, slinging it over his giant mane of hair. His flailing arms nearly clipped Taylor, who was scrolling through the clothing options in her Synth bracelet in search of a more appropriate outfit for their upcoming adventure. Cameron was doing the same up front.

"Watch those hands, Hairboy," Nova warned from her spot in the rear third row. She'd already changed and was wringing the last few drops of bathroom steam out of her own hair.

Eventually, Zack's head popped through the opening of his hoodie. He smoothed out a few wrinkles in the garment and settled back in his chair.

A few minutes elapsed in silence, broken only by the melody of early Saturday evening traffic.

From the corner of one eye, Zack noticed a pensive, almost despondent look on the blonde's face.

"What's up with you?" he asked. "Contrition?"

Taylor sat motionless with one palm beneath her chin. "I've never intentionally lied to Dr. Gosland before," she said softly.

Cameron turned back to look at her. "You didn't lie to her," he tried to reassure her. "We *are* about to grab some burritos, and I'm sure she *will* do great. And you can tell her *how* great she was with a clear conscience after we watch the playback tomorrow. Tonight, however, we all take a break."

Cameron grinned like an idiot before adding: "Tonight . . . we *t.Æ.k.2.*"

In the dimming natural light, Cameron saw both Zack and Nova roll their eyes and heard their combined groan of disgust. Even Emerson stifled the urge to react. Taylor didn't respond, but her face softened a fraction.

"Where exactly *is* Max?" Nova finally asked as the SUV pulled up to the O'Donnell Hoverail station. Contrary to Cameron's earlier claim, the burly teen had not, in fact, been in the basement garage at the agreed rendezvous time. Or, according to Cameron's internal scanner, anywhere else inside the Gordon Biogen lab.

"He'll be there," Cameron said confidently as he and the other teens exited the vehicle and ran to catch the departing 'Rail.

Of course, as the doors slid shut, all four of them shared the same unspoken thought:

Or . . . He won't.

CHAPTER 16

Center for Enhanthrax
Research and Treatment
Keaton Layer—8:00 pm

IN A CITY REPLETE WITH TOWERING AND GLAMOROUS edifices, the Center for Enhanthrax Research and Treatment was undeniably the pretty new kid on the block. And tonight, on the last evening in August, the block was *hot*.

In the space once occupied by the primary Gordon Industries corporate office building now stood a shimmering monument of glass and granite, a marvel of postmodern architecture. The newly renovated structure combined the best elements of Silver City's favorite family-owned philanthropic organization with the latest innovations in medical technology and genetic palliative care. Tonight, the upper echelon of the city's medical, political, and commercial communities, along with a select number of guests, were gathered together to celebrate the soft opening of the new facility.

Outside the Center, scores of valets parked as many luxury vehicles while their occupants were escorted into the lobby, which had been transformed into an opulent entrance hall. Light chillhop jazz music flowed through the lobby's speakers as smoothly as the wine and cocktails being poured from the long, winding reception desk-turned-open bar.

L'Tanya Gordon navigated her way purposefully around the room. She was a vision of contemporary nobility in her midnight blue velvet evening gown and matching opera gloves. Her freshly dyed burgundy hair was coiffed into a mildly subdued bed of cascading curls and her brown eyes sparkled brightly behind violet contact lenses. One hand kept a tight grip on her designer clutch purse while the other continually extended outward to offer a brief yet warm greeting to each arriving guest.

She extended her gaze across the lobby and observed Douglas and Debbie Andrews enter, both of them resplendent in their formal attire. Douglas had even tamed his naturally unruly golden locks into something approaching the term *suave*.

The sight of her long-time neighbors and fellow parents prompted L'Tanya to wonder where Cameron and the girls were. It had been an exercise in pulling teeth to force her son to accept that he was *not* going to that little pop concert he'd been yapping about for months. Family and company responsibilities always trumped minor personal desires, and Now was as good a time for the boy to learn that as any other.

To L'Tanya's supreme relief, Cameron eventually quelled his sulking and agreed to attend the opening without causing a scene—on the condition that he and the other teens catch a ride with Daddy, which was perfectly fine with L'Tanya and Perry.

A flash of suspicion suddenly darkened the woman's features. Even accounting for her son's legendary indecisiveness when it came to selecting formal attire, he should *be* here by now . . .

Just then, someone introduced L'Tanya to the recently appointed Acting Deputy Mayor Jared Moore, a dashing young man who possessed the most *striking* green eyes L'Tanya had ever seen, and all thoughts of her son and his friends were erased from her mind.

At the exact same moment, two layers below in the Cradle, Cameron, Taylor, Nova, and Zack strolled casually through the doors of Club Delerium, one of the few appealing venues located on Clooney; indeed, it was inexplicably one of the most popular venues in all of Silver City.

The teens passed by a long line of people waiting impatiently to have their digital tickets scanned, followed by a second line of patrons awaiting EX verification and, if necessary, nullification. Club security stood at the interior entrance to the concert hall, armed with handheld EX ion scanners like TSA agents ready to stop and wave down any person who failed to show his or her ion bracelet.

Without breaking stride, Cameron, Taylor, and Zack extended their banded wrists as they walked past the guards. Nova paused to flash her anklet—along with her third most seductive smile—at the closest guard, who returned it with a lascivious grin.

"You're stunning," he said to Nova.

"She's also *statutory*," Taylor called back.

Over the din of the rowdy crowd, Nova heard the poor guard's raging libido fall suddenly and permanently limp.

*   *   *   *   *

Back at the Center, Butch Fordsworth Jr. stepped regally into the reception party. His entrance was punctuated with a flurry of independent reporters all shoving their server microphones in his face, each of them hoping in vain to obtain a tasty soundbite from the medical magnate for tomorrow's society and gossip headlines.

At one end of the hors d'oeuvres bar, L'Tanya Gordon reached into her clutch to check the time on her server. She scanned the lobby again but still couldn't locate her father, her son, or any of the other kids.

She started to place a call to Perry and then abandoned the endeavor. The opening festivities were scheduled to continue for another twenty minutes, so there was no real hurry.

*   *   *   *   *

Down in the Cradle, Maximus Sylvester trudged through the chilled evening toward Club Delerium, his haphazard posture and gait perfectly conveying the sense of extreme discombobulation he was trying desperately to shake off.

Inside the club, the quartet of other teens rode an elevator to the top floor, where the VIP box seats were located. They stepped into Cameron's private room and Zack immediately dove onto the oversized loveseat. Cameron walked up to the massive wall-length glass window and stared down at the main auditorium, which was steadily filling with a writhing mass of subhumanity.

As Taylor riffled through a leatherbound menu in search of a suitable dessert, Nova occupied herself by adjusting the audio settings for the room. The entire club boasted a state-of-the-art sound system that fed the music from the stage mics directly into each of the upper-level private rooms, and Amanda Arroyo was a total audiophile; so, naturally, Nova wanted to do everything she could to aid in receiving the best quality experience.

Down the hallway inside a fancy single-occupant bathroom, Max splashed one final handful of cold water onto his face, turned off the faucet, and grabbed several paper towels to dry off. He wiped his palms and knuckles meticulously to ensure that he'd removed all traces of John Porter's blood before he flushed the paper towels down the toilet. One at a time, of course, to prevent clogs. Finally, Max killed the light and exited the bathroom. By the time he knocked on the door to Cameron's room, a fresh veneer of sexy indifference concealed his features.

*   *   *   *   *

Gordon Biogenetics Laboratory
Keaton Layer—8:05 pm

Perry Gordon opened the door to his office and walked airily into the darkened empty room. The dull *tap* of his walking stick was absorbed by the carpeted floor as he walked over to his desk, a large oak affair situated near the tall window at the opposite end of the office. Perry chose a room with a view in all his buildings, as it made the doldrums of daily work that much easier to endure.

Several moments elapsed before Perry realized two separate yet equally important facts: (1) the office *wasn't* darkened—the auxiliary canned lights were shining dully overhead—and (2) it wasn't *empty*, either.

Perry caught a flickering movement from the corner of his left eye. He snapped his head around and was greeted with the image of a young man who looked to be in his early twenties sprawled out on the small guest couch against the far wall. The man was twirling a black plastic device between his fingers. Perry recognized it as the remote control to his motorized office blinds. A second young man, perhaps only a few years older than his companion, sat leisurely in the dark ostrich leather office chair behind Perry's desk. Both men wore nondescript dark suits over faintly patterned dress shirts without neckties, giving them the appearance of a couple first-year marketing interns.

The Gordon patriarch froze in his tracks, stunned.

"Finally! Let's *do* this," the first man exclaimed with obvious annoyance as he wriggled off the couch. His face was soft, boyish, and his dark brown hair was cut short and slicked down with one visibly unruly cowlick rising from the center of his crown.

"Excuse me?" Perry asked. "Do what?"

The man sitting behind Perry's desk shook his head, clearly embarrassed. With his voluminous, retro-coiffed black hair, he could've given Zack Haynes a *serious* run for his money.

"*Manners*, Mitch," he said calmly.

The first man's face tightened. "I thought we said *No Names*, Josh!" he hissed through gritted teeth.

"Josh?" Perry said, pointing to the second man.

Josh looked at his companion remorsefully. "Sorry, bro. Got caught up in the moment. It just slipped."

"And *Mitch*," Perry said, looking at the younger man.

Mitch let out a quick and audible sigh, almost a groan. "Yep, and you're *Perry Gordon*, and that takes care of the names, and—" In one swift motion, he walked over to the office door, closed it, and fastened the deadbolt above the handle.

"—and now you have to die." Mitch's words were rapid, cold. Factual.

Perry raised both his hands in a mildly exaggerated gesture of noncomprehension. "Okay, okay. Slow down, son. You're going a little too fast for me. I know you just told me who you are, but that still doesn't tell me *who you are*. Or what brings you both to my office this evening."

Josh rose from his seat and walked around the desk, one hand extended to Perry in a gesture of cordiality.

"You're absolutely right," Josh admitted unhesitatingly. "He's absolutely right, Mitch. Our apologies, sir," he said to Perry.

"*His* apologies," Mitch corrected.

"Fine, just *my* apologies," Josh clarified as he grasped the old man's free hand, shaking it vigorously. "Now, Perry, I know you weren't expecting us, so I promise we'll be brief." Josh produced a small cylindrical tube he'd retrieved from a desk drawer. It was the case containing Perry's spare eyeglasses.

"You came up here to grab this, right? We know you did, we've been keeping tabs on you, and—and here you go." Josh slipped the case inside Perry's left lapel pocket, tucking it out of sight behind the silken white pocket square. Suddenly, his face twisted in an expression of anticipatory apprehension.

"But we also need to borrow something really important from you, something you're definitely *not* gonna want to give us . . . So we have to take it."

Perry didn't see Mitch press the button on the remote in his hand, but he absolutely heard the soft *whirr* of the aluminum privacy blinds sliding shut, obscuring the sun's final moments as it sank below the shoreline.

"And you have to die," Mitch said again.

"No he doesn't, stop *saying* that!" Josh exclaimed in irritation.

It was at that moment Perry Gordon felt the first inkling of unease, felt the first tingle of fear race up his spine.

Silence.

"What do you boys need from me? And what *exactly* do you mean, 'keeping tabs' on me?" Perry asked as Josh inched closer toward him. Unconsciously, the old man began backing away slowly toward the exit.

Suddenly, a flash of recognition brightened Perry's features. "Josh . . . Josh! I remember you. I *remember* you, you're with the—"

Without warning, Perry felt a jolt of searing pain at the base of his neck. Ugly white spots danced briefly in front of his eyes and he collapsed to the ground.

Mitch dropped the now-broken remote to the floor before reaching down to pick up Perry's fallen walking stick. He couldn't keep the anger out of his voice as he said to Josh: "He already knows your face?!"

"Whoopsie," Josh said tonelessly. He shook his head again, this time with feigned sadness, as he reached into his coat pocket and extracted a pair of black leather gloves. Josh slipped them on and motioned for Mitch to pass him the stick as Perry attempted, feebly, to pick himself up off the floor. He looked disoriented and was moaning softly for help.

"Sorry, Perry," Josh intoned as he swung the walking stick in a wide arc above Perry's head like a golf driver. The tungsten carbide bulb gleamed in the dull fluorescent light.

"Now you *do* have to die."

*　　　*　　　*　　　*　　　*

At exactly 8:20 p.m., Mira Arroyo and her daughter Amanda skipped joyously onstage amidst the roar of applause and the haze of a hundred holographic pyrotechnics. They took a few moments to shower the crowd with a double handful of tulips and candy, just like they did before every performance. At last, they turned to acknowledge each other with a quick curtsy before separating to find their instruments.

Inside the VIP room, Cameron and the other teens, including Max, cheered.

Mira sat down and fired up her massive keyboard setup while Amanda strapped on her custom single neck electric guitar/bass combo. Then, without asking the crowd below or the teens above for permission, the ladies set about their task of totally rocking the house.

*　　　*　　　*　　　*　　　*

Josh held out one hand as he and Mitch walked briskly down the hallway, leaving Perry's office in their wake. "Alright, gimme," he said absently.

Mitch mistook the gesture as an appeal for validation and casually slapped Josh's open palm in a low five.

Josh rolled his eyes and scoffed. "I'm serious, hand it over."

Mitch, who was several inches taller than Josh, whipped his head down and to the side to see the expression on his partner's face. It was not jovial.

"What? I thought *you* got it. You didn't get it?!" Mitch asked, his voice rising in alarm.

"Hold on," Josh said. He stopped in his tracks, turned around, and returned to the office, where the body of Perry Gordon lay in a heap beside his desk. Josh gave the body a quick but methodical pat down, careful to avoid touching the bloody parts, until he finally retrieved Perry's server from a coat pocket. Satisfied, he stepped over the body and walked hastily out of the office again, shutting the door firmly behind him.

Josh pretended not to notice Mitch's waiting glare as the two of them resumed their leisurely getaway, choosing instead to offer another lukewarm "Whoopsie."

On the main floor, they traipsed past several security guards and a woman wearing a fancy dress beneath a lab coat hovering around a coffee kiosk.

Mitch waved back amiably at the guards and then checked the time on his ion bracelet.

"You gonna make the call?" he asked Josh.

Josh lifted the edge of one leather glove to inspect his own ion bracelet. "Nah, let him grab one more cocktail."

Then the two DHS-EX agents exited Gordon Biogenetic Labs, but not before Josh added, rather impassively:

"It's showtime."

EPILOGUE

Center for Enhanthrax
Research and Treatment
Keaton Layer—8:35 pm

L'TANYA GORDON CONCLUDED HER OPENING REMARKS with an announcement that the video presentation chronicling the Center's journey from concept to completion was about to commence. Then she stepped away from the podium, the forced smile on her face crumbling fast. Beneath it was an expression of suppressed rage tinged with growing concern.

There was still no sign of Daddy or the kids, and L'Tanya had been forced to call an audible regarding the evening's schedule. She'd already placed several calls to her father's server, but all of them had been sent directly to voicemail. The same went for Cameron, but L'Tanya was less worried about that. She knew instinctively that her son and his friends had blown off Daddy and the Center's opening to go to their stupid little *concert*, which was perfectly fine.

I really hope they enjoy it, L'Tanya said to herself. *It's the last one they'll ever see.*

Inside the Center's reception hall, Fordsworth reached into his pocket and read the latest notification on his server:

It's done

On our way

Such a simple message, yet it was one that carried devastating implications.

Smiling, Fordsworth settled back in his chair and prepared to enjoy the show.

*   *   *   *   *

In the underground garage of Gordon Biogen, Emerson sat in the SUV waiting patiently for her boss. She'd dropped off the kids and returned in record time but Perry still hadn't come out.

As the minutes ticked by and Emerson's stomach began to rumble, she mused ruefully that she should've picked up a burrito for herself.

On the top floor of the building, something stirred in the faint moonlight filtering through the partially reopened blinds of Perry Gordon's office.

A swollen, broken, and pulpy mass wearing a tattered tuxedo trudged painfully across the carpeted floor. It hobbled past the broken walking stick and propped itself up onto one fractured arm in a desperate attempt to reach the phone resting on one sharp and bloodstained corner of the desk.

Fighting through a dense mental fog that threatened to envelop his entire being, Perry Gordon felt his hand close around something hard with curved edges. He hauled himself to one knee, lifted the receiver from its cradle, and heard the blessed dial tone drone in the one ear that wasn't already ringing. But the Herculean effort drained the last ounce of his reserves, and Perry Gordon uttered one soft, final groan before collapsing to the ground again. This time, he didn't move.

Above his head, the telephone receiver danced gracefully in the moonlight.

TO BE CONCLUDED IN

TEEN JUSTICE

JUSTICE HAS A CURFEW
BOOK THREE

ZACK STUDIED CAMERON'S FACE FOR A LONG MOMENT. He noted the expression of unwavering determination and knew *exactly* what his friend was about to do.

"Aww, come *on*, dude!" Zack exclaimed pleadingly. "The cops get *paid* to play hero. They get paid to *die* playing hero! Listen, I get where you're at right now, I really do, but . . . Do you seriously want to get killed tonight?!"

Cameron's face was granite.

"And *you're* gonna let him?" Zack asked the blonde.

Taylor's face was marble.

Before Zack could object any further, Nova stormed into the lounge. She was dressed in her twalium-reinforced neoprenium uniform, ready and eager for some action.

"We gonna go kill some cops or what?" she asked. The edge of darkness in her tone made it clear to everyone that there was only one right answer to *or what?*

"Not planning to," Cameron said. He meant it. "But if they try to stop me, then . . . we'll see." He meant that, too.

Nova's face was diamond. "Good," she said simply.

"Great, that's—that's just *great*. Now it's *three* corpses," Zack said sardonically. He turned to Gosland, the sole grownup in the room and, by default, the lone voice of reason.

"Doc?" he asked desperately.

"Nova, I know you're upset," Gosland began. "I'm upset, we're *all* upset. But you're not going to fix anything this way."

"I'm *way* beyond wanting to fix anything, Doc," Nova replied matter-of-factly. "Now it's time to blow some shit up." She turned to Cameron and Taylor.

"Whatever you're about to do, I'm in. Just remember—any badge I meet out there is a *dead* badge."

Cameron and Taylor gave her a subtle nod of assent.

Zack was outnumbered and out-crazied. He knew it was time to concede defeat. With a long, guttural *groan*, the tiny teen pulled off his hoodie to expose the top half of his own uniform.

"These things only protect *ninety percent of* our bodies, right?" Zack asked Gosland.

The scientist stared at each of her teens. She *also* knew what was about to happen, and the realization of her complete inability to prevent it both angered and frightened her.

"Yes," Gosland breathed.

"Well then, Doc . . . We're gonna need the masks."

BONUS MATERIALS

TEEN JUSTICE: JUSTICE HAS A CURFEW—BOOK TWO
Music Playlist
****All rights belong to the respective artists****

<u>Song Title / Artist</u>	<u>Scene Description</u>
1. **"Hammering in My Head"** Garbage	Tay's turn
2. **"Get Mine, Get Yours"** Christina Aguilera	Revelations and machinations
3. **"LEZGO"** Justin Martin & Ardalan	'Roid road rage / ruined rendezvous
4. **"The Trouble With Andre"** Shakespeare's Sister	'Roid road rage / ruined rendezvous (alternate)
5. **"All I Need (Clean Mix)"** Method Man & Mary J. Blige	Lindsey lip sync #1
6. **"Tha Crossroads"** Bone Thugs-n-Harmony	BONUS: Lindsey lip sync #2
7. **"Silence"**—Delerium ft. Sarah McLachlan	Nova'splosion
8. **"Little Man (Exemen Works)"** Sia	Superpowered montage mayhem
9. **"Little Man (Music Video)"** Sia	Nocturnal remissions
10. **"Summer Girls"**—LFO	Corporate beach bums

11. **"Let Me Blow Ya Mind"**   Super 8 sunset
    Eve ft. Gwen Stefani

12. **"Angels"**   *Melancholia Maximus*
    Wax Poetic ft. Norah Jones

13. **"Wannabe"**   Garage guilt maneuvers (remix)
    Spice Girls

14. **"Bye Bye Bye"**   Bribery before breadsticks
    *NSYNC

15. **"Feeling Good (Bassnectar   Welcome t.Æ.k.2. the Center
    Remix)"**—Nina Simone

16. **"H! Vltg3"**   Beat, Perry, Feint . . . RIPoste
    Linkin Park

17. **"Dog New Tricks"**   Teen Justice Theme
    Garbage

Playlist available on YouTube!

Just search for "Teen Justice Curfew Book Two"

ABOUT THE AUTHOR

C.A. Gordon credits fellow authors H.G. Wells, R.L. Stein, and K.A. Applegate with the inspiration for his cool writer's name. The product of two journalists (a poet and a musician), he spent countless childhood hours absorbed in stories. That was for fun. He also wrote many repetitive sentences and composed many in-depth research papers. *That* was for punishment.

Born in Seattle but raised primarily in Oceanside, CA, Gordon attended a Montessori preschool, spent his elementary school years in the GATE program, and triumphantly graduated from high school two years early. He spent the next twenty years earning a paycheck, landing boardslides and flip tricks, tap dancing, and, in his spare time, writing.

Gordon lives with his lovely wife and annoying dog in Northern California. He occasionally pines for the beaches, breweries, and exquisite cuisine in San Diego, but he's perfectly content with the variety of flora and fauna so close to his new home. Not to mention all the wineries.

Stay in touch with C.A.!

Website: cagordonauthor.wixsite.com/welcome
Instagram: instagram.com/cagordon_author
Facebook: facebook.com/cagordonauthor
Email: cagordon.author@gmail.com